"It's hard

Ian's blue eyes b[...]
whole body felt as if it had been brushed with
electricity. The man had a certain light about
him, something slightly bewitching.

"A man like me. Crude and shallow, a walking
embarrassment, a blight on the family name—
so unlike my parents—a philanthropist. It
sounds like a lie, doesn't it?"

She nodded, held speechless by the bitterness
and grief in his voice.

"Don't tell anyone, okay?" he whispered. "Let's
keep it a secret. You and me." His voice was a
purr, his gaze dropped to her lips and for one
shocked stupid second she would have bet
money that Ian Greer was about to kiss her.

And she, like a deer in headlights, couldn't
even move out of the way.

Her body was shaking—unused to such a rush
of adrenaline, a rush of anything. And it felt
good in a wild and uncomfortable way. Like
running full tilt downhill in the dark.

Dear Reader,

It's time to admit how I feel about the actor Christian Bale. It's not right how much I love him. As a married woman with two kids and a dog, I shouldn't feel like a teenager while watching this guy on-screen. But I do. And a few summers ago when the movie *Batman Begins* came out, I saw it, like, three times. I loved the remake of the Bruce Wayne character—a party-loving millionaire on the surface and crime-fighting, do-gooder at heart. What a character! What storytelling opportunities! How many times can we put Christian in a tux?

That summer the idea for Ian Greer was born: a scandal-loving party animal on the surface, a wounded do-gooder underneath it all. It took him a few years to find a book and story line that fit, but Ian Greer is my Harlequin Superromance version of Batman—without the cape or car. I did, however, give him a fabulous sidekick and a woman tough enough to force him out into the open.

Now, I should probably tell you how I feel about Gerard Butler....

Happy reading!

Molly O'Keefe

P.S. I love to hear from readers! Please drop me a line at Molly@Molly-OKeefe.com.

THE STORY
BETWEEN THEM
Molly O'Keefe

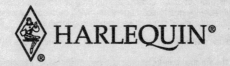

TORONTO • NEW YORK • LONDON
AMSTERDAM • PARIS • SYDNEY • HAMBURG
STOCKHOLM • ATHENS • TOKYO • MILAN • MADRID
PRAGUE • WARSAW • BUDAPEST • AUCKLAND

Recycling programs
for this product may
not exist in your area.

ISBN-13: 978-0-373-71542-8
ISBN-10:   0-373-71542-0

THE STORY BETWEEN THEM

Printed in U.S.A.

ABOUT THE AUTHOR

Molly O'Keefe, if she isn't sitting at the computer, can usually be found in the sandbox discussing the modern wonder of fire trucks with her three-year-old son, Mick. Luckily, between writing and fire trucks and her baby daughter, there is very little time for laundry or dishes. There is, however, always time for great television, good food with friends and the occasional walk along Lake Ontario.

Books by Molly O'Keefe

HARLEQUIN SUPERROMANCE
1365—FAMILY AT STAKE
1385—HIS BEST FRIEND'S BABY
1392—WHO NEEDS CUPID?
      "A Valentine for Rebecca"
1432—UNDERCOVER PROTECTOR
1460—BABY MAKES THREE*
1486—A MAN WORTH KEEPING*
1510—WORTH FIGHTING FOR*
1534—THE SON BETWEEN THEM

HARLEQUIN DUETS
62—TOO MANY COOKS
95—COOKING UP TROUBLE
    KISS THE COOK

HARLEQUIN FLIPSIDE
15—PENCIL HIM IN
37—DISHING IT OUT

*The Mitchells of Riverview Inn

CHAPTER ONE

JENNIFER STERN was a logical, sensible woman. And, she told herself, logical, sensible women didn't stand on chairs, screaming.

No matter how much they wanted to.

"Do you see it?" Deb Barber asked, from her position on one of the chairs.

"I can't see anything," Jennifer said, her own logical, sensible, stupid feet firmly planted on the floor. She had to yell in order to be heard over the cacophony of spraying water.

A geyser licked across the ceiling from the broken faucet then splashed onto the floor, creating a lake in the middle of the kitchen.

And while she couldn't see the snake, she knew it was somewhere between her and the water shut-off valve.

"It's just a garter snake," she said, inching around the fridge. "Right?" This is why she lived in cities. Cities with plumbers. Cities that didn't have snakes just roaming through kitchens.

"I have no idea," Deb answered, crouching and resting her hot pink wrist-casts on the back of the wooden chair. "All I know is it was big. A big snake in the middle of the kitchen."

Jennifer ducked under the geyser and stepped gingerly over the lake, with one eye out for visiting reptiles.

When she'd agreed to help out for two weeks at Serenity

House while her friends Samantha and J.D. went on a much-needed vacation she had not agreed to this.

"Tell me if you see it," Jennifer said, feeling vulnerable as she ducked under the counter and cranked off the water supply.

It was probably just a garter snake. Or, even more likely, a figment of Deb's imagination.

"I didn't make it up," Deb said, her voice loud in the sudden quiet. "I swear I saw a snake."

"I never said you didn't," Jennifer said quickly, wondering if Deb wasn't just a little psychic. She wouldn't be all that surprised. If Deb could sprout wings and fly, Jennifer wouldn't even blink.

Officially, Deb was in charge of Serenity since Sam and J.D. left. But a bad fall resulting in two broken wrists made doing anything required in the day-to-day running of a small community center pretty much impossible.

Which is why Jennifer was here. Deb was the brains, Jennifer was the wrists.

"Hey, wow, Mom, look."

At the sound of her son Spencer's voice, she jumped and smacked her head scrambling out from under the sink. "Spence, be careful there's a—"

Her eleven-year-old son, red curls catching the late afternoon sun, stood in the doorway to the kitchen holding a small, twisting green snake.

"Oh, dear lord," Deb breathed. "Honey, you need to put that thing down."

"Why?" Spence asked, glancing at Deb. "It's just a garter."

Daisy, Serenity's giant guard dog and Spence's constant companion when he was at the shelter, barked once as if to second that assessment.

"You're not scared of a garter, are you, Daisy?" Spence asked, dangling the snake over the half-rottweiler, half-whatever-lived-under-the-Munsters'-stairs beast. Daisy's tail didn't even twitch.

Jennifer collapsed against the counter because her knees were gone. And because she was so glad her son was a young biologist and knew he wasn't holding a cottonmouth, and because Deb looked absolutely ridiculous on the kitchen chair with her hot pink wrist-casts and ebony dreadlocks, Jennifer did something she hadn't done in ages. She laughed.

She laughed so hard she wiped her eyes.

She laughed so hard she kind of had to go to the bathroom.

"Mom?" Spence's blue-grey eyes were wide with wonder and a little fear. It had been so long, she realized, so long since he'd seen her happy like this. So long that uncontrolled laughter was scary. *Oh, Spence,* she thought, a sadness gripping her so hard it hurt, *have I been that grim?* "You all right?"

"I'm fine, honey," she reassured him quickly. "Deb thought it was a giant king cobra coming to eat all of us."

Spence's serious face cracked open and his laughter, not as rare as hers but sweet all the same, spilled over the kitchen and made her laugh harder until they were gripping their knees to stay upright.

"Jennifer? Spence?" Deb asked, looking at her as if she'd grown two heads. "You having some kind of fit?"

"Stop it," Jennifer cried.

"I mean, if it was someone else, I'd think you were laughing. But since in the whole year I've known you I've never seen you so much as giggle—"

"I laugh," she protested. "Spence? Don't I laugh?"

"Not like this you don't."

There hadn't been anything worth laughing about. Not in years. In fact, at some point two years ago, she'd been fairly convinced she'd never laugh again. Never feel joy again.

But here it was. Different than before, harder, sharper, almost painful. But everything was different than before.

Her. Spencer. Life.

But laughing again felt good. Like sex.

Though she was not counting on its return anytime soon.

"I'm going to take the snake outside," Spence said and was out the front door in flash, the screen slamming home behind him and Daisy.

A humid Carolina breeze trickled through that screen, making everything just a little stickier.

"When's the air conditioner going to be fixed?" Jennifer asked. Had she known there were going to be snakes, broken faucets and no air conditioner she definitely would have said no—no matter how much she loved Sam and J.D.

"Gary said it would take him a few hours, when he got here. Should be cool by tomorrow."

"Thank God." She sighed and took in the broken faucet, the giant lake and the water-splashed ceiling, and wondered where to start the clean-up efforts. She'd been here two days and already she had to wonder how Sam did this every day. It seemed like all she and Deb were doing was putting out fires. Snakes. Broken pipes. Hungry kids. Nutrition classes. Parenting classes. Book groups.

Deb ducked into the community center office/supply closet, tried to grab two big mops and ended up knocking both of them to the ground.

"Stupid casts," she muttered.

"Hey, I'm supposed to be doing that stuff," Jennifer said, and rushed in to get the mops and a big stack of towels. Being incapacitated wasn't easy on anyone but it was particularly rough on Deb, who was used to doing on her own since she ran away from home and right to Serenity House four years ago.

Deb was far, far older than her twenty-two years.

"What do you think about the pipes?" Jennifer asked, laying the white and green towels across the big puddle.

"Even if my wrists weren't busted," Deb said, "I wouldn't be able to fix that faucet. Sam's been holding those pipes together with string and hope for too long now."

"Figures it would fall apart when she was gone."

"Well—" Deb arched a plucked black eyebrow "—maybe with her gone we can actually get them fixed. Serenity House has a private benefactor who as far as I am concerned, doesn't do nearly enough benefacting."

Jennifer paused while mopping. "You're not suggesting we call—" dramatically, she looked left then right "—the mysterious number?" she whispered. When Sam left she'd given Deb and Jennifer this phone number that was only to be used in the case of extreme financial or legal disaster. At the time Jennifer had thought Sam was joking, but J.D. quickly shook his head, indicating the number wasn't something Sam joked about.

Deb tried to look stern, imitating Sam. "We don't make fun of the number."

"Has she ever called the number?" Jennifer asked.

"A few times." Deb kicked a towel over one part of the lake. "Once when there were some legal issues after that estranged husband broke in to the shelter and kidnapped his wife and child. And then other times when she wanted to build the classrooms onto the shelter and get computers. When the roof caved in." She shrugged. "That's it."

"Did the benefactor give you the money?"

"Right away," Deb said, like she couldn't believe it. "It was like he was waiting around for the chance to send money. Sam left a message and within two hours a banker was on the phone wondering where to wire the money."

"Wow."

"Right, wow." Deb was getting worked up. "And when we called with those legal problems, a lawyer contacted us right away and the whole thing just disappeared."

"Does she know who this benefactor is?"

"No idea."

And that, Jennifer thought, was the really wild thing about it. Money just arrived. Legal trouble got fixed. No obligations. No thank-you notes. Nothing. Like magic Sam called this number, left a message and her troubles vanished.

Who wouldn't call that number?

What Jennifer would have done for a number like that two years ago.

Though, she thought with the stabbing pain that had only gotten bearable in the past year, money wouldn't have saved her husband.

She heaved an armful of wet towels into the sink and turned around to look at Deb.

"Do we call this magic number?" she asked.

Deb sighed. "Not yet. Things need to get a lot worse."

AFTER THE KITCHEN disaster was handled, Jennifer went searching for her son, and found him in the garden with Shonny, Deb's three-year-old, and Daisy, who was rolling delightedly in the tomato plants. J.D. had started the garden at the beginning of the summer and had left Spencer in charge of all weeds while he was gone. It was a task her son took very seriously.

"Not that one," Spencer cried, as Shonny pulled out a young carrot by its leafy green top. "No!" he yelled when Shonny started to put it in his mouth.

She stood in the shadow of Serenity House and felt a breathless ache in her chest. A sense of distance far greater than the few feet of lawn that separated her from her son.

Her little boy was growing up. Growing away.

DNA, passing time, Doug dying, Sam and J.D.—they were all caverns between her and her Spence.

But more importantly, what had united them two years ago in ways that DNA could never touch were the wounds left on both of them by Doug's death. And Spence's were healing.

And hers…well, hers she was ignoring. Unable to look under the bandages.

She'd changed her life so she wouldn't have to look under those bandages.

"What's up, Spence?" She stepped out of the shadows toward the boys.

"Shonny's eating dirt."

"Kids will do that," she said, crouching down beside the boys. She smiled into the beaming dirty face of Shonny and wiped some of the dirt from his lips.

"He's pulling out vegetables, not weeds," Spence complained.

"You have to be patient," she told her son and revisited the wish that she and Doug had had a chance to adopt more children before he died. Spencer was in sore need of a little brother. "He's a lot younger than you."

"Three," Shonny chimed in.

"See." She looked at Spence. "He's only three."

"Fine." Spence sighed, long suffering.

His skin was damp under her hand and his curls felt like wire filament and she was suddenly desperately hungry for those days when she couldn't leave the room without him wondering where she was.

"Do you want to go swimming or something?" she asked, despite the deadlines looming over her shoulder. As a freelance magazine writer, there were always deadlines looming over her shoulder. "With me?"

"Nah," Spence said and her heart fell. "I want to help out in the garden."

"Do you need some help?" she asked, diligently trying to be a part of her son's life in a way he didn't seem to want.

He was getting older, needing her less, while she seemed to need him more.

Spence scratched on itch on his cheek with his shoulder. "J.D. left me in charge," he said, looking at her from the corner of his eye, telling her in his own language that this was something he wanted to do on his own.

And she could respect that.

She just didn't have to like it.

"All right." She stood, not wanting to beg. "I need to do a little work." Her knees popped, making her feel far older than her thirty-seven years. "I've got a deadline by five tonight. So, if you need me I'll be up in Sam's old apartment—"

"Jennifer?" Deb's voice rang out from around the side of the house. "There's something on the news you're going to want to see."

Good God, she thought, *what now?*

"FORMER FIRST LADY Annabelle Greer lost her battle with cancer last week in her home in New Hampshire." The newscaster's words took the strength right out of Jennifer's legs and she collapsed onto the couch. "Today is her memorial service."

She barely felt Deb's presence at her side.

Jennifer barely felt anything. She was numb with shock.

"First Lady Annie, as she was known by the millions of children who read the books she wrote while her husband was in office, leaves behind her husband, son and a grieving nation," said the blonde anchor with the perfect hair, shaking her head sadly.

And me, Jennifer thought. *She leaves behind me.*

"First Lady Annie and her New Horizons Foundation were instrumental in changing our country's educational system and the programs started during the Greer administration ten years ago have been credited for the spike in literacy numbers over the past decade. In her home state of North Carolina, literacy numbers have doubled."

Dry cold facts, she thought. Not even a hint at the beautiful, complicated woman who had died. Not a hint of Jennifer's hero. Her husband's godmother.

They showed a famous picture of her before the Greers were in the White House. It was after the release of her first book and Annie wore a pair of big, round, Jackie-O sunglasses and the high-necked mandarin suits that she had made so popular.

Jennifer sighed. The woman had been the picture of grace. Of elegance.

"In recent years, the only dark spot on the family's legacy has been Ian Greer." A shot of Annabelle's handsome son with a dark-haired actress—wearing less than a washcloth—on his arm, filled the screen. The blond man practically glittered, he was so handsome—the spitting image of his father. "Ian has become a regular in the tabloids—"

Angry, Jennifer reached forward and smacked the power button on the TV.

"The woman is an icon and all they can talk about is her son's social life?" she asked, so disgusted she was actually shaking.

"It's the way the media works. You know that," Deb said, her big brown eyes sympathetic behind her glasses.

"It's not the way I worked," she insisted, furious on Annabelle's behalf. "The last serious story about Annabelle and her husband was mine. Ever since then it's been nothing but tabloid garbage. The story is Annabelle, not her—" her voice broke "—son."

"The boy's gone wild."

"Boy!" she cried. "The guy is my age and he's acting like a teenager." Jennifer shook her head, wondering how much her son's behavior must have wounded the intensely private Annabelle. "So disrespectful. Remember last year when he showed up drunk at the White House when his father was getting that medal for public service."

"Oh, I know. The whole thing was being televised and he showed up with that actress who doesn't wear underwear."

"It's just so gross," she said, baffled that a woman like Annabelle could have a son like Ian.

Her skin began to itch and buzz, starting at her scalp, working down her neck across her back to her arms—an old indicator that she sensed a story here. She could do a follow-up, the right kind, one that focused on Annabelle. Her life. Her lessons.

Stop. Stop it. Jennifer put her head in her hands, counted to ten until the feeling stopped. *You are not that person anymore.*

In the past year it was like she'd developed this wicked sword and any time some part of her started reaching for the person she'd been, or the way things were before Doug died, that sword cut off the inclination at the root.

She didn't do hard news anymore.

"I'm so sorry this had to add to an already bad day," Deb murmured. "I know you really liked her."

Jennifer laughed, a short burst of grief and incredulity. "I barely knew her," she said. "She was Doug's godmother. She came to our wedding and then I didn't see her again. Not until—" She sighed. The interview. The interview a year ago that had inspired her to utterly change her life.

"You have to embrace the dark things in your life," Annabelle had said, looking so regal on her sunporch in New Hampshire. "You have to embrace the sadness and the anger and the hurt or you have to cut it out. Remove it from your life or it will take over everything. But if you embrace it, live with it, it just becomes a part of your life. A part of you."

Jennifer put her head in her hands. One interview, a two-second sound bite and Jennifer changed *everything*.

Changed? She nearly laughed. *Changed* didn't even begin to describe what she'd done with her life.

Massive overhaul was more like it. *Extreme Makeover, Life Edition*.

She'd sold the condo in Baltimore with all of her furniture, most of her clothes and anything Doug ever wore, used or touched.

Moved to Asheville.

Quit her writer-producer job at the NBC affiliate in Baltimore. A job she'd loved. A job that had been a huge part of her identity. In fact, with Doug gone, it was all she had left. Besides Spence. And she knew, as a single parent looking for a new identity, the job had to go.

Now she wrote women's magazine articles about home spa remedies and natural household cleansers so she could go to every soccer game of Spence's. So she could be home every night to help with homework. So she never ever had to think of who she'd been and what she'd lost two years ago.

She reinvented herself instead of facing what was left of her life without Doug.

And the craziest part was it worked.

The Oprahs out there in the world might have a beef with Jennifer's methods, but it was the smartest thing she'd ever done. Bar none.

And if she were really smart, she'd write a book so other

widows could do the same thing. Why try and pick up the pieces of a shattered life? Why not get new pieces?

"My son is going to be so sad," she said, covering her eyes with her hands. "He loved her books."

"Shonny's beginning to get in to them, too."

They sat in silence for a few moments. And Jennifer was grateful for Deb's quiet company even though the woman no doubt had a million other things to do. In fact, Jennifer needed to get back to work. That deadline wasn't going to meet itself.

A knock on the screen door interrupted her pity party and both women turned to look over the back of the couch at the man standing on the front stoop.

"Can I help you?" Deb asked, walking to the door.

"I am looking for Sam Riggins, J. D. Kronos or Deb Barber."

"I'm Deb," she said, popping open the screen door.

A blue envelope of paper flew through the open door, landing on the hardwood floor and skidding over to the couch where Jennifer sat.

"You've been served," the man said with a smirk and then walked away.

CHAPTER TWO

"This is from the Conti family?" Jennifer said, trying to make sense of the outrageous claims made in the nearly undecipherable legal language on the court papers.

"Looks like it," Deb agreed, from over her shoulder. "Frank Conti is in jail but it looks like Mom Conti is coming after us for...damages and the loss of a diamond ring?"

That's what it looked like to Jennifer, too. Doug had been a lawyer specializing in media law and when he got carried away with lawyer talk she tended to zone out unless it had something to do with one of her stories.

Now she wished she'd studied every word he'd said. The bad news was piling up around Serenity and as the person who was supposed to be helping take care of things, she wished she could make this go away.

"I knew that girl was going to be trouble," Deb said, clucking her tongue. "Coming in her with her fancy jeans and lies."

Last year Christina Conti, the pregnant sixteen-year-old daughter of Frank Conti, who was a thug in the Gamboni crime family, had arrived on Serenity House's doorstep.

Jennifer had been way too wrapped up in her own breakdown to take much notice in the girl, but Christina and Spence had become friends of a sort. And according to Spence, Christina had lied about her age and her identity, but she was running from real trouble and Sam and J.D.

did everything they could do to make sure she and her baby were safe.

Including getting Christina and her boyfriend into the witness protection program. In return, Christina and her boy-friend gave the FBI all the information they had on Frank.

It was enough to put the guy away for life.

Spence had watched the news religiously all last fall.

And Jennifer, trying to amputate the hard-news journal-ist in her, had turned her face away from the screen so she wouldn't die of envy.

Even now, just thinking about the Conti story made her jealous. The stupid story unfolded right under her nose. She could have scooped everyone. She could have scooped everyone to a Peabody.

But that was a different life. A different person.

And you don't care, she reminded herself. *Not anymore.*

"You know what we need to do," Jennifer said, stroking Deb's shoulder.

"Yeah," Deb said, nodding her head so her rhinestone glasses slipped back on her nose. "I do. Go get the number."

Minutes later, Jennifer sat at the desk in the cluttered office, the cordless phone in her right hand. The scrap of paper with the handwritten, magic number in her left.

"You talk," she said, trying to pass the phone to Deb, feeling a sudden attack of nerves. "I'll dial."

"No way," Deb said, sitting back, holding her wrists out in front of her, a hot pink phone barricade. "You talk. You're a journalist, for crying out loud. You're better with words than me."

"Okay." Jennifer licked her lips. Took a deep breath. "What do I say?"

"That our pipes are broken. We got legal trouble and Gary's too slow with our air-conditioning."

"All right. Here goes." She dialed the number and cleared her throat while it rang.

"Leave a message," a robotic voice said then there was a long shrill beep.

"Hi. Ah…this is Jennifer Stern, at Serenity House. Sam Riggins is on vacation and her assistant Deb and I are in charge of things here while she's gone." Deb whirled her hands in a universal signal to get on to the good stuff. "Right. Anyway. We're having some problems with pipes and the air-conditioning and don't have the funds to cover both. So, we need some money. I—"

How much? she mouthed.

"Five grand," Deb said and Jennifer scowled. "Time we got central air," Deb insisted.

"A few thousand should cover it," Jennifer said into the receiver. "But more importantly, the shelter got served today with some legal papers that we are ill-equipped to handle and we—"

Jennifer was cut off by another shrill beep then the phone went dead.

She removed the receiver from her ear. "Should I call back?"

Deb shook her head, leaning back in her chair with a heavy sigh. "You said enough."

"So? That's it?" Jennifer looked at the phone and the number as if there should be more involved. Magic potions or something. Chanting. Spells.

"That's it. Makes you think Sam's got a screw loose for not calling that number more often."

"Well, it does seem pretty easy."

And frankly, pretty exciting. Her hands tingled and Jennifer couldn't remember the last time she'd been nervous about something.

"Anyhow—" Deb looked up at the wall clock "—I've got a class on pregnancy and nutrition in ten minutes."

"And I need to get this article done. I'm going to be pushing hard for my deadline as it is."

Jennifer met Deb's eyes and smiled. Shrugged. "We just wait for our knight in shining armor to call back?"

"Shouldn't be long. Two hours tops."

UPSTAIRS IN Sam's old apartment, Jennifer checked the phone for the third time in the past hour and a half to make sure the thing worked.

Ringer was on.

Dial tone working.

But it had been silent since she'd made the call.

Two hours, she reminded herself. It still hadn't been two hours.

She forced herself to focus on the task at hand—edifying the women's-magazine-reading public of the untold benefit of using olive oil in your hair.

She kept out the part about how it made her look like a greaseball for three days. And her son had wondered what that smell was every time she'd come in the room.

An instant messenger balloon popped up on her screen.

KerryWaldo: Stop hiding from me.

Jennifer's heart stopped at the message. Her old producer. Her old friend, from her former life. Even seeing the name brought back memories she didn't want—a job she loved, work she was good at, a life she adored.

The pain was excruciating. Just as it was every time Waldo contacted her. Two weeks of ignoring Waldo's phone calls and e-mails and the woman still didn't get the picture.

But that was Waldo and Jennifer was going to have to deal with it. Mentally, she unsheathed the sword and typed:

I'm not hiding. I'm busy.

KerryWaldo: I read your last story about how to get rid of soap scum in your shower. Life-changing.

Jennifer smiled. Waldo would think she'd fallen a long way, but the truth was Jennifer made a choice. She chose soap scum because it was easy.

Stay tuned. Working on a fascinating piece about the many uses for olive oil.

KerryWaldo: And I've got a piece on a teenager starting a business to clean up Chesapeake Bay. Contract work. Two days in the office. Come on. I need you.

A barrage of questions filled Jennifer's head. A teenager? How? Why? Is it working? Was she funded?

But then, with brutal sword efficiency, she stopped. She stopped the questions, the curiosity, the skin-itching enthusiasm to get to the heart of a story.

The sword methodology would be discussed in chapter three of her new widowhood book.

I'm busy, she wrote.

KerryWaldo: You can't be happy. Writing that fluff? No way the Jennifer Stern I knew is happy.

Happy? Jennifer nearly laughed. Oh, man, Waldo had it so wrong. This wasn't about *happy.* It was about survival. About not going crazy.

I'm busy. Fluff doesn't write itself.

KerryWaldo: You hear about Annabelle Greer? I'll give you carte blanche for a follow-up on her life.

Jennifer's heart stopped and it took a while, but with shaking fingers she typed:

Gotta go.

She closed the messenger window, shutting down the program. She almost closed her computer and threw it out the window.

That's how much she was tempted. That's how much she yearned to tell the Annabelle Greer story.

But opening up that door would let in any number of memories and nightmares. And she hadn't worked this hard to cave now. She had a new life. She was a new person.

And she had a job to do. It wasn't her old job. It wasn't the greatest job, but it was hers. So, after a couple of deep breaths she stayed in her seat and finished a thousand words on olive oil. It wasn't much, but it was something to be proud of.

An hour later, she e-mailed the story to her editor at *Ladies' Home Journal,* and quickly distanced herself from the computer as if it were a snake that might bite.

The temptation to do a little research, surf the Net about the New Horizons Foundation and Annabelle Greer hadn't faded in the past hour.

Leave. It. Alone, she told herself. But the demand didn't help with the craving.

Instead, she faced Sam's empty apartment, searching for distraction. The unit on the top floor of the community center had been emptied when Sam moved out a year ago. At the same time Deb and Sam decided to focus more of their attention on community day programs rather than offering shelter to women, since the demand had diminished.

And since that decision the shelter had radically changed. Gone were the security cameras and bullet-proof doors. Cops no longer spent nights on patrol outside, watching for angry husbands and boyfriends. Now there were screen doors and a vegetable garden. Kids played in the front yard and women held evening book-group meetings and cooking clubs. The floodlights on motion sensors were still around, although now only raccoons and other nocturnal animals set them off.

Twice last night, to be precise. Not that Jennifer was counting.

There were still three bedrooms downstairs. But instead of the protective haven they'd once been, the rooms now served more transitional purposes. Women newly arrived or between jobs. They still housed women leaving relationships but only on the condition the former partner would not hunt them down. And when someone was living in one of the rooms, either Deb or Sam stayed in Sam's old apartment.

Jennifer and Spence had that privilege for these two weeks. A bed. Dresser. Pull-out couch. A card table. A broken coffeemaker. That was the sum total of the apartment's contents.

Home sweet home, she thought, smiling. Oddly, enough, the sparseness was all right. There was something about Serenity that superseded the lack of material comforts.

The skin on the backs of her arms itched. *Now,* she

thought, *that's a story*. The life of a shelter. How Serenity had changed and adapted to the needs of the community.

Stop. Just stop.

That was the last time she responded to Waldo. Conversing with her made the door on the past that much harder to close. And shone a spotlight on the fact that soap scum and olive oil weren't satisfying in the least.

Phone in hand, Jennifer ran down the stairs and found an empty kitchen and an empty common room. Pushing through the door toward the classrooms she heard the shrieking laughter of a bunch of kids.

Smiling, her heart like a bubble high in her chest, she found Spence, Shonny and three other kids playing Twister on the colored mat in the middle of a circle of watching women.

"Hey," Deb said, coming to stand next to her. "Heard from our knight?"

Jennifer shook her head. "Not yet. Should I call again?"

Deb wrinkled her nose. "Let's not be pushy."

Spence howled and fell sideways, right into the legs of a blond woman sitting next to a little girl Jennifer hadn't seen when she'd walked in the door.

"Sorry," Spence said, pushing his mop of red curls off his forehead. "Wanna play?" he asked the girl.

The girl seemed to shrink, despite the mother urging her forward. After a little struggle the mother smiled sweetly at Spence. "Maybe later. She's just a little shy."

"She's my sister!" a girl about Spence's age with the same white blond hair said as she reached her right hand out for a red circle. "She never plays."

Spence gave the smaller girl another look. "You can do the spinner."

The girl shook her head, practically crawling into her mother's side.

Spence shrugged and took over spinner duties.

"What's this class?" Jennifer asked, filled with pride over Spence's efforts.

"It's sort of an empowerment class for kids," Deb said.

Jennifer rolled her eyes before she could stop herself. Empowerment class for kids? Really? Was that necessary? Sometimes Deb and Sam got a little "feel good" for her tastes.

"Jennifer," Deb said, her voice a shade tight. "All the women in this room have been beaten by men they loved and their children saw that. These women got out but who knows what's lingering in their kids' minds? Who knows what kind of damage has been done? These women are trying to make sure their kids don't fall into the same traps they fell into."

Oh, man. Jennifer hated it when Deb proved just what an unfeeling, blind idiot she could be. "I didn't think of it that way," she said. "I'm sorry."

"I know you are," Deb said, nudging Jennifer. "Why don't you go talk to that mother? It's her first time here."

Jennifer stepped forward, smiling slightly when the blonde looked up.

"Hi," Jennifer said. "My name is Jennifer. That's my son, Spencer." She pointed to Spence as he tried to reach his foot in between two kids to get to a yellow circle.

"I'm Laura," she said with a smile, revealing teeth so white they looked like pearls. Her long hair fell in the perfect waves that only women in hair commercials had.

"That's my daughter Madison—" she pointed to the girl on the mat "—and this is Angelina." Laura gave the girl beside her a squeeze.

"Mind if I—" Jennifer indicated the free chair and Laura

quickly moved her purse out of the way. "I understand you are new here."

Laura nodded. "You?"

"Oh, I am helping Deb run the place for two weeks," she said. "I'm friends with the couple who operate Serenity."

Laura nodded. "We just moved here to be closer to my sister. She doesn't have any children and since school hasn't started, I thought this might be a good way for the girls to meet some kids."

You've never heard of a swimming pool? Jennifer thought, but didn't say. Empowerment classes for the children of abused parents seemed like a strange place to try and set up playdates, but what did she know?

Laura leaned closer and dropped her voice. "I didn't read the class description before I signed up," she whispered. "Otherwise I might have gone to the pool."

Jennifer smiled, wondering if mind reading was something people did in the South. "Well, then I am glad that you aren't—"

"Abused?" Laura whispered, casting a quick glance to Angelina, who was watching the Twister game and ignoring the women. "Good God, no. I married the gentlest man on the planet."

Well... Jennifer thought of Doug, his hands, his heart. *Not the gentlest.*

"Either way," Jennifer said, "we're glad you're here."

"You know, we are, too." Laura gave Angelina a jostle. "Maybe it will help this one come out of her shell."

"I don't live in a shell," Angelina was quick to say and Laura leaned down, kissing the crown of her head.

The phone Jennifer had tucked in her pocket rang. The sudden shrill noise caused half the kids on the mat to tumble sideways.

She met Deb's excited eyes across the room and scooted out the door, the phone in her hand.

In the hallway she read the caller ID—unknown caller. Made sense. Wealthy benefactors wouldn't want their numbers out there for the world to know.

She took a deep breath and lifted the phone to her ear while hitting the talk button.

"Hello," she said. "Serenity House."

"Jennifer!"

Jennifer collapsed against the wall at the unexpected sound of Samantha's voice. "Hi, Sam. You know you're not supposed to be calling."

"J.D. went to go get drinks so I've got about five minutes before he catches me."

"Is this how you relax?" Jennifer asked, incredulous, but not totally surprised. "You're on a beach. I can hear the waves."

"How am I supposed to relax? I've had this pit in my stomach all day. Something's happened, hasn't it?"

Jennifer thought about the pipes and the AC and being sued and calling the magic number. And she considered J.D. and how excited he was about this vacation he and Sam were on. How badly both of them needed it.

"Nothing's happening," she said. "The place is practically running itself."

"Are you lying?"

Jennifer laughed, knowing if Sam were in the room she'd know right away that she was. "No," she lied. "I'm not. Everything's fine."

"What about the—crap. Here comes J.D."

The line went dead.

Deb's head poked out the door. "Well?"

"It was Sam," Jennifer said and both she and Deb deflated a little. "Maybe it won't work this time," she said, voicing her worst fears. "Maybe we need to figure this out on our own."

Behind Deb there was a yell and a thump and Deb glanced that way. "We'll talk more at dinner," she said. "Right now my son is biting one of those blond girls."

Deb vanished and Jennifer walked toward the office and Sam's Rolodex with the vague hope that there would be some regular phone numbers in there that might help.

Starting with a good lawyer.

AFTER DINNER, Jennifer put two mugs of tea on the kitchen table and sat in front of the Rolodex and phone she'd placed there. Deb was putting Shonny to bed in one of the three bedrooms off the kitchen and when she came back it was time to face facts.

It was 8:00 p.m. Their knight had stood them up.

Spence was in the common room watching *Spider-Man* for the tenth time. The bright lights of the movie illuminated the dusk-filled rooms.

Night was falling all around Serenity House and at this hour of the day she really missed the city. She really missed the noise that let her know she wasn't totally alone.

The dark silence that closed in around the community center was, she was embarrassed to admit, a little scary. It was just so dark. So quiet. So…foreign.

Shaking off her city-girl nerves, Jennifer pulled out the numbers of the four plumbers and two lawyers she'd found earlier.

Deb walked into the room. "What did you find?" She dropped into a chair.

Jennifer didn't know how the woman did it. Raised a toddler on her own while doing everything she did at Serenity, all at an age when Jennifer was staying out late, drinking martinis and falling in love with her husband.

She shied away from the memories, immediately setting up a distance that made it seem as if those events had happened to someone else. So that thinking of them wouldn't hurt.

"Do you know these plumbers?" she asked, pushing the cards toward Deb.

Deb craned her neck and scowled. "Crooks. Every one of them."

"You have some other suggestions?" Deb was quiet and Jennifer sensed her frustration. "He hasn't called," Jennifer reminded her. "And we can't keep doing the dishes in the bathroom."

Deb smiled. "What about—"

There was a crash at the front door. And another.

"Mom!" Spence cried, running into the kitchen. Daisy went ballistic.

Adrenaline surged up Jennifer's spine and she scrambled from her chair, grabbing her son and throwing him behind her.

"What the hell is that?" she asked Deb, who was staring, wide-eyed at the front door.

"No clue," she breathed.

The heavy pounding practically shook the house. Daisy's barking took on a fevered pitch.

"Go—go upstairs," she told Spence, trying to push him toward the door to their apartment, but he wouldn't let go of her.

Fear scurried along her nerve endings and at every knock on the door she jumped. Twitched. Wanted to leap right out of her skin.

"Well, good God," Deb said, standing. "They're going to wake up Shonny."

Jennifer, despite her fear, knew she couldn't let Deb go answer that door alone.

"You stay right here," she said directly to Spence's pale, panic-stricken face. "No matter what. You don't move."

He nodded and Jennifer whirled and grabbed a knife from the block on the counter. She caught Deb's eye and expected her to tell Jennifer that she was overreacting.

The pounding started up again and the windows shook.

"Good idea," Deb said, holding out one of her casts. "Give me one, too."

Jennifer gave her a knife and they stepped—side by side—from the bright kitchen into the darker common room. Jennifer felt her heart beat in every inch of her skin. It was all she could hear.

The *Spider-Man* theme song was a surreal musical accompaniment and Jennifer hit the off button with a shaking finger as they crept past the TV.

"Down, girl," Deb whispered and Daisy stepped back as they approached the door. Her ruff was at attention and the barking downgraded to a truly terrifying growl.

"You good?" Deb asked as she put her hand on the doorknob.

Good for what? Jennifer wanted to ask. A knife fight? No. Definitely not.

Instead, she clenched her fist around her knife and nodded.

Deb crossed herself and yelled through the door.

"Who's there?"

"My name is Andille," a deep voice answered.

Jennifer rested her head against the door, as her body sagged with a new surge of terror. She had hoped it wasn't a man. A man pounding on a door like that couldn't be a good thing.

"I am looking for Jennifer Stern."

Panic zinged through her and she lifted her head only to meet Deb's big eyes.

"Any reason you'd have a man named Andille pounding on a door for you?" Deb asked. Jennifer shook her head, her mouth too dry to speak.

"Look," the deep voice named Andille said, "I'm not here to hurt anyone or steal anything. So, it would be a real favor if you could open the door."

"I don't know any Andille," Jennifer said. Through the heavy wooden door they heard someone groan. Andille grunted, there was a thunk and another groan.

Daisy barked and Deb quickly shushed her.

"Could you open the door?" Andille said, his voice strained and growing angry.

"Andille," she said reasonably, or as reasonably as one could, terrified and yelling through a door, "I mean no offense, but there's no reason for me to open this door."

Something slid and crashed against the portal. Another groan.

Jennifer and Deb both jumped back. Daisy lunged forward.

"Lady," Andille said. "You called us."

Deb and Jennifer both paused, stock-still as if pinned in place by utter bewildering astonishment.

"No," Deb whispered, shaking her head.

"I only called one person today," Jennifer said.

"You think that guy is our knight?" Deb asked, jerking her thumb toward the outside.

Confusion spiked the fear cocktail in Jennifer's blood and for a second she thought she might giggle. Or cry.

"Daisy," she commanded. "Back. Sit." The dog reluctantly obeyed but Deb put her body between the dog and the door just in case.

"Only one way to find out," Jennifer said, pretending to

be far braver than she actually was. She reached for the door and slowly turned the knob. Once the catch was free the door swung toward them as if there were a big weight pressed against it.

A big weight about the size of a full-grown man.

"Whoa, whoa there," Andille said, grabbing the man who was sliding backward into the common room. Jennifer stepped out of the way, dragging Deb with her and holding up the knife in between her and Andille.

Andille, who was roughly six and a half feet of night condensed, handled the smaller, seemingly unconscious man back into an upright position.

"Is he hurt?" Deb asked, her eyes narrow and watchful behind her glasses. Jennifer got the real impression that Deb could handle herself in a knife fight.

"No," Andille said, a brilliant white smile splitting the black of his face. "But he will be tomorrow."

"Is this Serenity?" the smaller man asked in a slurred voice, his head bent sideways on his neck, a flop of blond hair over his face.

At the sound of the blond man's voice, Daisy's growl resumed, her lips lifting from her long fangs.

"Sure," Andille murmured, eyeing Jennifer's knife and Daisy. "But it's not quite like I imagined it."

"Good." The man pushed himself upright, away from Andille, and Jennifer realized he wasn't that small. Without the contrast of Andille the giant, the guy was terrifyingly big all on his own.

The man swept his blond hair off his forehead and both she and Deb leaned away from him, nearly overcome by the smell of alcohol radiating from his pores.

"Ladies," he said, sweeping his arms out, "I am here to

solve your problems." He smiled and Jennifer nearly dropped her knife.

Even in the darkness he was recognizable. His eyes so blue, his hair so perfect and golden blond. His cheekbones, those lips. The dimple, even. He was perfection. As handsome as handsome could get.

He was last year's sexiest man alive, the man on the cover of half a dozen tabloids, the man whose behavior on this day, of all days, defiled his mother's memory.

"You're the benefactor?" she whispered.

Ian Greer, drunk as a skunk and son of the former president of the United States, nodded and stumbled across the threshold of Serenity.

CHAPTER THREE

A FULL BODY BUZZ started under Jennifer's skin and she couldn't ignore it. Couldn't stop it. It was so powerful it nearly lifted her off her feet, blew off the top of her head and her mind went in about twenty directions at once.

This, her instincts howled, *is a story.*

The urge to know more, to dig deeper, gripped her so hard, so fast, she couldn't breathe, she couldn't pull the sword to cut off this sudden and thrilling fascination.

Ian Greer. Here. Drunk. On the day of his mother's funeral. Claiming to be the millionaire silent benefactor of a community center in rural North Carolina.

Really. It doesn't get any better than this.

Her giddy instinct was to let him in, sit him down, ply him with more booze until the whole story spilled from his gorgeous chiseled lips.

But Deb was here, and children, and Jennifer was supposed to be taking care of Serenity, which was in danger of falling down around their ears. Not hunting down stories.

"Wait a second," Jennifer said, standing in the way of Ian Greer's progress. It was weird. Really one of the most surreal moments in her life but she was stopping Ian Greer—sexiest man alive and the hottest news story in America right now—from entering the shelter.

"You can't just walk in," Jennifer said. "Not without an explanation."

Deb stepped up beside her, holding her knife like Andille was a steak, and Jennifer, who wasn't scared anymore—not really—wanted to tell Deb to relax.

"I'm sorry," Andille said, snagging Ian's jacket and pulling him back outside. Ian balked, catching himself on the doorway. "We can get a hotel," Andille insisted. "There's got to be one around here somewhere."

"There isn't," Ian said and Jennifer and Deb shared a quick astonished look. The guy was right.

"There's a Motel Six about forty miles west of here," Deb said.

"See," Ian said, facing Andille. "I told you nothing ever changes around here."

Andille sighed and closed his eyes as if gathering his strength.

From the direction of the bedrooms Shonny cried out for Deb, who went ramrod-straight at the sound. She exuded a mother-bear instinct that was pretty terrifying. Daisy caught Deb's vibe and went back to attack mode.

"Come on, Ian," Andille said, watching Deb warily. "Let's go. We can talk in the morning. We're waking up children."

"We're not here to hurt you," Ian said, as if he were offended by the notion. But his whole aura of injured pride was ruined by the fact that he couldn't stand up straight. "We're here to help. Because you called."

Ian was right. The situation was ridiculous but it wasn't dangerous. "Go," she urged Deb. "We'll be fine and you don't want Shonny to come looking for you. And take the dog."

Deb cast one more measuring look at the men.

"Deb," Jennifer insisted. "We're fine." Reluctantly Deb left to comfort her son, taking the growling beast with her.

"I'm sorry about the knives and the dog," Jennifer said, turning back to the men. "But you've taken us by surprise. I mean…you're Ian Greer."

"I am."

He stared at her, his ice-blue eyes impenetrable. Drunk as he might be, she couldn't tell what he was thinking. Which was utterly disconcerting. As was his sudden taciturn silence. The guy was drunk, for crying out loud. First rule of interviews—drunks babble.

"You've…been drinking."

"I have." His lips quirked and her temper flared. This wasn't a joke. And she wondered if maybe Ian Greer, besides being drunk and disrespectful, wasn't a little dumb.

"Well," she said, "oddly enough, the son of the president of the United States doesn't often show up on my door claiming to solve all our problems."

Her new guess was that Ian Greer couldn't solve any problems. She had a sinking feeling that his arrival here had less to do with their phone call and more to do with his constant search for publicity. It was so ludicrous that Ian was the benefactor. Perhaps his father was? And he'd intercepted the call? That made more sense.

His eyes narrowed. "What exactly are you asking?"

"How do we know you're who you say you are? To us." He didn't answer and so she put it out on the line. "And this isn't some stunt. Of yours."

Ian blinked at her and for a second it seemed like the fog cleared and he was really looking at her. Really seeing her. And she saw him. Through his fancy suit and messy hair she saw him. Her skin buzzed and burned. He wasn't dumb. Or as drunk as he seemed.

He was in a lot of pain.

It was there, buried deep in those blue eyes.

"Three years ago there was a legal issue regarding a man who kidnapped his wife and child from Serenity," he said, his voice a low, rough growl that swept up her spine and across her skin, making everything feel too tight. She was transfixed by his words, his sudden intensity, the ice blue of red-rimmed eyes. "I settled out of court. A year before that I gave you the money to fix the roof. Three years before that I funded the classroom addition. I'm the person on the other end of the number you dialed. I've been that person for fifteen years."

Okay, Ian Greer was their knight in shining armor. Or rather, rumpled Armani. But that was only the beginning of her questions.

"But what are you doing here?" she asked. "You've never shown up before. Sam Riggins, who has been here for ten years, has no idea that you—" she laughed slightly "—that Ian Greer is the benefactor."

He blinked, sagged slightly against the wall and Andille pushed a big hand against Ian's shoulder to keep him upright. "If you'll just give me the directions to that hotel," Andille said, giving her a quick smile, "I'll get—"

"It's hard to believe, isn't it?" Ian asked, as if Andille had never spoken. His eyes bored into hers and her whole body seemed to wake up under his gaze, as if brushed with electricity. Even drunk and nonsensical the man had a certain light about him. Something approaching bewitching. "A man like me. Crude and shallow, a walking embarrassment, a blight on the family name—so unlike my parents. A philanthropist. It sounds like a lie, doesn't it?"

Jennifer nodded, unable to speak. Held motionless by the bitterness and grief she heard in his voice.

He lurched forward, bumping against her shoulder, and she dropped the knife so she could put up her hands to catch him. "Don't tell anyone, huh?" he whispered, his eyes lighting over her face. "Let's keep it a secret. You and me." His voice was a purr, his gaze dropped to her lips and for one shocked stupid second she would bet money that Ian Greer was about to kiss her.

And she, like a deer in headlights, couldn't even move out of the way.

"Whoa there, Casanova," Andille said, hauling Ian back by the neck of his jacket. Andille tossed him lightly against the wall and Ian slumped, his eyes closing. Jennifer stepped away, sucking in big breaths because she'd stopped breathing for a few minutes.

Her body was shaking, unused to such a rush of adrenaline. A rush of anything…to be honest. She lived in a deep freeze and the past few minutes had been like being dropped in boiling water.

And it felt good—in a wild and uncomfortable way. Like running full-tilt downhill in the dark.

"Are you okay?" Andille asked.

She nodded, and then, because really, it was all just so strange, she laughed. Again.

"I'm fine," she assured Andille, who looked as if he didn't quite believe her. "I feel like I've stepped down the rabbit hole but I will survive."

Andille grinned. "Welcome to life with Ian Greer. Normally he's not this bad. But—" He took a deep breath. "It's been a hard day."

The funeral. Right. She looked at Ian, who seemed to be holding onto consciousness by a thread. This sad drunk man said goodbye to his mother today. His grieving process left a lot to be desired but Jennifer knew everyone handled pain differently.

Andille slung Ian's arm over his shoulder as if to carry

him to the car but Jennifer held up a hand to stop him. "There are beds here," she said. She knew Deb would absolutely flip out but the reality was Ian and Andille were in need of shelter and they had shelter to give.

The guy had practically paid for it anyway. She could not in good conscience let Andille haul their knight in rumpled Armani to a Motel Six. It would serve Ian right getting drunk on the day of his mother's funeral, but Andille looked exhausted.

For Andille and Annabelle, she would do this.

Part of her screamed a warning. The part that had cultivated this new life and wielded the sword with cold efficiency and was so terrified of feeling something again. That part wanted to slam the door and lock these men out in the night, where they couldn't entice her, couldn't nearly kiss her, couldn't beguile her with stories and blue eyes.

This is a mistake, she told herself. *You won't be able to go back from this.*

"Are you sure?" Andille asked and she could tell he wanted her to be sure. She could tell he wanted to collapse on a flat surface as soon as possible.

"Let me get you a key."

"You DID WHAT?" Deb whisper-yelled. She was not happy. Not at all.

"What was I supposed to do?" Jennifer whispered, looking over Deb's head to the hallway toward the rooms.

Not let him in, she answered her own question. *Send him to a hotel.*

But it was too late now.

Andille, who in the light of the kitchen had been even bigger than he'd seemed outside, had half carried and half dragged Ian to one of the spare beds. Deb had passed them in the hall and she and Jennifer had engaged in a whisper fight as soon as the men had been out of sight.

"The guy's mother died. It's late. They are clearly exhausted. I couldn't just—"

"Yes," Deb said, dreadlocks flying, "you could. Have you forgotten this is a women's shelter?"

"But it's not anymore, Deb." Jennifer was getting into semantics at this point but it was about all she had. "We haven't had women stay here like that for over a year. We're community-focused and frankly, I think the guy needs more help than we do."

"So, Ian Greer's going to spend the night? A drunk, womanizing—" Deb glanced at Spence, who stared wide-eyed in the corner "—man. Just bunking down in a former women's shelter?"

"He's the benefactor, Deb," Jennifer whispered back. "He practically owns the place. If he wants to sleep here, I don't think there's a lot of choice to it."

"He's the freaking son of the freaking former president of the United States," Deb whispered back. "He probably owns a hotel nearby he could stay in. This is nuts. And who is that Andille guy?"

"A bodyguard or something," Jennifer answered.

"What are you guys talking about?" Spence asked in a normal voice that sounded like gunfire in the quiet house.

"Shhhhhh!" Jennifer and Deb both turned on Spence.

"Who were those guys?" Spence asked, dropping his voice to a whisper. "What's going on?"

"Nothing." That big deep voice of Andille's echoed through the room and everyone snapped around to face him. Spencer grabbed on to Daisy.

Andille smiled and his face showed something so calming, so reassuring, that Jennifer nearly gasped. Without the drunken weight of Ian Greer at his side, the guy's vibe was positively serene.

Jennifer, in her other life, had interviewed Maya Angelou. Andille was about thirty times bigger than Maya, but he carried himself with the same peace. The same calm.

"Nothing that you need to be scared of," he said. "I promise you."

A diamond earring winked in his right earlobe and he wore a black suit. An incredibly well-tailored one, with a crisp white shirt and a pink tie.

The guy, tired and slightly road-wrinkled, was gorgeous.

Deb sucked in a breath, her whole body tight and still and radiating a certain fear and distrust.

"May I?" He gestured toward the kitchen and Jennifer realized the man was asking permission to join them.

"Sure," she said, waving him in.

He indicated her hand. "Mind if I ask you to disarm first?"

"Oh, my gosh, right." Jennifer laughed awkwardly and shoved the knife she'd picked up from the common room floor back into the block on the counter. Deb was still watching him out of narrowed eyes and Jennifer appreciated the woman's skeptical nature. It was hard-earned, but her holding that knife wasn't helping things. So she took the knife from Deb's weak grip and put it away.

"My name is Andille Jabavu-Fushai," he said, striding through the room to tower over Deb.

"What kind of name is that?" Deb asked, with all the graciousness of a half-starved guard dog.

"A family one. With a long history and a complicated spelling," Andille joked and Deb still scowled.

"I am Jennifer Stern," Jennifer said, putting her hand in Andille's giant paw. "This is my son, Spencer."

She turned slightly to include Spence, who stood, slack-jawed, at the table. Jennifer gave him a little jostle with her elbow and he lifted his hand in a wave, but didn't pick his jaw up off the floor.

"It is good to meet you," he said to Spence as if little boys stared at him all day long. "And your name?" Andille asked, throwing his considerable vibe toward Deb. She didn't even crack a smile. She eyed him up and down as if she'd seen such men a million times before.

Which couldn't be true. Jennifer had a hunch about Andille, that he was one of a kind.

"Deb Barber," Deb finally said.

"I'm sorry we scared you," he said, shaking Deb's hand, cast and all. "It's been quite a day."

Deb pulled her hand free and crossed her arms over her chest. "I guess so. Is that really Ian Greer back there?"

Andille nodded.

"And he's really the benefactor."

Andille nodded again.

Deb harrumphed.

"He usually makes a better first impression," Andille said, then yawned, covering his mouth with his fist. "Sorry. I've been driving for hours."

"There's one more room back there," Jennifer said. "You should feel free to go sleep."

"I will," he said with that deep voice and kind smile, and Jennifer found herself really liking the guy. "And we appreciate it. We do. I just want to reassure you that we mean you absolutely no harm. Ian got your call this morning and after the funeral, when the paparazzi started dogging him, he decided he needed to hide out and we decided to come here. Killing two birds with one stone."

"It's fine," Jennifer said and Deb shot her an incredulous look.

"We won't be here long," he said. "We'll clear up your banking and legal issues and be on our way."

"We appreciate the help," Jennifer said.

"Well." Andille locked eyes with her and Jennifer saw something scared there. Something worried and unsure and it stunned her. Shocked her. "We appreciate the break. After today…" He stopped and shook his head as if redirecting his thoughts. "After today a good night's sleep will be welcome."

"Let me get you the key to that room," Jennifer said, waving him toward the office where they'd gotten the key for Ian's room.

"No," Andille said, holding up a hand to stop her. "I'll bunk in with Ian. We've troubled you enough."

"You guys are our knights," she said, wanting to ease what she'd seen in his eyes. "It's the least we could do."

Andille laughed. "That's not anything I've been called since I was a kid, but it's nice you think so." He nodded slightly at her and then at Deb, like he was actually a knight, then turned and left the kitchen.

Spence let out a big breath and Daisy beside him seemed to relax, licking her nose. "Is he like a basketball player or something?" he asked.

"I have no idea," Jennifer said with a smile. "But I really like him."

Deb's head flipped around. "You bought that line of crap?" she asked.

"Crap?"

"I don't trust that man as far as I could throw him." Deb scowled. "Lock your doors tonight."

THERE WAS SOMETHING pounding in Ian's head. A hammer. Or a drum. Something loud and terrible. And painful. An army of hammers.

Fully clothed, in a suit even, he rolled—carefully trying not to anger that army—onto his back and found himself staring up at an unfamiliar ceiling.

Hmmm. He was alone in the bed under that unfamiliar ceiling and that was a very good thing. He could not handle anyone, naked and probably good and pissed off at him for any number of stupid things he might have done last night.

The sheets were rough. He poked out a toe and found the edge of the bed. The single bed. So, not a hotel. At least not a very nice one.

This was getting worrying.

His eyes were filled with sand and his mouth tasted dead and furry. And those hammers—the terrible pounding in his head—were his own blood.

Ten years clean and sober and apparently the wagon backed up and rolled over him a few times when he fell off of it.

"Andille?" His voice was a soundless rasp and he tried again. "Dille?"

"We're at Serenity House in North Carolina."

The name sounded familiar and Serenity certainly sounded better than jail.

Ian turned his head to see the mountain of his best friend under the sheets on a single bed on the other side of the narrow room.

"You acted like an ass and the women are nervous," Andille said, rolling onto his side. "Don't talk to me until noon."

"The funeral?" Ian asked, his skin prickling with dread and a pain so big, so thick and real it felt like fear. It felt like losing her all over again.

"You ruined it."

Ian rolled back over and grinned at the ceiling.

CHAPTER FOUR

TWO HOURS LATER Andille's snoring and the scent of coffee drove Ian from the small bedroom. The house was quiet, the narrow hallway he stood in was bright and shabby in the way that a lot of the shelters he'd toured and helped over the years were.

He followed the bitter tang of coffee into the kitchen where a woman—blond, thin and elegant—sat at a laptop on the table.

A shaft of sunlight illuminated her, gilding her hair, turning her pale skin into something…otherworldly.

His breath caught in his chest. She looked angelic. Like she truly belonged in a place called Serenity.

And she was talking to herself.

"At Serenity House the need for shelter," she mumbled, "was quickly usurped by the need for education and—" She paused. Grimaced. Tilted the screen to the laptop and thunked her head on the edge. "Stupid," she muttered. "Stupid."

"I don't think it sounded that bad," he said into the silence and the woman jumped, clamping the laptop shut.

A dog—a monster, really—leaped from the woman's feet and charged Ian, teeth bared and saliva dripping. Ian froze, prepared to be ripped apart.

His misbegotten life flashed before his eyes.

"Daisy!" the woman cried. "Stop!" The dog slowed but

didn't stop and was soon standing on Ian's feet, growling low in its throat. But not killing him. For the little things, Ian was grateful.

"Daisy?" Ian asked. It was like calling Godzilla sweetie.

"Yes." The woman cleared the table and got a hand on Daisy's collar, pulling her out the kitchen door. "She's our guard dog."

"She seems to like her job," he joked, feeling like he'd lost about five years of his life.

"Sorry about that," she said, shoving the dog onto the lawn. Her eyes, wild and brown—or rather amber, like whiskey—looked over him from top to bottom and frankly, scared the bejesus out of him.

Sharp. Focused. Being the attention of that gaze felt like being under a scalpel—without anesthesia. She looked at him and took him apart at the same time.

Then she blinked and the scalpel was gone. Instead there was a soft, stunning, slightly rumpled woman looking at him, a little detached, only vaguely curious.

The change made him dizzy.

He felt naked and he wished he was sober. Wished he smelled better. Wished he felt half as clean and pure as she appeared.

"No problem. It's probably handy to have an animal like that around a place like Serenity," he said, running a hand over his bed head. "I…ah…understand I owe you an apology."

She waved her hand between them. "You were drunk and tried to kiss me."

"I did?" His voice squealed slightly in his horror. This is why he didn't drink. Why he'd stopped ten years ago. He was an absolute idiot every time he did.

"Happens all the time. If I had a nickel for every time the sexiest man alive tried to kiss me, I'd be a rich woman."

He chuckled, relieved that he'd made an ass of himself with a woman with a sense of humor.

"I am so sorry," he said. "Truly. I was—"

"A mess," she supplied with a grin that was totally enchanting. And, transfixed, he found himself staring at her for a moment too long.

"So, you're our…secret benefactor?" she asked, looking away to fiddle with the corner of her laptop, because clearly this apology was going so well.

"I am," he answered, snapping out of his daze. "I am the benefactor of about a dozen community centers and women's shelters in North Carolina and another dozen in New Hampshire."

He saw the disbelief in her whiskey eyes. To be honest with himself—and he believed in being honest with himself because he wasn't honest with anyone else—he saw every headline, every tabloid photograph of him at a party with his arm around some actress, he saw every rumor and every scandal.

Really? her eyes said. *You?*

He nodded, answering her silent question. "It's complicated. My—" he swallowed the bitterness in his throat that never seemed to go away "—father was a lawyer here before he became Governor of North Carolina. I grew up not far from Northwoods."

"That explains it, I guess," she said, her voice indicating his answer didn't explain anything, which is what it was designed for.

The conversation stalled and he knew he should say something, but he was distracted by her hair. It was beautiful. A blond curtain, straight and shiny, and all one color. No highlights or lowlights or blue streaks or whatever else the women he usually spent time with did. Just a waterfall of real hair and he wanted to touch it, run his hands through it.

"Well, then." She cleared her throat and he told himself to get it together. "Welcome to Serenity. We're really glad you're here. We've had a little run of bad—"

He stopped her, crying surrender. "Coffee first, if you don't mind. I am more than ready to help, but I can't do it without coffee."

"I totally understand." She stepped away from the table toward the counter and the coffeepot that sat there, and he, because he was hungover and a terrible cad, checked out her long, long legs under the khaki shorts she wore.

She turned, steaming cup of salvation in her hand, and he, trying not to be caught staring, stepped toward the sink as if to wash up.

"The pipes are broken," she said. "We had to turn off the water. You can wash up in the bathroom."

"Coffee first," he said and took the mug from her.

He noticed the blue court papers on the table and gestured toward them, like they were a life raft and he was drowning.

"The legal problem?" he said.

At the same time she said, "Can I ask you something?"

"I'm sorry." He laughed. "I'm sure you have questions. Go ahead." Not that he would answer them. He took a sip of coffee and waited.

"Why—?" She paused and he had to hope she didn't finish the question. Why did he anonymously donate thousands of dollars to women's shelters? Or why did he show up drunk at his mother's funeral? Either way he wasn't going to tell her and they were on shaky ground already.

"Why do you let the world think the worst of you?" she asked.

A chill ran down his spine. His skin prickled uncomfortably. That was a first. What did she see in him that made her ask that question—that question that no one asked? That he no longer asked himself.

"What makes you think this is the worst?" he asked, forcing himself to meet her razor-sharp gaze.

"You're not what I expected," she said, her shrewd eyes narrowed as if she were squinting to see him better. "The stories in the tabloids don't match the guy who gives away thousands of dollars to community centers."

"Like I said, it's complicated." He took another sip of coffee and pretended he wasn't shaken. No one, not in a long time, had doubted those stories, the persona he showed the world.

Jennifer licked her lips and seemed, in his highly hung-over and possibly still intoxicated state, to be battling something. Arguing with herself. Something he used to do all the time before he beat his better sense into submission.

Don't do this to yourself, he wanted to say. *I'm not worth it.*

But after a second she waved her hand. "Never mind. It's none of my business," she said and pushed the papers across the table. "We're not too sure what the possible grounds are for Mrs. Conti to want to—"

Able to breathe again he tucked the papers in the pocket of his jacket. "I'll have a look," he said. "You don't need to worry about it anymore."

Her teeth caught her lower lip and he shouldn't have been turned on. Not by such a doubting gesture and because the blood pooling in his lap was mostly whiskey. But there it was. She bit her lip and he wanted to kiss her.

Cad. Cad. Cad.

Sweat ran down his back, cold and clammy, and he shrugged out of the suit jacket he'd slept in, trying to pretend he wasn't shaky and sweating in front of this woman, who seemed as calm and cool as a northern lake.

"I'd forgotten what kind of heat you have down here." It

reminded him of growing up and just the thought of his childhood down here made him raw. Aggravated.

"It's not usually this bad," she said. "Our air conditioner is broken."

"I guess I'll take care of that."

"I guess you will," she agreed.

If he shot himself in the foot, it couldn't get any worse. He struggled for conversation.

"You met Andille?" he said, watching her over the mug.

She smiled a different smile. An illuminating smile that only proved how false her earlier ones had been. And he could blame it on low sugar levels, his pounding headache, five years of celibacy, whatever, but that smile went right to his blood.

He wanted to swear at his own predictability. Hot actresses with loose morals and gorgeous pop stars dressed in less than nothing with Kama Sutra-like invitations in their eyes left him cold.

Give him a nice girl. A good girl, no doubt with white cotton underwear under those sensible khaki shorts, and he got excited.

You're sick, he chastised himself.

It's why he avoided these shelters. Helped them from afar. Because stepping foot into a place like Serenity was a guarantee he'd fall head over heels.

Sick and stupid, he amended.

"Andille was very gracious. He's—" She paused, as if searching for the right word.

"I know," he said, relieving her of that impossible task. "There's something about the guy that defies description. He's been like that since we met. Let me guess, the dog loved him."

She laughed. "Well, she didn't attack him."

"Dogs and kids love that guy."

"Have you known each other long?" She tilted her head, her scalpel eyes back.

"Since I was fourteen and he was ten," he said. "We met at boarding school. Within two weeks he was practically running the place."

She laughed then stared at her hands again and the air in the kitchen got heavy. Uncomfortable. All that charm he'd been blessed with was nowhere to be found. And for the first time in a long time, he floundered. Tongue-tied, he couldn't even make polite conversation.

Something in him just wanted to stare at her until he felt better. Like she could do that for him.

"I'm sorry about your mother," she said, her voice quiet and husky. "She was—"

He set the cup down with a thunk and she jumped.

"What?" he asked, his voice biting. Hard. He couldn't stop it. Couldn't call it back. His grief, his anger, was an animal out of control. Running him into corners.

"An inspiration," she whispered, those gorgeous eyes wide.

His lip curled and he shook his head. "You don't know my mother," he said.

"I met her," she protested. "I interviewed her two years ago."

"Interviewed?" His eyebrows clashed. "You're a journalist?"

She nodded. "I worked for the NBC affiliate out of Baltimore."

Oh, sure. Of course. He remembered the story— Camelot's Golden Years. A couple of news shows had picked it up and after years of not seeing his parents in the press, he'd sat, sick through the whole thing, watching his mother and father sit side by side on a couch, smiling. Pretending.

The woman running the interview had been sharp. All angles and corners—hardly recognizable from this soft, messy woman in front of him. Except maybe those eyes. The scalpel eyes were the same.

"That was you?" he asked, his voice hard, and she flinched slightly, but her chin came up, her eyes shot sparks.

"Your mother changed—"

"Your life?" he asked, mocking. He hurt, ached and bled in all the old places, and it was making him crazy. Hurtful. "Let me guess, she said something so wise. So smart and kind. And it did something to you. It changed the way you looked at the world. The way you looked at children or husbands or the way you wanted to live your life?"

"Yes," she answered. "That's exactly what happened."

He nodded, regret and anger burning through his veins like poison. Like acid. God. His mother. She was dead. Gone. And all she'd left behind was this legacy of lies.

"No one," he said, looking right at this woman and knowing he was taking something she valued and throwing it against the wall. "No one knew my mother. Not really."

And he left.

He left before he fell apart right in front of her.

STUPID, JENNIFER THOUGHT, opening her laptop. *That was incredibly stupid. Talking to him like that? Asking questions? Caring? What is wrong with you?*

Without a second thought, being ruthless and cold and hard-hearted, she deleted all the notes for the Serenity story she'd started working on early this morning. If only getting rid of her curiosity over Ian was as easy. But the sword wasn't working like it did yesterday. And Ian lingered in her head like a leech, unshakeable.

How many times do I have to tell you, she thought, *that life is gone? Those stories are no longer yours to tell.*

She should not have let him in. Her instincts had been right and now, stupidly, disastrously, Ian Greer was here.

he said. "There he was, ... I'm not ... the morning I.?
... a spacel ... ... Those damn phone lines ...
She should be Ban it him in his face, she had
right and was already on them in. Ian Greg and here.

CHAPTER FIVE

EARLY THE NEXT MORNING, leaving Spence still sleeping on the couch, Jennifer came downstairs looking for coffee and a reprieve from the morning heat. She'd wrestled with bad dreams and sleeplessness all night long, but with the sun's arrival she was determined to make the best of the Ian situation.

And by "make the best" she meant she'd stay out of his way and keep her mouth shut.

"Hey, Deb," she said, reaching for the coffeepot.

"Sink's still broken," Deb said, not looking up from the paperwork she was filling out at the kitchen table. She flipped a page decisively. "Air conditioner still isn't fixed and the two men you let stay slept all day yesterday." She sniffed. "Some benefactor."

"Message received," Jennifer said, lifting her hands in surrender. "But Ian and Andille are here and things should get fixed soon." Not that she knew that for a fact. After his tirade yesterday morning she hadn't seen hide nor hair of their benefactor all day long. Which was fine. More than fine. But it would be nice to get the pipes fixed. "Did you see them at all yesterday?"

"I saw Ian briefly," Deb answered. "Coming out of the bathroom, looking like death. And Andille spent most of the afternoon outside on the lawn on his phone." She snorted, and Jennifer wasn't sure if Deb disapproved of Andille or cell phones or lawns or the world in general.

Jennifer filled the coffeemaker with coffee and almost asked Deb what she thought of Ian, but it would have been useless. She knew what Deb would say and Jennifer had spent hours last night convincing herself she didn't care.

Shonny ran into the room and Deb stood, giving off enough chill that if she stayed mad long enough they wouldn't need an air conditioner.

"It's Sunday," Deb said. "We'll be outside."

The door slammed behind them and Jennifer, cursing under her breath, grabbed the coffee carafe and headed for the bathroom.

She ran smack into Ian's naked chest.

Every wall she'd built in the last two years fell down. Those things she'd told herself about men and dating and sex and how she wasn't interested were proven, in one heart-rending moment, to be utter lies.

After a two-year sleep her body woke up.

She went hot then cold as she took him in—all of him, every bare inch of him—in a heartbeat.

His skin, fresh from the shower, smelled clean. Masculine and foreign. Drops of water clung to his neck and the thick blond tips of his hair, and as she watched, one drop ran down his shoulder and she couldn't look away. She actually couldn't breathe as she waited to see where that drop would go.

He was muscled and smooth and her hand, her whole body, itched with the desire to touch him. To test the velvet texture of his skin.

"I...ah," Ian stammered, his hand clutching the knot of his towel. His hair clung to his forehead, making him look, of all things, like a boy, endearing and sweet—not at all like the drunk man who had shown up here.

Who are you? she wondered, caught up in this man's tide, her body out of control. *Who are you really?*

"I left my clothes in my room," Ian finished.

She should look away. Walk away. Tear out her eyes. But she couldn't. Doug had been thin, smallish. His chest had hair and it had been years since she'd touched it. Years since her skin burned like this. Years since she'd wanted another man. And she stood here, shaking and trembling for Ian Greer.

The realization was horrific. Terrifying.

What am I doing? she thought, disgusted with herself. Comparing this man to her husband? What was wrong with her?

I'm a married woman.

"Don't worry," she snapped, waving it off as if naked men wandered the hallway all the time. "Just be careful Deb doesn't see you."

Her balance thrown, her equilibrium gone, her body burning for reasons she'd been sure were left behind two years ago, she turned and left. Mentally, she reached for that sword. It was gone. Burned to ash by the sudden heat. The shock was astonishing. She felt betrayed. Out of control.

Having Ian Greer here was tearing her carefully constructed world apart.

DEB BELIEVED in prayer. She loved prayer, actually. She wanted to eat it, drink it. She wanted to roll herself up in it and wear it every day like her nana's sweater.

She loved prayer as much as she loathed church.

Daddy had been a preacher and that man was enough to put anyone off religion.

But despite Daddy and his evil, Deb saw God everywhere. In Shonny. In Serenity. In the sky and dirt and broken-down cars.

And since she didn't go to church, she took her son outside every morning, had since he was a baby. She could laugh about it now, the way God had worked in her life, because she had been stepping outside at Serenity House to the old willow tree out front in order to praise and thank God since she was a twenty-year-old kid. Since she'd been beaten so badly by Daddy that she nearly lost her baby.

That willow tree was her church now. Shonny all the congregation she needed.

And this morning she needed some prayer. She needed to ask for some strength and some guidance because there were men at Serenity House. After years of a man-free life, a life she cultivated and cared for like a garden, they were suddenly underfoot, and had been for two days and it was giving her some grief. Andille Jabavu-Fushai, with his charm and sly grins, was screwing up her calm.

The morning sunshine warmed her neck and the smell of asphalt heating up under the Carolina heat made Shonny sneeze.

"Bless you, baby," she said, following her son as he led her to the willow. He darted under the long, whip-thin branches that hung nearly to the ground and she parted them with her cast, stepping into the shadowed cave.

"I'll sing!" Shonny yelled, jumping up to try and grab some of the dangling branches.

"Lay it on me, son," she said, sitting in the dirt and roots, her back against the trunk.

Shonny launched himself into "This Little Light of Mine." He sang like he did everything, with his whole body, and screaming at the top of his lungs. Deb sat back and drank it in. At some point "This Little Light of Mine" morphed into "Go Tell It on the Mountain" and he looked at her as if he knew something wasn't right.

"Keep on going," she urged, trying to teach him at this very young age that keeping on in the face of your mistakes was the only thing to do.

"Go tell it on the mountain." A voice so deep it resonated through her belly and down her legs, like it came up from the very center of the earth, joined Shonny's high childish soprano. That voice could only belong to one person and Deb jerked upright, reaching for her son, just as Andille parted the willow-branch curtain and ducked in.

"That Jesus Chri— Oh." Andille stopped singing and he stood upright, the top of his head nearly touching the lowest branches. The long willow leaves hung over his shoulders. "I heard singing," he said, flashing that wicked smile that made Deb feel as though there were a hundred bees under her skin dying to get out, "and couldn't resist."

"We're praying," Shonny said and Deb tugged him closer, stroking his arm. She didn't like that man so close to her boy. So close to her. Frankly, she wouldn't like that man if he went back to where ever he'd come from.

Lord, please give me strength and patience. Help me to deal with this man.

There. Praying done. Time to leave since the sanctity of her altar had been messed up by this man barging in.

"I see," he said, smiling at Shonny. "I'll let you get back to it." He turned to go and she noticed his clothes. Not as fine as the suit from two days ago, but the man still looked good. The suit had been replaced by cargo shorts, a red-and-blue plaid shirt and a pair of running shoes. The earring was still there, twinkling against his skin.

Temptation, her father's utterly unwanted voice rang through her head. *Sinful temptation.* The diamond and the man.

Andille was handsome, more handsome and more manly

than a man had a right to be, but life had taught her to distrust the packaging when it looked so good.

"Deb?" he said, turning back before leaving. "Have I offended you in some way?" His brow furrowed. "I am sorry for the way we arrived and I can certainly understand how Ian's behavior might be—"

"I'm not offended," she said, truthfully. Part of her froze in sudden fear at his questions—a little something left over in her head from Daddy. And while she didn't want to answer this man's questions, she wasn't going to run. Not her. Not anymore.

"Really?" His lips twisted at the corners. "Because you're acting like you don't like me."

"I don't know you enough to like you or not like you," she said.

"Well," he said, "there's something about me you don't like."

"I don't like you here," she snapped and something in Andille paused. He lost his shine and she guessed not many people didn't like being around the man. "Shonny, baby, why don't you go inside and get yourself a banana. I'll be in in a second." Her boy was off like a shot. Deb stood and brushed off her pants, gathering up every scrap of herself to stand in the face of this man who upset her balance. The balance she protected at all costs.

"You called us here," he reminded her.

"We called you," she agreed. "But we never expected two men on our doorstep to stay for two days."

"Ah," he said, his eyes getting wide. "So, it's not just me. You'd be throwing off this kind of attitude to any man who came here."

She wanted to scoff at his generalizations. Like she was that textbook. But, frankly, she was. She knew that. She was trying to work on it and having this man here wasn't helping her.

"That may be," she said, knowing the truth when she heard it. "But my job is to protect the women who come to this shelter."

"I mean no harm," he said, his face thunderous.

"Then help us," she said, "and get on your way."

He stared at her for a long time, taking in her dreadlocks and her rhinestone glasses and hot pink casts, and for a second under that man's chocolate gaze she lost herself. All those things she wore and did that made her feel so good, so in control and in charge of herself, faded and she was sixteen again, wanting just one man in her life to be kind.

And she hated it. And she hated him for making her feel that way again.

"I need to go," she said.

She parted the willow branches and stepped out into the sunlight, and behind her she heard Andille murmur, "I guess we do, too."

JENNIFER AND SPENCE were headed to the classrooms for the children's empowerment session when someone pounded on the door.

"Go ahead," she urged her son, who was excited about this class. She had a feeling his enthusiasm was more about Laura's older daughter than it was about Twister or any other game. "I'll be right there."

He took off at a run and she backtracked to the common room and the front door.

She opened the door to a man wearing a grey coverall suit holding a clipboard. A patch over his chest read Bob.

"Can I help you?" she asked.

"Yeah," Bob said in a thick Jersey accent. "We're here to look at the central air."

"We don't have—"

"Hey, Bob," Ian said from behind her and she felt every muscle tense. Every bone go rigid. Since his appearance in a towel this morning she'd been hoping maybe he'd disappear—fall into a hole, or some starlet's arms—and she wouldn't have to see him ever again. Apparently, no such luck.

"Come on in." Ian stepped up beside her, pushing the screen door open farther, and she stepped away from the heat of him before there was even a chance of them casually touching.

"We don't have central air," she reiterated.

"Not yet," Ian said and before she could stop herself she glanced up at him. His golden beauty was undiminished by a day-old beard and rumpled clothes. He wore jeans and a T-shirt and his wattage was up full blast.

She remembered his chest. That drop of water.

She looked away before she was blinded. Or embarrassed.

There had been enough of that in this man's company.

Her reaction to him this morning had been simple biology. She was bound to be attracted to someone at some point. The only strange thing was that it was for a man so unlike her husband.

She was simply a woman alone for too long. A woman who missed her husband.

Another man approached the front door wearing a ball cap and carrying a toolbox.

"Hiya, Ian," he said, as if they were old friends.

"Hey, George. Problem's in the kitchen," Ian said, jerking his thumb in that direction. "Unless," he asked Jennifer, "you have some other leaks you need looked at?"

"No," she said. A plumber and an air-conditioning guy,

on the same day—maybe Ian would be gone sooner rather than later. "It's just in the kitchen."

George stepped past her, tipping his hat slightly on the way toward making their faucet problems disappear.

Bob stepped in and started talking about duct work and furnace rooms.

"I'll show you," she said quickly and led him to the furnace room in the bedroom wing of the house, eager to be out of Ian's company.

Bob clucked and murmured at the duct work and the furnace.

"Is there anything I can do to help?" she asked.

"Nah," he said. "We've been updating these shelters across Carolina for months now," he said, tapping at the silver square ducts with a penknife. "This one is in pretty good shape. Should have a system in here in no time."

Ian's other shelters, she realized. He'd grown up here, which explained why he had decided to fund shelters in North Carolina instead of in, say, Montana. But it didn't explain anything else about him.

There's more to him, she thought. *More to him than being the sexiest man alive. More to him than his smile and blue eyes.*

And you, she told herself, ignoring that itch and tingle down her neck, *don't care.*

But she wasn't even close to believing it.

IAN WATCHED Jennifer leave, hoping the quick addition of central air would be a good enough apology for his tirade yesterday. And that shower thing this morning. But frankly, the way she'd ogled him, maybe she should apologize to him.

She'd walked away this morning and he'd headed back to the bathroom for a cold shower. Just thinking of the way she'd looked at him—the naked desire and raw heat in her eyes—had him breathing deeply for a minute.

In the silence of the common room, the dark screen of the television beckoned. He had to believe his mother's death and whatever scene he'd caused at her very public memorial would still be news.

Eager to see what the world thought of his latest escapade he searched for the remote.

"We need to leave," Andille said, stepping into the house and, for just a moment, blocking the sun.

"What do you mean leave?" Ian asked, finally finding the remote and turning on the TV. "I've got Bob here putting in central air, George looking at the pipes and I haven't even read the legal papers."

"Trust me," Andille said. "We can fix Serenity's problems on the road. These women don't want us here."

Ian paused in his search for CNN. "I know what I did," he said, thinking of Jennifer. "But what did you do?"

"Well—" Andille scowled "—apparently I was born a man and that was enough to give Deb a reason to hate me." He narrowed his eyes. "What did you do?"

"Besides show up drunk and try to kiss Jennifer?"

Andille nodded.

"And then hide out, hung over most of the day yesterday?"

Andille nodded.

"I might have flipped out on Jennifer when she told me she was sorry about my mom."

Andille sighed and looked up at the ceiling.

"Maybe you're right," Ian said, scrolling through the channels. "We can do all this stuff on the road. We don't—"

Fox News had him. Or rather a picture of him passed out in the back row of the memorial service. His arm around a woman he didn't even know.

Excellent.

Then the still picture changed to a live press conference. And it was Jackson Greer standing behind a podium, looking as presidential as ever. He smiled, smug and self-righteous while flashbulbs went off all around him. There was not a strand of gunmetal-grey hair out of place. His red power tie was straight and tied perfectly. Looking at him, you'd never ever guess that just days ago, his wife of thirty-eight years had died after a painful battle with cancer.

There was not an inkling of grief. Of regret. Remorse.

Looking at him, Ian's blood thickened with anger and it hurt as it pounded through veins that were suddenly too small. His vision blurred and a numbness was spreading through his body, clearing the way for the blinding rage that was sure to follow.

"What the hell is he doing now?" Andille said, coming to stand beside Ian. Andille took the remote from Ian's numb hand and turned up the volume.

Ian's father, the former president of the United States, slid on a pair of reading glasses, cleared his throat and the whole room went silent.

Ian bared his teeth, waiting for the latest from dear old Dad.

"In the wake of Annabelle's death our son, Ian, has checked himself into a rehab clinic in California." Jackson lied right into the camera and Ian's breath escaped in a surprised gust. Jackson's polar-blue eyes seemed to reach right through the distance and glass to curl around Ian's throat, cutting off even the possibility of taking in another breath. "Realizing that his behavior was an embarrassment to his mother's legacy, he understood that the only thing he could do was clean up his act. He has my support in this decision and, I hope, the support of all Americans, who will see his behavior on the day of Annabelle's funeral as that of a man with problems and grief outside of his control."

Parasitic journalists swarmed Jackson Greer and he held up a hand, displaying all the gravitas of a former leader of the free world. Magically the journalists shut up and stepped back, letting Jackson walk away, unscathed. His lies unquestioned.

Andille swore and Ian swayed slightly on his feet.

The image on the screen changed and showed an aerial view of Ian's apartment in Manhattan, where there was nothing less than a three-ring circus. Crowds of people stood at the front gate, which was practically choked by flowers and teddy bears.

"Dear God," Andille murmured.

"I can't go home," Ian said, watching the screen. "There are helicopters circling my apartment. Thanks to my father."

"Well," Andille said, turning to face him, leaning his bulk against the couch, "you aren't exactly innocent. You put on quite a show at your mother's funeral."

Ian chewed on his lip, his hands shaking as he ran them through his hair.

"He thinks he's won." Ian sneered, the edges of his vision going dark. "He thinks I won't come out and prove him to be a liar. A fraud."

"What do you want to do?" Andille asked. Ian turned to him, saw the weariness and concern there, and it pissed Ian off. Andille thought he should stop. Everyone thought he should stop.

"You want to tear up a club in New York City?" Andille asked, like he was bored of the whole thing. "Show up pretending to be drunk at some charity event your dad will be at? What's your move, Ian?"

"We've done all those things," Ian said and Andille laughed, but it was humorless and tired.

"You can leave anytime, Dille," Ian snapped. "I haven't asked you to stay."

"How can I leave?" Andille asked, standing upright, a reminder of all that could go wrong in the world. A reminder that the world could be a brutal place.

Not that Ian needed any more reminders.

The silence between them was charged. Electric.

"I owe you more than I can say," Andille said. "So, I can't leave and watch you run yourself into the ground for this vengeance you crave."

Ian smiled despite the tension. Andille's tribal heritage appeared in the strangest places. Andille hadn't lived in his country since he was ten and, though he'd been raised by European and American boarding schools, he was still bound by a tribal African system of checks and balances. Earthly favors and cosmic retribution.

"So, you're going to stay and watch me run myself into the ground?" Ian tried to joke.

Andille didn't laugh and Ian suddenly felt so old. So tired. Years in the spotlight were taking their toll. This chess game he engaged in with his father was wearing him down to nothing. He couldn't keep taking these weak shots at the old man. He needed something final. Something that would end this nightmare once and for all.

Ian looked back at the television, where pictures of his mother flashed across the screen.

His mother at readings. At state dinners. With Ian on her lap. Standing beside her husband. Those sunglasses. The high mandarin collars. Each picture a slice across his skin, a burning reminder of why he needed to destroy his father.

She was gone. He could remember her face, her smell, the touch of her hand across his forehead as if she were right there with him. And the fact that she wasn't and would never be again was crushing.

Wait a second.

Static buzzed in his head.

She was gone. His promise to her was void. He was freed, suspended for a moment in a disbelief so profound, he could barely think. Then he could only laugh as the bittersweet joy of his emancipation bubbled through him.

"Ian?" Andille asked, clearly wondering if he'd totally lost it.

"Andille," he said, grabbing his friend's shoulder. "I know exactly what we're going to do." He smiled into Andille's confused face. "And it's going to kill him. End him. He will be totally and utterly destroyed."

"What's your plan?" Andille asked warily.

"I'm going to tell the truth."

CHAPTER SIX

SPENCE WAS IN LOVE. He was sure of it.

Last night he'd written about Madison Jones in his notebook and when he wrote stuff in his notebook it was for real. Carved in stone, as his mom would say. And last night he'd written *I love Madison Jones.*

"Where was your mom today?" Spencer asked as he and Madison walked toward the kitchen for a snack after the class. Deb had told them to go because she had another class to teach and Madison's mother still hadn't shown up to get her.

"She didn't feel well," Madison said, pushing her long hair off her face. It was, like, the blondest hair he'd ever seen. One of his reasons for liking her.

"So, how come your sister didn't come?" he asked.

"Angelina doesn't go anywhere without Mom," Madison said with just a little sneer. "Do you have a little sister or brother?"

Spence looked over his shoulder at Shonny, who followed, picking his nose. "Sort of," he said.

"Him?" she asked, glancing at Shonny. "He's black."

"So?" Spence asked. His best friend in Asheville was Claude, a kid from Haiti who had two moms. The world is a different place, his mom always said.

"Is he like, adopted?"

"No," he answered, "but I am."

"You are?" she asked, turning to him like he was something exotic at the zoo.

He nodded, uncomfortable.

"Wow." She sighed. "I totally wish I was adopted."

It was such a weird thing for her to say that he didn't know what to say back. "It's all right" was finally what popped out of his mouth.

"So, Deb is his mom," she said pointing to Shonny. "Then who is your mom?"

"Well." He sighed. This stuff got so complicated. "My *mom* mom is Jennifer Stern. But my birth mom is Samantha Riggins. She usually runs Serenity but she's on vacation."

Madison nodded then turned to Shonny, who stood grinning at them.

Madison smiled. Her front tooth was missing and it was his second reason for liking her. "So do you live here?"

"Not all the time."

She looked at him directly and Spence's heart beat a little faster. She was so pretty. Her eyes were green. Like grass. He'd never met anyone with grass-green eyes before.

"You like it here?" she asked.

"I love it here," he said. "We've got a swimming pond. And there are a bunch of trails out back and I can ride my bike—"

"My dad says this place is for losers."

"Losers?" Spence asked, not getting it.

"Yeah," she said. "He says that only women who are total losers and don't know how to handle their lives come here."

"You and your mom come here," he said.

She bit her tongue so it poked out through the gap in her teeth. That was cool. "You're right," she said and started walking again. "What have you got for a snack around here?"

"Well—" They pushed through the swinging door into the

kitchen, where all the pipes under the sink had been taken
out, and he paused at the sound of that guy Andille's voice.
He was arguing with someone in the common room.

"Ian," Andille said. "There aren't any journalists who are
going to take you seriously."

"They don't have to take me seriously," another voice said.
"They just have to take the story seriously. This is the biggest
story American politics has seen since Monica Lewinsky."

Spence grabbed Madison's shirt and started to pull her out
of the kitchen. She yanked away from him and held a finger
up to her mouth. Slowly she snuck along the wall toward the
common room.

She was going to spy!

She waved at him to follow, but he shook his head.

Mom said no spying. He'd made a promise because she
hated it so much. She said if there was something he wanted
to know, he should just ask. But spying was sneaky and mean.

Mom had a real thing about mean.

"Don't be a baby," Madison mouthed at him and his skin
prickled. He loved her and she was calling him a baby. He
didn't know much about girls, but he was pretty sure that wasn't
a good way to get her to be his girlfriend. He looked at Shonny,
who watched him with big eyes, and decided just this once
wouldn't hurt. It's not like they were spying on Mom or Deb.

He held his finger up to his own mouth so Shonny would
know not to talk then tiptoed after Madison. His heart
pounded hard in his chest.

Man, if Mom found him he'd be so busted. But he got up
close to Madison and her bare arm pressed against his and
he totally forgot about mom.

"*Sixty Minutes, Twenty/Twenty,* even *Dateline* won't do
it," Andille said.

Spence knew those shows. His mom watched them.

"This is boring," Madison whispered.

"Yeah," he agreed, happy for a reason to get out of the kitchen. He turned, ready to leave.

"Jennifer Stern is a journalist, isn't she?" Ian said and Spence whirled back around and elbowed Madison out of the way to get closer.

They were talking about Mom. His mom.

No way he was leaving now.

"Is she?" Andille asked then laughed. "I doubt she'd do the story, either. Not after all you've done."

"I'll worry about that," Ian said in a tone that made the hair on the back of Spence's neck stand up. "A journalist will forgive a lot of things for a scoop."

One of the men stepped toward the kitchen and Madison yanked on Spencer's arm, trying to get him back to the hallway. He pushed her away, wanting to hear what else they were going to say about his mom, but Madison was really strong and she got a good hold of him and he was dragged backward even while he strained forward.

They hit the swinging door and she tripped and he lost his balance and they both fell onto the floor in the hallway.

"Are you nuts?" she asked, laughing. "You were going to get caught!"

"You did get caught." He heard his mom's voice and slowly turned to see Mom, Deb and Shonny watching him.

"You were spying, weren't you?" Mom asked, crossing her arms over her chest. Oh, boy. She was mad. "On our guests?"

"No," Madison said.

At the same time, Spence confessed. "Yes."

"Spence…" Mom was talking but her lips weren't moving, which was never a good sign. Last time that happened he'd been grounded from his skateboard for a week. "What did I say about—"

"Spence," Deb said, cutting in on Mom. "What were they talking about?"

"Deb!" Mom cried.

"I'm just saying if he heard something, we should know." Deb looked back at Spence. "So? What did you hear?"

Spence wondered for a second what was happening with these two men here and what they would want with his mom, who could be nice. And could be cool. But mostly she was just Mom.

"They were talking about you," he told her.

IT TOOK A SECOND for Spence's words to compute. "What do you mean?" Jennifer asked. "What were they saying?"

Spence shrugged and she knew he was uncomfortable having been caught and now being forced to tattle.

Frankly, she was uncomfortable, too. This went against all her parenting rules. But when Ian Greer is talking about you behind your back the rules are different.

"I don't know," Spence said. "He was talking about journalists and how he had a story."

A story. Again, with her skin, itching and buzzing along her hairline, making her fingers numb.

It's probably a story about how he screwed some actress. You're not interested.

Oh, but she was. She really really was.

"The other guy was saying no one would believe him," Madison offered, apparently comfortable in the role of tattle and spy.

"Yeah," Spence said. "He said it was a big story. Bigger than—" He couldn't remember it all. "Something Lewinsky."

"Monica?" Jennifer asked, her voice breaking over the sudden excitement.

"Yep." Spence nodded. "He said it was bigger than that."

"He said it was a scoop!" Madison added helpfully.

Jennifer's head spun. Bigger than Lewinsky? Perhaps it was a story about his father's love life. Or political career. That would be big, but it would be dirty.

But a scoop?

Her blood pumped hard, deliciously hard, and she knew the man was devious. A liar, no doubt, but she couldn't help herself. The journalist in her was salivating.

A scoop. From Ian Greer. She should at least hear him out.

"This whole thing is getting weirder the longer they're here," Deb said.

"You're right," Jennifer agreed, preoccupied with what this story could be. "I think I need to have a conversation with Ian Greer."

"I'll take the kids out back," Deb said, ushering the three kids toward the exit. Jennifer charged right into the common room, smacking the door with her palm and interrupting whatever conversations about her Ian and Andille were having.

Ian looked startled before he put on his charming smile. A mask, she realized. That smile and that charm were all a mask.

A handsome one, her hormones reminded her, noting how the day's sunlight seemed to gild Ian all over.

But what was he hiding behind all that charm?

"We need to talk," she said.

Andille sighed wearily, and she wondered what had happened that had aged him since the last time she'd seen him, because he seemed older. Smaller somehow, like the weight he carried was wearing him down.

"I'll be in our room," he said to Ian and headed down the hallway.

"If it's about the sink—" Ian gestured to the mess in the kitchen "—George went to get some parts. He assures me it will be fixed by tonight."

"This is not about the sink."

Ian turned up the wattage on his smile and she held up a hand to stop him before he could even get started.

"I want you to understand that we appreciate all that you do for Serenity." That didn't quite cover it and she wanted to be honest. Nothing but honest, so that hopefully he would do the same. "Without you and the money and the help you're providing, we wouldn't be here today. And we thank you."

Ian looked slightly baffled. "It's my pleasure," he said. "Sincerely."

Right, she thought, his record of helping shelters seemed oddly suspicious. Like a man desperate to balance his karmic scales.

"And we have no problem with you and Andille staying here should you need it." She stressed the word *need,* because frankly, the guy could afford the penthouse suite at any Hilton within a hundred-mile radius. He didn't need to be here.

"Ah." Realization dawned across his handsome face and she knew that for all of his faults, the guy wasn't dumb. "You're wondering why a man of my wealth is choosing to sleep here? Right?"

"Well, you have to understand that your choosing to is…odd." She smiled. "I've slept on those beds back there. And doing so for more than one night could be considered masochistic."

He didn't laugh. He didn't even smile, this man who smiled through life. Instead, he watched her through suddenly cool blue eyes and she felt assessed by his gaze. As if he were taking her apart bit by bit and examining what he'd found.

Her skin prickled in sudden heat. She was all too aware of him, standing just an arm's distance away, emanating a certain controlled speculation. A barely harnessed power. Her chest was tight and she'd never in her whole life felt so naked.

The guy was a shark and she had the distinct impression she was dinner.

"I saw that interview you had with my parents. It was good," he said, changing the subject so totally it took her a second to regroup. But once she did, energy and adrenaline surged through her.

"Thank you."

"But why you?" he said, tilting his head. "My parents didn't give interviews after Dad left office. And Mother rarely did them during."

"She was my husband's godmother," she said with a shrug. The words were sticky in her mouth and she realized she didn't want to talk about Doug, not with Ian. Not with anyone. She'd left this grief behind. New life and old life were getting muddled and she didn't like that. Wanted to run screaming from that.

Ian's brow furrowed. "Godmother?" he murmured then smiled. "Doug Stern is your husband?"

Was, she thought, but didn't say. Instead she nodded, because her throat was so tight. So dry.

"When I was little my mom and her best friend, Missy—"

"Doug's mother," she said, her voice reed-thin so she smiled to bolster it.

No one talks about him anymore, she realized. *Not even Spence.* So, it was doubly strange to talk about him with Ian.

"Right. We would spend a week on the shore every summer," he said. "Doug's a little older than me, but wow—" He laughed, incredulous. "Small world, huh?"

She nodded.

"Where is he now?"

Jennifer sucked in a breath, wondering where all the oxygen had gone.

"Jennifer?" Ian placed his hand on the bare skin of her

arm and it was as if every molecule of her body jumped. Leaped. She felt his heat through her blood, across her skin right to the tips of her hair, like an electrical current, and she jerked away from him.

To feel Ian while talking about Doug—what the hell was wrong with her?

"He's dead," she blurted, shocked by her body.

Ian stood there, his arm out as if he were still touching her, his face fallen. "I'm so sorry," he whispered.

And God, it was all so real—his sincerity and remorse—that it infuriated her. She didn't need this right now.

"I don't understand what any of this has to do with why you're choosing to stay at Serenity," she snapped and his hand dropped. His face changed, all that warmth and earnestness vanished, and the shark was back.

"Did you know my father?"

She shook her head, clenching her hands together, trying to rub feeling into her fingers. "He was only part of the interview and even then he didn't answer many of the questions."

Ian took a deep breath and stepped toward her and she was locked in place by the appeal in his eyes. "What I am about to tell you, I haven't told anyone, except Andille. Ever."

The air was filled with thick heavy currents that she didn't understand and she had the distinct impression that, whatever was about to happen, whatever was about to fall from his lips, might just change her life. She couldn't have moved if she wanted to.

He was magnetic. Hypnotizing.

"Hello!" a woman cried from the hallway leading to the classrooms. "Anyone home? Madison?"

But whatever life-changing event was going to happen was interrupted.

Jennifer sagged and Ian stepped back, all that magnetism banked. All his shrewdness gone. She blinked, stunned by his transformation. The shark was gone, affable Ian Greer was back.

She wanted to scream from the tension in her stomach.

"Anyone— Oh!" Laura burst into the kitchen in a cloud of long blond hair and sunglasses. "Jennifer," she said, frowning slightly. "You're here. I can't find Madison." She glanced over at Ian then did a double take. "Do I—"

"Madison is out back," Jennifer said, directing Laura toward the door, for some reason wanting to protect all of them from the fact that Ian Greer was actually standing in her kitchen. She simply didn't have the energy. "Deb has all the kids down by the pond."

"Great. Thanks again for keeping her a little later," Laura said, ruffling her bangs so they fell over her sunglasses in a fancy sweep.

"It's not a problem, but we're not a babysitting service," Jennifer said, perhaps a bit more sharply than she intended, but she was having a pretty tough time keeping things all together.

Laura's back went straight and her perfect smile faded.

"Right," she said, subdued, and Jennifer felt bad. Truly bad. The woman was new in town.

"I'm sorry, Laura," she said quickly. "It's been one of those days. I really didn't mean to take it out on you. Madison is welcome anytime, she and Spence have really hit it off."

"Oh, I understand," Laura said, her good graces seemingly restored, though it was hard to tell with those sunglasses. "I'll go get her out of everyone's hair."

Laura left in a swirl of hair and perfume and Jennifer steeled herself before facing Ian.

"One of the shelter's abused women?" Ian asked, his face a white mask. Expressionless.

"Laura?" she said, taken aback by his question and suddenly stony demeanor. "No. Not at all. She's just new to town."

"Is that what she told you?"

"Yes, but—"

Ian's laugh was cold and they both turned to watch Laura and Madison walking through the backyard. Laura was practically dragging a reluctant Madison across the lawn.

It wasn't a pretty scene.

"She was hiding bruises under those sunglasses," Ian said and Jennifer turned to him, exasperated.

"Isn't that a bit cliché?" she asked. "You see a woman at a shelter in sunglasses and you assume she's hiding a black eye."

Ian's eyes were ice blue and they froze her to the spot. "It's a cliché because it's true. A woman has to go out in the world. Pick up her children. Get groceries. And when that woman has a black eye, sunglasses cover it up."

"How would you even know?" she said. "Laura told me—"

"I know," he said, stepping toward her, his voice a burning whisper, "because I saw it a million times. I know because my mother had to do it."

Jennifer blinked, reeled back a step. So stunned by his sudden intensity, his sudden vulnerability, that the words he said didn't make sense. "What are you saying?"

"My mother used to hide the bruises her husband gave her under sunglasses and high-necked suits and heavy makeup."

"Her husband? You mean—"

"I mean Jackson Greer, former president of the United States, abused my mother. For years. And I want you to help me tell the world."

CHAPTER SEVEN

IAN COULDN'T FEEL his hands. Actually, the more he thought about it, he couldn't feel his body. It was as if he'd vanished. Dissipated into mist.

He wanted to sag onto the floor and relish this freedom. Finally. Thirty years of harboring this terrible secret. Of carrying it like stones that only got heavier. That only got bigger. More and more unmanageable. Finally it was gone.

He took deep breaths and fought the urge to laugh, knowing it would make him look even more crazy. Relief, adrenaline and a strange kind of fear bubbled through him like champagne and he wanted to hug Jennifer. Thank her for letting him tell her.

Mom, he thought, feeling so much he could hardly contain it. He wanted to laugh. Cry. *Mom, I'm sorry, but I just can't keep this secret anymore.*

What he really wanted, more than anything, more than ever before, was to see his father. To look him right in those cold, callous eyes and tell him the truth was coming after him. Finally. The real Jackson Greer was going to be revealed to the world.

Ian had never realized it before, but he'd been living for this. Breathing. Sleeping. Working to start this ball in motion for thirty years. All of his efforts to embarrass his father, to bring terrible shame to the Greer family name, had been preparation for this plan. This moment. Thirty years. Since he realized what those sounds from his parents' bedroom really were.

"You're making this up," Jennifer said. "This is just—" She stopped and stared at him, openmouthed. Bright red flags lit up her pale cheeks and her hands were clenched into hard, bone-white fists.

"Crazy?" he asked. "Preposterous?"

"Insane."

"I know," he agreed. "Trust me. I know."

She shook her head. "This is some kind of trick of yours. Some kind of—"

"I wish it was." He swallowed a lump in his throat. "You have no idea how many times in my life I wished I was wrong. That I had made it all up or dreamed it. But—"

Jennifer still wasn't buying it and his emotions, wild and out of control, slowed down. His heart stopped pounding. He saw his situation for what it was—precarious. "I swear," he told her looking as deeply into those guarded whiskey eyes as he could, "that this is true."

"How could she have hidden it?" she asked. "He was the president!"

"By the time they got to the White House my father had stopped." He thought of that summer between terms when he'd convinced his mother to come visit him in New York City and the bruise on her arm that they didn't talk about. "Mostly."

Jennifer stared at him then put her head in her palms, fisting her hair in her hands.

He'd expected this reaction. He'd have been stupid not to. And he knew that loading her down with this information then trying to force her to believe it wouldn't work.

She would need space. Time.

But hopefully not too much.

"I know this is hard to assimilate," he said. She laughed roughly in her throat. "I know you'll need time—"

"Time will make me believe you?" she asked. "You showed up here drunk on the day of your mother's funeral and now you're telling me she was abused through her whole marriage. A marriage that the whole world saw. That millions emulated. That I emulated." She laughed. "Let me tell you, time isn't going to make me believe you."

"What will?"

"Do you have proof? Doctors? Someone? Anyone?"

"Other than me?" he asked, knowing sadly that the reputation he'd cultivated was what was making it hard to believe him.

She nodded, her eyes hard and flinty, and he saw the journalist in her and it warmed him. This was the right decision. She would believe him, in time. She had to.

"Our family doctor has all our records," he said, leaving it vague, scared of telling her more without her promise to tell the whole story. His way.

She stared at him, blinking, and he could see the wheels turning. "This is the story my son heard you talking about?"

Ian blinked, caught flat-footed. "I was talking about this, I wasn't aware he was listening."

I wasn't aware you had a son.

"This is your big scoop?" she said, as if checking.

He nodded. "This is a big story." He took a step toward her. "You know that."

"If it were true it would be huge!"

They were at a standstill, and he knew there was nothing he could say right now that would convince her.

"I'm going to check on Bob and the air-conditioning," he said. "I would ask that you not talk to anyone about this."

"Who would believe me?" she asked.

He chewed on his lip, feeling awkward. Vulnerable. "The press and most of the world believes the very worst about me," he said. "And I live with that. But if this story got out in a way that I couldn't control…" He thought of all the ways he'd hurt his mother, all the times she'd looked the other way while he tried to draw blood from Jackson Greer. If the world thought this was just another stunt of his, it would kill him. "I couldn't live with myself," he told her.

She didn't say anything. She didn't appear to be breathing. Or blinking.

"I'll be around if you want to talk," he told her, hoping he'd done enough. That he'd not made the biggest mistake of his life.

"Ian?" He turned back to her, hope surging in his chest.

"Did you love your mother?" she asked, stripping him bare.

His eyes burned and he had to look away from her, had to gather himself together because she'd scattered him to the wind, blown him into pieces. He couldn't find himself anymore, not without the secret he'd harbored. The anger he'd cultivated and carried. But he knew the truth—*his* truth—like a bright, white light guiding him on. "More than anything," he said and he left.

He left his entire fate in Jennifer Stern's hands.

ON AUTOPILOT Jennifer went upstairs, her mind blank, her body buzzing. She found herself standing in the middle of the living room, long afternoon shadows falling across her feet.

The entire world was skewed. As Jennifer looked out the window, the earth tilted under her feet and trees grew sideways and birds flew backward and nothing—absolutely nothing—was as it should be.

Annabelle Greer, First Lady Annie, had been abused by her husband, the president of the United States.

There was no part of that sentence that made sense, much less could be true. It was the height of ridiculousness. And really, considering Ian Greer's track record with scandal and the truth, it made perfect sense that he would make up a story like that.

And to think she'd gotten excited about that scoop. Was, frankly, stupidly, still excited. Good lord if this were true...

But it couldn't be. It couldn't.

Still, she had never seen a man so vulnerable as Ian before he left her. He'd been stripped bare, his sparkle gone, the charm and the grin nowhere to be found. He was simply a man worried and naked.

The journalist in her wanted to believe him.

The woman in her wanted to help him.

That vulnerability, that heart-rending guilelessness, appealed to her, called out to something soft and nurturing in her, and she wanted to help him. She wanted to touch him. Brush that hair back from his forehead and tell him she'd help him make things better. She wanted to touch her fingers to his lips, to ease away the sad set to his mouth. She wanted to run her hands across his eyes, down his cheeks to erase the solemn cast to his beautiful face.

Those walls he'd blown over this morning with his bare chest and that towel were not going to be rebuilt. She saw that now.

This attraction to Ian was only getting worse, because where the nurturer stopped, the woman took over, and there were other things she wanted to do to him. Other ways she wanted to touch him.

"Crazy!" Jennifer said, shaking herself free from where she'd been rooted on the floor, staring vacantly out the window. "Absolutely nuts."

There was nothing for her to do upstairs, no way to

occupy her hands and head. Already the small apartment was
too filled with her anxiety and misplaced desire. Spence
and Deb were outside and she turned, ready to go back
downstairs, but then she heard the rumble of voices through
the floorboards.

The dark timbre of Ian's voice sent gooseflesh across her
back and over her scalp. Bob answered, she could tell by his
Jersey accent.

They were in the kitchen and she needed to stay away
from Ian. To just wait it out, while he was down there.

Suddenly, stupidly, the image of Annabelle with those big
sunglasses popped into her head. Her skin prickled as if a
draft blew over her.

Tentatively, wondering if she were simply validating a
lunatic's wild accusations because she was so unhappy with
her life, she reached for her laptop and clicked onto the
Internet using the wireless that J.D. had set up.

A messenger window popped up.

KerryWaldo: You're like one of those people who has a
huge house but only uses one room. Do you know what
carte blanche means? Annabelle's son is in rehab, though
no one can find out which one. Jackson Greer is all over
the news again—if you're going to do a story about Annabelle, you need to do it now. You should want to do
it now. The Jennifer I knew would leap at this chance.
Come on. Don't leave me hanging.

Jennifer stared at the screen, dumbfounded. Waldo no
doubt meant something fluffier than what was happening
here with Ian. Waldo…the whole damn world…had no idea
what Jennifer could do with this follow-up story. The
tsunami-sized ripples this story would make.

Waldo, Jennifer knew, would commit crimes for this story. Murder. Mayhem. She'd chop off heads for this scoop.

With a calmness she was so far from feeling Jennifer closed the window.

Swallowing hard she searched pictures of Annabelle Greer and within seconds she had that black-and-white photo from Greer's first term as governor of North Carolina.

Annabelle had just released her first children's book to rave reviews and the couple was suddenly all over the newspapers. The photo was taken outside, in the spring. Sunlight made a halo around her shiny pageboy, and she wore those big glasses and that mandarin collar.

Jennifer peered closer, as if better study of the photo would reveal its secrets. Her mind swung like a pendulum from doubt to wonder—was she? Wasn't she?—without ever getting closer to a decision.

Looking harder at the photo, she realized Ian stood in the corner. At ten he'd already been handsome—striking, really— with dark lashes around light eyes. He stood beside his mother, watching her.

His eyes, his whole face, so terribly, terribly sad.

What was true?

And she realized, if she could just get that answer, and it was the right one, there would be no stopping her from writing this story.

JENNIFER MANAGED to avoid Ian for a while. Or maybe he was avoiding her. Either way, there were no accidental run-ins in the kitchen, or outside the bathroom.

She and Deb taught classes, ran a book group, ordered supplies. They rejoiced over the fixed faucet, speculated on life with central air and didn't talk about the men living in the back room.

Instead it was just Jennifer and the thoughts spinning in her head nonstop.

Finally, crying uncle the next afternoon, Jennifer headed outside to the pond, where she knew Deb would have the boys cooling off during the hottest part of the day.

She needed to breathe fresh air. Needed to be outside. Needed to be out of her damn head.

She broke through the treeline onto the dirt rim of the swimming pond. Spence, stripped down to his cut-off jean shorts, was sailing out over the water on the rope swing J.D. had built years ago.

Spence had been practicing his trick off the rope and he managed to get half a somersault in before belly-flopping into the water.

He came up howling and she winced in sympathy. Her boy caught sight of her and lifted his hand up in a wave.

"Did you see that?" he cried.

"Yep," she said. "You almost got it."

Spence swam for the shore and was soon scrambling up the rough bank, reaching for the rope again, the flesh of his belly pink from hitting the water.

When did he get so brave? she wondered. He certainly hadn't learned it from her. Doug had been brave in his way, taking everything head-on, even sickness and death.

If Spence and Doug could do that, what could she do? What could she face? Another fluff piece? Sure, if she had to. What about Kerry Waldo's assumption that Jennifer's life was over because she wasn't writing hard journalism?

Or the possibility that Ian was telling the truth?

If it were true—and that was such a huge if—the story would electrify the world. The story would electrify her career.

The career she'd left behind. The career she'd left for dead.

"Hey," Deb said and Jennifer broke out of her thoughts to find the woman playing in the sand with Shonny.

"Hi," she said, scrambling around the pond to get to Deb.

"Ian and Andille are still here," Deb said, cutting to the chase. "They gonna start paying rent, or what?"

"Central air is still getting fixed and Ian hasn't said anything about the lawsuit."

Deb pursed her lips and looked down at Shonny and his scribbles in the sand.

The sound of bugs buzzing through the grass and bushes filled the quiet between them. Jennifer closed her eyes and let the warm Carolina wind blow over her face, wishing it could blow away the weight she felt on her shoulders.

"You okay?" Deb asked, shielding her eyes from the sun as she glanced at Jennifer.

No, she wanted to say. She actually wanted to tell Deb everything Ian had told her, but she'd promised and she knew what Deb would say anyway.

Deb was no fan of Ian Greer.

"I'm okay," she said. "Tired."

"You snapped at Laura yesterday?" Deb said, raising her eyebrow and smiling just slightly.

"What did she say?" Jennifer groaned, feeling bad again for the way she'd dealt with her.

"That you were snappy and that she'd never count on us for babysitting service again."

Jennifer sighed and put her head in her hands. Really, she was batting a thousand. "I'll apologize," Jennifer mumbled.

"Don't," Deb said. "She was plenty snippy in return. Walking back here with her nose so high in the air it's a wonder she didn't fall."

"Did she take off those sunglasses?"

Deb looked at her askance. "No. Why?"

Jennifer stared at her hands, wondering if she were a fool for even contemplating this. Ian was a scandal monger and this could be his biggest scandal, his greatest success, and she was getting sucked in.

"Jen?"

"Do you think—" She sighed and just said it. "Do you think Laura is abused?"

Deb blinked at her. Watched her. Then shrugged. "She says no."

"She could be lying," Jennifer said then wondered why she was pursuing this.

"Sure," Deb said. "But we have no reason to believe otherwise." She drew a series of stars in the sand for Shonny to exclaim over.

"Fire truck!" Shonny demanded and Deb began to sketch a fire truck.

"When I first came here," Deb said, "and for the year that I stayed, I thought every woman was a victim and every man an abuser. Everywhere I turned. And I realized at some point you have to take people at their word or you'll make yourself crazy."

Jennifer turned, slack-jawed, to face Deb, wondering if she was even aware of the huge hypocrisy in what she was saying. "So, you're totally over that?" she asked sarcastically. "You don't believe every man is an abuser?"

Deb's head snapped around at Jennifer's tone then she seemed to catch on. She relaxed and smiled ruefully. "I'm trying," she insisted.

"Like you're trying with Andille?"

Deb's lips tightened and she stared at the fire truck sketched out in the sand. Her small body radiated tension.

"The man has given you no reason not to trust him," Jennifer said, wondering if maybe she should leave well enough alone, but somehow unable to. "And you're treating him like he's personally assaulted you."

Deb wiped her cheek on her shoulder and they both looked up at the sound of Spence screaming out over the water. He landed in a huge cannonball and Shonny cheered.

"I know." Deb sighed. "It's just that I had no chance to get used to him. No chance to get used to the idea that a man like that—"

"Like what?"

Deb was so still. So quiet. "Big," she said. "Real big. And handsome, like my father was. And charming like him, too."

"He's not your father," Jennifer said softly.

"I know that." Deb scowled. "In my head, I'm clear on that. But when I see him, something happens. Some alarm goes off that—" She stopped. "I can't ignore," she finally whispered.

"You don't want to spend your life hiding from men, do you?" Jennifer asked. "Hating all of them for what your father did?"

Deb watched Shonny, her heart in her eyes, and Jennifer's heart bled for the woman, it really did. "No," Deb finally said. "And I tell myself to try. I tell myself not every man is my father. Not every man will hurt me. I'm telling myself that right now, about Andille, who has been nothing but kind." She sighed. "But it's hard."

Jennifer slung her arm around her friend. "I hear you," she said, knocking her head lightly against Deb's.

"What about you?" Deb asked, pulling away.

"What about me?"

"You've been doing a pretty good job of keeping yourself clear of men for the past few years."

Jennifer reeled back, her heart pounding. "My husband died," she said.

"So, you're done?" Deb asked. "Thirty-seven years old and you're giving up?"

"It's not about giving up."

"Yes," she said, laughing slightly, and Jennifer bristled. "It is. Men make up fifty percent of the world and we've both been avoiding them. Not that we can any longer with two of them right under our feet, for who knows how long."

Jennifer wanted to protest, but she knew Deb was right. The problem was Jennifer was in no hurry to stop.

She thought of all the reasons she didn't like Ian Greer. The secrets. The way he'd shown up drunk on her doorstep after his mother's funeral. The way he'd spent so many years defiling his family's good name. She really didn't like the way he'd saddled her with this secret…or lie, depending on what was true.

But what really bothered her, what really sunk under her skin and made her itch, was her reaction to him. The way her body went liquid at the sight of him. The way his gaze could hold her and stop her heart. His smile and the way his jeans fit and his shirt hugged the muscles of his shoulders made her feel womanly again. He made her want to be desired and feel desire.

It made her want Doug. It made her want Ian.

It made her want to have her hormones surgically removed.

To her horror, part of her—the part out of the control of her brain and her grief—was ready to join the living again. At least in some capacity.

Behind them leaves rustled and branches snapped and Jennifer and Deb both stood to see what was running through the woods.

Ian sprinted from the treeline. He stopped when he saw them, panting and panicked.

Adrenaline surged through her at the sight of him.

"We've got a situation," he said.

CHAPTER EIGHT

IAN WAS NO GOOD with hysterical women. They made him nervous. Andille said it was because he wasn't in touch with his feminine side, which made Ian inclined to believe maybe Andille was a little too in touch with his feminine side.

Luckily, Andille was right at home with hysterical women. He had seven sisters after all and a mother to try to keep happy. So, when the hysterical woman toting two hysterical girls knocked on the door of Serenity minutes ago, Ian left them in Andille's capable hands and went to find Jennifer and Deb.

Jennifer and Deb, who were such pros they took one look at his face, gathered up their kids and were on the trail back to the house before he could catch his breath.

He brought up the rear, behind a red-headed boy in dripping wet cut-offs. The boy turned and walked backward, watching Ian.

"Hi," Ian said, after a moment. In his effort to give Jennifer her space to make up her mind about him and his story, he'd been avoiding all the residents, including this kid.

"Who are you?" the boy asked, stepping over a root as though he had eyes in the back of his head.

"My name is Ian." He was no good with hysterical women but he really liked kids. His mother, before his father was ever in office, had taken Ian to orphanages and shelters to volunteer on weekends. It was something he did all through his teens and only stopped once it began to contradict this image he worked so hard to present to the world. "Who are you?"

"Spence." Spence swiped at a mosquito that hovered close. Twilight was coming and with it the swarms of southern pests. "Is Andille a basketball player?"

"Nope. But he's very good at soccer."

"He is?" Spence asked, his eyes lighting up.

"Not as good as me," Ian said with a grin. "But pretty good."

"I play soccer."

I bet you do.

"Well, then, sometime we'll have to have a game."

"Me, too!" the toddler over Deb's arm shouted.

"You, too," Ian agreed, feeling so good he almost forgot about the screaming woman.

Spence stumbled slightly, but didn't slow down. "My mom doesn't like you," he said quietly.

"I'm not always a real likeable guy," Ian said. He rarely wished things were different, but walking with this kid he felt the bite of remorse.

Spence harrumphed and Ian wondered if that noise was a good opinion, or bad.

As they neared the house, the wailing of those little girls could be heard and Ian felt a terrible surge in his blood pressure. Lord, he hated crying.

He wasn't an idiot, and knew it went back to his mother. Who, oddly enough, didn't cry. She never got hysterical. No matter what—and there had been plenty for her to cry over.

But he knew that her total and utter control in the face of all things was why he was never prepped for tears. He simply didn't have the tools to deal with them, like trying to go after a nail with a socket wrench.

Jennifer and Deb took off running at the sound of the crying and, without many options, Ian followed.

The woman, who looked a bit like the woman who'd been here yesterday with the sunglasses, was right where he'd left her. Sitting on the couch, the two girls clinging to her.

At the sight of Deb and Jennifer the girls cried harder.

Andille stood useless in the corner and Ian gave him a pointed look, wondering why he hadn't handled this, and Andille shrugged. Apparently this situation was beyond his calming capabilities.

"Madison?" Jennifer asked, coming to crouch in front of the girls. "What's going on?"

Deb sat on the couch and stroked the blond heads and murmured comforting things. *Ah,* Ian thought, *that's what you're supposed to do.*

"I'm sorry," the woman said. "My name is Sarah. I'm Laura Jones's sister."

"What's happened?" Jennifer asked and Ian could see the strain and stress on Jennifer's face and he felt the utterly bewildering desire to help her. To relieve those fine fragile features of their concern.

But, sadly, he didn't have the tools for that, either.

He really was useless sometimes.

"Laura's been arrested," Sarah said. "Marcus is in the hospital."

Oh, but this situation was starting to look like familiar ground. Perhaps he could be of use after all.

"What?" Jennifer breathed. Madison cried harder and the other girl's screams hit a fever pitch.

"Come on." Deb stepped in. "Let's go see if we have any cookies in the kitchen." It took some doing but she managed to pry the girls away from Sarah. But then Shonny started crying and finally Andille earned his keep by sweeping the boy up in his arms and giving him a little jostle to make him laugh.

Deb stiffened like Andille had taken a bat to the boy but after a long tense moment, she relaxed. Barely.

Spence, still dripping and looking about as shell-shocked as Ian felt, followed everyone into the kitchen.

Pat heads, whisper comforting things and, finally, find cookies. The ABC's of grief counseling, Ian filed it away for future use.

Daisy brought up the rear, sparing a growl for Ian as she walked by.

With the children gone the silence was heavy and Ian felt like an interloper on a scene he didn't even want to see. Since he knew this story, knew it better than he wanted to having lived it for so long, he knew it would be handy for him to stick around.

He was, under the tabloids and scandals, a damn good lawyer.

"What happened?" Jennifer asked, stroking Sarah's shoulder.

"No one is sure," Sarah said, her eyes wide and wet. "Madison called nine-one-one because her parents were fighting. And by the time the police arrived Marcus was unconscious."

"Because Laura finally fought back?" Ian asked quietly. Both women turned to him. "Does she have legal help?" He stepped into these shoes with ease. "Self-defense can be hard to prove in these cases, but I have experience and I can help. She—" Something in Sarah's eyes made him stop. A shame and an anger.

It took him a second but he finally read between the lines.

"She wasn't defending herself, was she?" he asked, his

stomach in his shoes. Those glasses weren't hiding a black eye, they were hiding guilt.

Please don't let me be right, he prayed.

But a heavy sob rocked Sarah's shoulders and she nodded. "Laura's always had all this anger," she finally said. "Since she was a teenager. She used to—" She bit her lips then waved her hands as if to erase what she'd been about to say. "We thought that with Marcus she had finally gotten it under control. She'd been going to therapy and bringing the girls to the empowerment classes, but she's been deliberately hurting him for years. None of us knew or even suspected. I mean…" Her wide bewildered eyes searched his and he wished he had answers for her. Something that would make this better, because this was way past the cookie remedy. "She's half his size. Who would guess?"

"Has she hurt the kids?" he asked, aware of Jennifer's eyes on him like searchlights. Her curiosity and confusion were palpable, but he didn't know how to explain himself.

"My instinct," Sarah said, "is to say no. Absolutely not, but after tonight?" Sarah's face crumpled a little and Jennifer held tight on to the woman's arms, giving her as much support as she could.

"I…ah…" Sarah sighed, wiping her eyes with the palms of her hands. "I have to go back to the hospital and then to the jail. I…don't know what to do with the girls tonight. I don't want them to see—"

"They're fine here," Jennifer said quickly. "They're fine here for as long as it takes."

"Thank you." Sarah sighed and then turned to him. "If we need it, will you still help?"

"Your sister?" he asked and she nodded.

He was a man of very few principles, but this was one of

them. Ian shook his head. "I'm sorry," he said softly. "I don't help abusers."

Sarah looked resigned, as if expecting that response, then took a few moments to pull herself together.

Jennifer's eyes, sharp and wary, met his over the top of the woman's bowed head.

How did you know? her eyes asked.

He smiled, sadly. *I've seen it all before.*

He wondered how all this silent communication was possible, but when she took a deep breath and nodded slightly, he knew exactly what it meant.

His heart surged. Jennifer Stern was going to listen to his story.

JENNIFER'S CHEST HURT, her heart was pounding so hard. Her throat was dry, dry all the way to her stomach.

Watching Ian walk to the door with Sarah, telling her what she could expect from the legal process in the next few days, Jennifer felt like she'd been rolled over. Hit by a car.

Who was the real Ian Greer? The man in the tabloids? The drunk man on her doorstep? The angry man at the breakfast table? The vulnerable one, talking about his mother?

Or this man?

This compassionate, considerate and intuitive lawyer. This man of principle with the terribly wounded eyes. This man whose whole demeanor spoke of a dark knowledge about the many facets of abuse and betrayal.

This man who was pushing her, shoving her back into a life she'd left behind. She was going to listen to him and her motives were so muddled even Waldo would tell her to pass on the story. To walk away. As of this moment she was emotionally invested.

But she could no more walk away right now than she could fly away.

There was a softness at her core, a tenderness and heat that was beginning to throb, like a sore tooth. Aching more with every encounter.

Nothing about this man was what it seemed, and the more she found out, the more attracted to him she was.

Oh, lord what a mess.

"Jen?" Deb's voice snapped her out of her fog and she turned, hoping none of her attraction, none of her stupidity, was showing on her face.

Deb would pick up on it like a bloodhound.

"Maybe you and Spence should move downstairs and we'll put Andille and Ian upstairs?" Deb asked as she stood in the doorway.

"Good idea," Jennifer said, standing. Happy to have something to do with her unruly body. Maybe moving furniture would rid her body of this pull. Maybe she'd start marathon training. Tonight.

"And we need to think about dinner," Deb said. "It's already past six and we're—"

"I've got dinner," Ian said from the front door and Jennifer's eyelids flinched and her body squeezed tight, holding onto itself in those empty places. Those lonely places.

"Kids like pizza," he said. "Right?"

She told herself not to turn, not to catch his grin, that glow in his eyes, that relief and gratitude on his face.

But she did it anyway.

Somehow, she'd tied herself to this man. Agreeing to listen to his story would only put her in his company with greater frequency.

What am I doing? she wondered, lost for a moment in the endless blue of his eyes. *Why you? After all these years?*

The answer was in the way his eyes blazed, as if he'd sensed her attraction.

"Sounds good," she said brightly, falsely, like he was bagging her groceries. Then, coward that she was, she ran upstairs to safety.

FOOL. FOOL. FOOL, Deb thought, shaking her head while she watched Jennifer run for upstairs like a horse with its tail on fire. Deb would laugh if it were funny rather than a little sad, but a mere hour ago Jennifer had said she wasn't interested in men.

And now, the air in the common room was practically on fire.

Interested, Deb thought with an internal snort, *doesn't quite cover it.* In heat, the two of them, was closer to it.

"I'll…ah, go pack our stuff up," Ian said, nodding briefly at Deb but unable to make eye contact as if he'd been caught doing something he shouldn't.

And, frankly, in Deb's opinion he was. He was messing with a good woman's head.

They were both gone but the sparks of their attraction still lit the air.

Deb was torn, truly torn, between being happy for Jennifer and wanting to protect her from the pain a relationship, no matter how brief, with a man like Ian would bring to a woman like Jennifer.

Jennifer was rock-solid. A woman who tried to make things better. For herself. Her son. Her friends.

Ian was… Deb considered what she knew about the guy, which wasn't much and wasn't good, and decided Ian Greer was negligent.

And a negligent man could be as cruel as an evil man.

Ah, well, she thought with a heavy sigh. Jennifer was a

big girl and if she wanted to get herself in knots over a man like Ian, so be it.

Turning back to the kitchen she was paralyzed by the sight of Andille on the kitchen floor, his back against the cupboards and his lap filled with Shonny and Angelina. Andille's chin was buried in their blond and black curls and he pursed his lips and tried to blow some of it from his mouth.

He had his palms out, the light brown skin stretched taut over big muscles and bones, and the children, their hands so small, their fingers so fragile, were tracing the lines of his hands while he sang in their ears.

The alarms went off in her head, shrill and loud, and her body spasmed with the need to heed the warnings.

Get the kids away from that man.

But she forced herself to remain where she was. To take deep breaths. To see what was happening with her eyes rather than her sick, twisted instincts.

Andille's deep voice was a low murmur but it still filled the kitchen. She didn't understand the words and after a stunned second realized they were foreign. Totally unfamiliar, but it didn't matter. Not to the kids in his lap. And not to Madison and Spence at the table, drinking glasses of milk and listening. Watching.

Certainly not to Daisy, the vicious guard dog, curled up between the man's spread knees.

Angelina, her hair so blond, her face red and blotchy, her eyelids swollen from crying so hard and so long for her mother, leaned her head against Andille's shoulder then turned her face so she rested her forehead to his neck. Her little fingers curled around his thumb and held on.

Deb's stomach twisted. Her heart squeezed. Tears bit hard into the backs of her eyes.

Not all men are my father. A reminder she didn't really

need at the moment, considering her father would never have done what Andille was doing. Sitting on the floor. Holding hands. Singing songs.

"What's that song?" she asked quietly, not wanting to disturb anyone.

"A lullaby," Andille said. His eyes, when they met hers, were liquid with emotions she knew all too well. Emotions that kept her at Serenity in order to help other people.

His beautiful eyes were filled with grief and sympathy. And anger.

"I don't know the words," she whispered.

"It's African," he said. "My mother sang it to me when I was a boy. It's about the sky at night being a blanket and the stars are friends who watch over sleeping children like lions making sure no one will hurt them."

Deb nodded, unable to speak for a second. "That's a good lullaby," she finally said, her voice gruff.

Andille's smile split his face and his laugh was as comforting as the song he'd been singing. "Yes, it is."

"You are—" she looked down at Angelina, who now was sound asleep, and Shonny, who was measuring his three-year-old hand against Andille's "—good with kids."

"I have seven sisters," he said. "Much younger than me. I've had to sing a lot of lullabies."

He smiled, but it wasn't happy and his attention drifted back down to the sleeping girl in his arms. His hand, so wide, big and capable of untold things, terrible and wonderful, lifted, his finger scooped back a curl of hair from her sleep-flushed face.

So gentle, this man. So careful.

She stared at them for far too long and Andille caught her, his brown eyes too knowing and suddenly the kitchen was too small. North Carolina was too small.

"Deb?"

She jumped for the phone book, unable to look at him any longer. "What do you like on your pizza?"

"MOM?" SPENCE ASKED as he got ready for bed that night.

"Yeah, hon?" Jennifer said, pulling back the sheets on his bed then flipping on the small bedside lamp. She'd stopped, years ago, doing these kinds of things for him, but tonight she wanted to. She wanted to care for him, wrap him up and put him in her pocket.

He climbed in bed, his curls drying in a wild, fine halo around his head. "What did Madison's mom do to her dad?"

Jennifer sat next to him and lifted the sheets up to his chin, which he batted back down to his waist. "I'm not too sure, exactly," she said.

"She hurt him?"

"Pretty bad."

"Why?"

She sighed. "I don't know. I don't know why some men hit their wives and I don't know why some women hurt their husbands."

"Why didn't he just run away?"

"Probably because of his daughters," she said, reaching forward and pushing the hair off his forehead.

"I would just run away," he said. "If a girl tried to hit me, I would just run and run."

She smiled, happy that her son's world was so simple. "That's a good plan," she said. "But you don't know what Madison's dad felt like or why he stayed, so try not to pass judgment on him."

"Okay," he said and her heart was so swollen, so full it hurt.

"Good night, honey," she said, standing up after kissing his cheeks. "I've got a little work to do."

The door closed behind her with a soft click. Behind the other two bedroom doors there was silence and she truly hoped everyone was asleep and, thinking of the two girls, that their dreams were sweet.

The rest of the house was dark and she walked in shadows into the kitchen, planning to knock on Ian's door and get some answers.

"Jennifer?" Andille's voice, deep and smooth like dark chocolate, curled out of the darkness and she whirled to find him staring out the kitchen window toward the woods behind the house.

"Andille," she said with a smile. "What are you doing?"

He glanced back at her and smiled briefly. Again, she got that sense that he was tired. Sad. "Waiting," he told her. "It's what I always do."

"Can you—" She paused, wondering how much Andille knew about Ian's secrets.

"You're looking for Ian?" he asked. "He's very excited that you've agreed to listen to him."

"Then you know?" she asked. "About his parents."

Andille looked back over the yard, the moonlight that turned everything silver and gold. "I don't know what I know anymore," he told her, sadness lacing his words.

"Is it true?" she asked, her voice a whisper.

Andille hung his head and laughed. "It's his story," he told her. "And yours. What's true is up to you."

He leaned over and opened the kitchen door, the smell of grass and heat and night and mystery and secrets wafting in the door.

"He's out by that pond," Andille said. "Go talk to him. See for yourself."

CHAPTER NINE

THE OLD JENNIFER was in charge. The journalist elbowed herself to the forefront and she was rolling over questions in her mind. Taking over. Staking claim.

And, God, it felt so good.

As she walked the path toward the water, Ian and an unknown future, she planned her attack. The sequence of questions. The tone. Professional but approachable. Skeptical but not jaded. Reserved, but willing to be persuaded.

She wanted him to know that she didn't totally believe him, there was still a lot of doubt in her mind. But at the same time she wanted him to trust her enough to try to convince her.

Fine lines. Good journalism was all about fine lines and she was so eager to be up on the tightrope again.

She was just worried, scared actually, of being up there with Ian.

A good interview. A good exposé like this required a lot of trust on both sides and right now she didn't trust Ian. She wanted to hear his story. And she desired him.

Neither of those things required trust.

The treeline ended and she stepped onto the sandy banks that surrounded the water hole and she found him, unerringly. As if there were something in her body tuned directly to him.

Standing in the shadows between the beach and the rope swing he was barely visible. But she looked right at him.

And he looked right at her. Even across the distance and the doubt, she felt his eye contact deep in the core of her body, between her stomach and her womb.

He began to walk toward her and she toward him. They met at the beach. The moonlight so bright she could see the blue of his eyes, the black of his eyelashes.

"Hi," he said.

She smiled. "Hi."

"Long night," he said, making conversation, and she wondered how the sexiest man alive could be so awkward. So unsure. And she wondered how she could find it so attractive.

Questions, she reminded herself. Fine lines. Journalism.

"I want—"

She held up her hand, interrupting him. This had to be on her terms.

"I have some questions," she said. "I'm willing to listen, but I'm not committed to writing this story. And I make no promises about believing you."

"Your eyes," he said with a bewildered smile. "They'd scare the devil into confession. How do you do that?"

"Do what?" Jennifer asked, blinking.

"Change on a dime. One minute just a beautiful woman, the next a terrifying journalist."

The beautiful-woman thing shook her, but she ignored it. "I'm a journalist," she said. "I don't know about the terrifying part."

"All right," he agreed and gestured to the log Deb had been sitting on this afternoon before everything blew up. "Let me hear your questions."

He sat and faced her, his elbows on his knees, leaning toward her just slightly. Just enough that she could feel the heat of him, smell the warmth and spice of him. And she leaned backward, to maintain her equilibrium.

"You mentioned a family doctor," she said, hauling herself back in line. "And records."

He nodded. "Dr. Engle has been our family doctor since my parents were married. He treated my mother every time she needed more help than heavy makeup could give her."

"And he would share those records?"

"He can't open her records, but he would answer questions."

"Why?" she said. "Why hasn't he done it before? Why haven't you done this before?"

He swallowed, his adam's apple bobbing in his throat, and he stared at his hands, tracing the lines across his palms and she watched the movement so intently she could feel his touch on her own flesh. "It sounds so ridiculous now," he said, shooting her a look through his lashes, "but she made us all promise. Me. Dr. Engle. Her assistant, Suzette Williams."

"Promise not to tell?"

"She believed—" He sighed and pushed himself upright, his eyes boring into hers. "She believed that the good of what my father did, the good of what they were able to do together, was bigger…more important than what happened between them privately."

She sagged, understanding how a woman like Annabelle might believe something like that.

"And she could be really persuasive. So all of us promised."

"And then she died," Jennifer said.

"And then she died and I decided that I couldn't keep this promise forever. If she wasn't here to see it, then my part of the deal was over."

"But you've caused so much scandal," she said, wondering about his motives. "The past few years you've done nothing but heap gossip and speculation on yourself and your family…your mother."

He laughed humorlessly, his head tipped back. His throat

exposed, his eyes closed. He sat that way for a second as if turning his face to the sun for warmth and peace. But it was the moon and there was no peace in him. She could feel the tension radiating off him like cold from ice.

"I wanted to hurt him," he finally admitted. "I wanted to shame him and scar him and drag his name and his legacy through the mud. I wanted the name Greer to be associated with disgusting things."

Oh. She bit her lip. It all made sense. Sick, sick sense.

"That couldn't have been easy," she finally whispered.

He shrugged. "I hung out with the wrong kind of people. I drank too much until I got sober." Again that disarming smile, again the pulse of her reaction. "Believe it or not until I showed up on your doorstep, I hadn't had so much as a sip in years."

"All those events you showed up at?" she asked, wondering how complex this ruse could get. How deep this public persona. "The press conferences when you seemed so drunk? So—"

"Fake," he said. "Toward the end I barely had to pretend the press was so eager to believe the worst about me."

And they still would. She thought about the uphill climb Ian would have to make people believe this story.

"So, everything—the parties and the women, the sexiest man alive stuff—"

"Not real. Well, the magazine was real, but the interview in it I pretty much made up."

"So, what is real?"

The question seemed to take him off stride and he blinked at her, frowning slightly. "It's hard to say anymore. You do something long enough and well enough it becomes the truth. I never believed in what I was doing but I did believe in why I was doing it."

"Your father."

He nodded.

She noticed he didn't answer her question and she wondered if maybe, after all these years, he simply didn't know who he was anymore.

"And no one knows the truth?" she asked, stunned that he'd duped so many people, including himself.

"You did," he said. "That first morning you asked why I let the world believe the worst of me. You knew I was lying."

She wanted to deny it. Wanted to pretend that she didn't know him at all, but she couldn't. An electrical current flowed through her and she nearly stood to leave she was so flustered.

"But you are a lawyer, right?"

"I am. I am a lawyer and Andille has advanced degrees in international finance. Between the two of us we try to keep our karmic balance in line."

It was so close to what she'd thought about him just a few days ago that she laughed. Unbelievable that she could be so wrong about the man and so right at the same time.

"Anyway," Ian said, "all of it—the lies, the press, the drinking—was far easier than what my mother went through."

Right. The real story. Ian, as compelling as he was, was not why she was out here.

"What did she go through?" she asked. "Exactly."

"Exactly?" He shook his head. "I'm not sure I could tell you. They were very private and she never talked about it. Even when it was obvious. When she was bleeding or in so much pain we had to take her to Dr. Engle. Even then the only thing she would talk about was our promise not to tell anyone."

"You need more than that," she told him, confronting him with the facts of what he was up against. "You've got media that aren't going to take this seriously and a lot of public perception stacked against you. And you're going to need some cold hard facts to make the story. Otherwise it just looks like another one of your efforts to embarrass your dad."

She watched his jaw tighten, the muscles clench and relax all along his cheek, into his hairline. She could see his pulse pounding in his throat and could feel the reluctance in him. He wasn't sure about telling her.

"You have to trust me, Ian," she said. "You've come this far." He glanced at her with a knowing smile.

"Trusting you isn't the problem," he said, watching her, studying her. "I trust you more than I've trusted anyone but Andille for years." Their gazes clung and the warm Carolina night got hotter. She didn't know what to do with that information, where to file it. She had a story, a husband she missed so much she couldn't think about him and a desire for Ian Greer that could burn down mountains.

"I've never told anyone any of this. Even Andille," he said, after clearing his throat and breaking the moment. "Ever. But if I tell you—" he licked his lips "—these stories, I have to know you trust me. I have to know you believe me. That you'll tell my story."

Oh, man, the guy was smart. Smarter than she'd given him credit for. He wasn't going to give her all the marbles without knowing where she stood. And, oddly enough, just the fact that he was so careful with this story—with his mother's legacy and truth—sealed the deal for Jennifer.

"I believe you," she said. "And I will do everything in my power to tell this story in a way that it is truthful and respectful of your mother."

His eyes glistened in the moonlight and his emotion touched her. She forced herself not to reach between them and touch his hand. Not that touching his hand in and of itself would be unprofessional. No, it was the way she felt about that touch that made it wrong. Where she wanted that touch to go, what she wanted it to lead to.

She'd committed to this story and there was no room between them for desire.

"Please," she said, tucking her hands under her thighs. "Tell me your story."

"I would hear them at night," he said, looking out over the water. "For as long as I could remember, I could hear the muffled sounds of yelling and things getting thrown. And then—" he swallowed "—I didn't know it at the time, but I heard them having sex."

Jennifer's throat tightened to the point that she couldn't breathe. She tilted her head up and sipped at the air, dreading the worst of what was going to come out of his mouth.

"One morning, when Mom called Suzette to her room, I snuck down the hallway and sat at the doorway, so scared. So—" His voice shook and her heart broke for the boy in that hallway and this man in the starlight. "So scared for my mom. Suzette asked Mom if he'd raped her and mom said—" He faced her, his eyes burning brighter than the moon. Brighter than anything she'd ever seen and she couldn't look away. Couldn't resist the pull of him. "It's not rape if it's your husband."

"Oh, my God." The words fell out of her mouth.

"Suzette could tell you more," he said. "I was a kid and she sent me away once I started trying to defend her or get between them."

They sat in silence, all of her questions blown apart. Her determination to stay professional in jeopardy of tumbling to ruin around her. She wanted to touch him. Comfort him. Press her lips to the heartbreaking line of his.

"That must have hurt so much," she said.

"The rape?"

"Your mother sending you away."

He blinked, his face blank, and she wondered what was happening behind his eyes, what he wasn't telling her. "I hardly think about it, to be honest," he said with a shrug.

She couldn't believe it. No one recovered from that kind of childhood betrayal without some serious scars. She opened her mouth to press further, but he interrupted.

"Do you think that's enough?" he asked, genuinely unsure, and she nodded, clenching her hands and her heart against the urge to reach for him.

"I'll need to talk to Suzette. Otherwise it's just your word against your father's."

"Right." He laughed bitterly. "And that's gone so well for me."

She smiled in sad sympathy. After a moment she stood and he looked up at her.

"Let's talk more tomorrow," she said. "I'll need to get in touch with Suzette, but we've had enough tonight, I think."

He didn't say anything, didn't move. His eyes were locked on hers until the world fell away. The past, future, her son, his mother, everything vanished and it was just them and the hushed quiet and warm air that cocooned them.

She felt him sitting there like he was the moon calling to her and she was a wave looking for a beach to crash upon. As much as she wanted, *needed* to walk away, she couldn't. Finally, equally scared by him and her reaction to him, she turned, needing to be free of the magnetic push-pull he had over her.

Ian grabbed her hand and the rough abrasion of his palm against hers drove the air from her lungs, the thoughts from her head, and he slowly tugged her back around.

Resist, she told herself to no avail. *You know no good will come of this. Remember the story.* But the truth was she didn't care. She didn't care at all. Right now a fever gripped her.

His hand brushed from her palm to the fragile sensitive skin of her wrist and her body bloomed with a humid heat. A sudden desire.

His gaze was so hot and everywhere it touched—her face, her lips, her neck—she burned. This wasn't right. This feeling. This moment. Nothing about this was as it should be.

But she couldn't fight it. Couldn't even figure out how to try.

His thumb stroked her pulse point and he stepped closer. Then closer still. His hand touched her face and her eyelids fluttered, her breath broke on a gasp, her nipples hardened in a wild rush of need.

Please, please kiss me, she nearly whimpered.

And then he did.

His lips were dry. Warm. Reverent, almost. As if unsure. And she wondered if this was it. The sexiest man alive kissed like a monk.

But he pulled her closer, her body cupped lightly by the sway and heat of his. His hand caressed her waist, scalding her through the thin cotton of her T-shirt. His breath was sweet, his lips sweeter, and she hung suspended between frustration and bliss.

The kiss was chaste and she didn't want chaste. She didn't need chaste. Chaste allowed her to think. She needed mindless. She needed heat and sweat and sex and feeling.

She opened her mouth, invited him in. And with a groan, as if giving in, he took her up on her offer. In spades. They gripped each other, fists in shirts, fingers curled against sensitive flesh like two survivors of a terrible storm.

So long. So, so long since she'd felt this hot bite, this ache and pulse. Dams inside her broke, shattered, and longing she couldn't fight pounded through her.

Someone moaned slightly and his grip changed and she

stepped closer, needing more. Wanting him. She was ravenous, starving from years of subsisting on memories and fantasy. And now this man, this wild sexy man whose very touch promised things she'd forgotten, was here. In her arms.

Hot and wet the kisses grew, multiplied, one kiss into a thousand. Circling her arms around the wide muscles of his back, she crushed herself against him. His tongue stroked hers and she stroked him back, closing her teeth on his lip, pulling his hips hard against hers. Needing pressure, needing pleasure so badly it was a pain in the heart of her.

His laughter ruffled over her nerve endings and he leaned down to kiss and bite her neck. He shifted a knee between her legs, hard and high where she hurt the most. Groaning, she leaned back, letting him hold her up.

A cool breeze drifted between them, lifting her hair, blowing across her skin, down her shirt.

The cool breeze shattered the moment.

It gave her a second and that was all her mind needed. Her better sense, anesthetized by craving, leaped into action.

She blinked. Jerked. And realized the groan against her chest was a shade too deep. A shade too rough. The hands at her back were too big. Too hard.

The hair on this man's head was too light.

Doug.

This was not Doug.

And this was wrong in about twenty different ways.

She shoved away, trembling and horrified. He fought her for a moment, obviously not reading her struggles, but when he looked up into her eyes he released her.

What he saw there she didn't know. Couldn't even guess at. But he looked horrified.

"I'm sorry," he breathed. "I thought—"

She was willing? She had been. She was. She would

probably continue to be every time she saw him. Oh, God. Oh, lord, what had she done? What was she doing? Her body ached and her hand shook and all she could think was Doug.

"My husband—" she breathed then stopped, unsure of what she'd been about to say.

"I thought he died."

Oh, that he would think Doug's death made what they'd just done right made it worse. And that she thought the same made her sick.

"Jennifer?" He held out a hand for her and she retreated. His face, all that naked need and appreciation, turned to stone.

"I'm sorry," he said and because she was a coward and couldn't figure out the right words to say, she turned.

And ran.

CHAPTER TEN

MORNING, DEB THOUGHT, opening one eye, *comes too soon.* It wasn't always the case, but having spent the night in bed with two little girls who alternately curled against her and kicked at her in their sleep, the morning light cutting across her face like a laser beam was a cruel joke.

"Mommy?" Shonny stood beside the single bed where she was sandwiched between the girls.

"Hi, honey," she whispered, smiling at her boy and his afro.

"What are you doing?"

"Well—" she sighed "—I guess I'm getting up."

"What are you doing with them?" he asked, pointing at the rumpled blond heads next to hers.

"They couldn't sleep, honey," she said. "You know how sometimes you like me to lay down beside you when you have nightmares?"

Shonny nodded. "Did they have nightmares?"

"They did," she said. She didn't tell her son that part of her wanted to be in here with them, because she knew all too well what those nightmares could be like. And how lonely and scary a place like Serenity could seem in the middle of the night.

"Why doesn't their mommy sleep with them?" Shonny asked.

Deb flopped her head back down on the pillow, conceding to the Good Lord that sometimes being a good mommy and a good Christian required three more hours of sleep and a pot of coffee.

And honest answers to the tough questions were just going to have to wait.

"She's busy," she said and began to ease out of the bed, no easy trick with the casts. "Let's get some breakfast going."

"Andille's already doing that," he said and she paused, crouched over Angelina.

"He is?" she asked, like an idiot.

Shonny nodded and leaned down to the floor. "He told me to bring you this."

Her little boy straightened with a steaming mug of coffee. Sent to her by Andille.

Her heart practically stopped.

She told herself it was just kindness. It was just empathy and generosity from a place she didn't expect it and that there was no reason for her to feel so silly about it all. Like the coffee was roses or something.

But it felt like it. Oh, dear God, it felt like it.

"Well," she said, "let's go thank him."

She made it out of the bed with barely any noise and was, quite frankly, pretty amazed by that. But when she turned back to the bed, two little girls were blinking their green eyes at her.

"I'm hungry," Angelina said.

"Me, too," whispered Madison.

Deb smiled at them, stroked their cheeks. "Then let's go eat."

"Can we see our mom today?" Angelina asked and again, Deb told God she was sorry and she'd try better later before she said, "I'm not sure. We'll have to see what happens. Why don't we go see what Andille is cooking for break—"

She jumped out of the way as the girls hurtled themselves from bed at the mention of Andille's name. They raced out the door and moments later she heard from the kitchen the deep rumble of Andille's laugh.

"Well, Shonny, should we—" She looked down and realized Shonny was gone, too. All that was left was the cup of coffee steaming at her ankles.

I guess that just leaves me, she thought, leaning down to pick up the mug with both hands, balancing it between her casts.

She stepped into the hallway and took a sip of coffee, expecting the bitter bite of black coffee and was stunned to taste the sugar. Lots of it.

He'd known, somehow, how she liked her coffee.

And that really was roses.

DEB WALKED INTO the kitchen just as Andille filled the coffeepot at the kitchen sink.

"It's fixed?" she asked, thrilled.

"It is," he said, "And—" he stepped over to a box on the wall that hadn't been there last night "—Bob finished the central air this morning."

"It's ready?" Deb could have cried. Seriously. Central air where there hadn't been any before. She nearly sprinted to the box and, throwing caution and bills to the wind, she cranked that sucker up.

It was time to get cool.

Andille laughed at her and she sent him an arch look, but grinned a little herself. This was turning into quite a day.

Andille made scrambled eggs with bacon and salsa and tortillas and he showed the kids how to make burritos.

They were making a mess, but the girls were laughing and Spence, who'd stumbled into the kitchen not long after Deb, was smiling, too.

It was, Deb thought as she leaned back and enjoyed her second cup of coffee, worth a mess just for these kids to have a good time.

"You don't like burritos?" Andille asked, his voice behind her ear and she jumped, sloshing coffee down the front of her T-shirt.

"I'm so sorry," Andille said, reaching past her to hand her a napkin. "I didn't mean to startle you."

She whirled around and glared at him, snatching the napkin from his hand. "Then don't go around sneaking up on people," she snapped.

His brown eyes were soft and warm and contrite and her stomach did stupid things when they were on her. "I'm sorry," she said, blotting at the stains. "I shouldn't snap."

"It's all right," he said, his voice that thick rich purr that oozed and melted along her nerve endings. "I was just wondering why you weren't eating." He pointed to her plate, the eggs, bacon and salsa sitting on the open tortilla.

She held up her casts with a rueful smile. "Folding burritos is beyond me," she told him.

He winced. "Of course." Before she could protest, he reached forward again, his arms, so big, so strong she could see the ridge of his muscles through the light blue of his T-shirt, mere inches from her face.

He smelled clean, like soap and sunshine, and she fought the urge to close her eyes and breathe deep, absorb some of this man into her body.

"There," he said and she jerked away from his arms, looking at the burrito he'd rolled up, tucked in a napkin and held out to her.

Oh no, no, no, no. First the coffee. Now this.

"Please," he said when she hesitated. "You need to eat." Her stomach grumbled in agreement and she reached out, her fingers brushing his and sending nearly painful shocks and sizzles through her body.

Now who is the fool? she thought angrily. Jennifer had nothing on her, that's for sure. Feeling this way about a man she knew less than nothing about because he was good to kids, made her coffee and was easy—she looked into his face then back at the burrito—*so* easy on the eyes.

"Hey, Deb?" Spence asked and she turned gratefully to the boy. "Can we go outside and play soccer?"

"Yes," she said fast, standing up even faster. "Excellent idea. Let's go outside."

The kids all ran out the door, leaving behind a mess and Andille. Daisy lingered under the table, inhaling the scraps.

Deb paused, breakfast in her hand, coffee and sugar and this new attraction buzzing through her body. "Come with us," she said, before she could think.

"And leave this mess?" Andille asked, putting a white tea towel over his shoulder so he could grab dishes. "I don't think so."

He did dishes, too.

"Leave them," she insisted, knowing somehow that everything would be more fun, for the kids and for her, if he was outside with them. "Please."

He stilled. His gaze had weight and she wanted to shrink from it, like she used to when any man looked at her. She lived her entire childhood not wanting to be noticed. Not wanting to be seen. And now she had hot pink casts and blond-tipped dreadlocks and rhinestone glasses.

People were going to look. She'd planned that. She'd wanted the whole world to see how far she'd come, even if they didn't know where she started from.

But Andille was different. He looked at her and she felt

like he saw the scared kid in her, the unsure child, and it made her sick with nerves.

"Ian can clean up," she said.

"Now, that would be a first." Andille laughed, the sound rolling over her like a wave. "Ian cleaning up after me." And he threw the tea towel on the table. "Let's go play soccer."

Deb laughed as she walked out the door into sunshine so bright it felt like God smiling down on her.

And she hoped he was.

JENNIFER WOKE to thoughts of Ian.

Her dreams, filled with every fantasy she'd harbored in the years of celibacy, had been hot. Even if she couldn't remember much past skin and sweat, she flushed at the XXX-rated memory of them. And as sleep faded her body ached. Her body ached because it was totally unfulfilled. Empty.

She felt as if she'd been hollowed out in the night. Deep caverns of loneliness ached and pulsed with need she'd pushed aside for so long it had stopped coming around.

But desire, lust and passion were all back. With a vengeance.

She glanced across the room, relieved to find her son gone. The room was empty. Quiet. Sunlight lit dust in the air and made it glitter. It seemed as though she was the only person in the house. The only person in the world. Just her and the aching memory of those too-hot dreams.

For a moment, her hands stretched flat across her belly, felt the soft skin and muscle and heat, and she considered taking care of this ache herself. Something she hadn't done in years as her body had entered a grief-stricken, deep freeze. But she was lonely and it was quiet and she wanted so badly to banish Ian Greer from her mind.

She felt awkward, skimming her hands just under her shirt, testing her eagerness, but even that seemed to conjure

Ian to her bed. Because as she closed her eyes, it wasn't Doug's hands she imagined. Or George Clooney's. They were Ian's. Right where she didn't want them.

It was weird, and she was disappointed in herself, but she was also relieved. If she could maybe manage these feelings by ignoring them, pushing them aside then pretending they weren't there until they vanished, it would be easier than bringing lust and desire back into her life when there was nowhere for them to go.

If she could cut the grief over Doug out of her life, she could cut this out, too.

She was tough like that.

Pushing aside her blankets she sat up and immediately shivered against the cold air pumping through the room.

Well, well, she thought, the air-conditioning was installed. And apparently in celebration Deb was turning Serenity into the arctic.

Shivering, she pulled on a long-sleeve T-shirt and a pair of yoga pants. She paused at the door, wondering if Ian would be out there. Waiting for her with his blue eyes and wicked tongue. And suddenly she remembered how he'd tasted like soda and something spicy. Something dark.

Stop it, she thought, angry and annoyed with herself. *Just stop it.*

She grabbed her day planner with her producer's phone number and went out to the kitchen to grab a coffee and get to work.

There were phone calls to make. Ian needed to give her the numbers of Annabelle's doctor and assistant. She needed a better time line, a better sense of when the abuse started and how long it lasted.

Finding the thermostat, she cranked it back to something reasonable and headed to the coffeepot.

She needed— She caught some movement outside on the lawn from the corner of her eye. On tiptoe she leaned over the sink to peer out the window where, much to her total shock, it looked like there was a soccer game going on.

A soccer game Deb was playing. With pink casts and rhinestone glasses and a smile. A pure smile of—if Jennifer allowed herself to be a bit melodramatic—joy.

"Get out," Jennifer breathed. Then as Andille came running into view Jennifer nearly fell over. "Get. Out."

Deb was playing soccer. With Andille.

Spencer then Shonny came careening around the side of the house, kicking wildly at the ball, and Deb tipped her head back and howled with laughter. Jennifer's heart swelled to twice its size and she was so profoundly, deeply happy to see her friend happy.

Daisy whined at her side and she opened the door to let her join in the fun.

"Jennifer?" Ian's voice behind her sent her heart into her feet. A cold chill broke over her and all that happiness vanished as if it had never been, replaced with an anxiety that put her stomach in knots.

"Hi, Ian," she said, giving herself a moment of cowardice to pour a cup of coffee and not face him.

"Jennifer." His voice, his tone, was beseeching and she knew when she turned around his eyes, those gorgeous eyes, would be liquid with sympathy and concern and she hated that. And hated his pity.

Sugar swirled into her cup, and she wondered what he must think of her—throwing herself at him one moment, the next bringing Doug between them before running away like a little girl.

His hand grazed her arm. An electric sizzle ran from her elbow to her fingers and the spoon clattered on the counter.

She whirled to face him, taking a step away and forcing herself to meet his eyes and to steady her reaction, to control the leap of her blood.

That man…those hands…the lips. Her heart staggered and chugged and she took a deep breath, trying to find her balance amongst all the tumult.

"Jennifer—"

She held up her hand. "Ian, let me say something first." She barely waited for him to nod before forging on. "Last night was an anomaly. We were both emotional and wound up in what had happened and things got out of control."

"Things?" His blue eyes glowed briefly and she couldn't tell if he was mad or laughing and she didn't care.

"Yes, things," she snapped. "And it's done. We've got a job to do, a story to tell and I don't want anything to get in the way of that."

"Neither do I, but—"

"No buts, Ian. If we were to have any kind of personal relationship, it would jeopardize the integrity of the story, to say nothing for my reputation and what is left of yours."

"You're right," he said, solemn and still. "And I'm sorry about the kiss. It was out of line. I don't—"

"Ian," she said, uncomfortable with his apology, "let's forget it. Please."

He blinked at her, holding her in the gaze of those blue eyes that could be so penetrating, that could see right through her. What did he see? At one time she wouldn't have had a doubt. She'd known who she was down to her DNA. But now, his scrutiny taking her apart piece by piece, she didn't have a clue.

"All right," he said, quietly. "It's forgotten."

"Good," she said with a definitive nod. She grabbed her coffee and opened her planner. "I'm going to need some phone numbers," she said. "Your family doctor and your mother's assistant."

"Suzette," he said and took his phone from the front pocket of his faded, well-worn jeans. "Let me call them and give them the heads-up. I don't want to spring this on them."

"Fine," she said, sweeping her organizer from the counter. "I need to make a call myself." She paused. "We're good?"

He laughed, a merry sound that nearly stopped her breath. "You are unlike any woman I've ever met," he told her.

Words failed her and she wanted to ask him what he meant and if that was a good thing. But she couldn't, so she nodded— which was stupid—then left. Finding solace in the small office off the kitchen, she closed the door and leaned against it.

And pressed her hand hard to the ache pounding in her chest.

TWENTY MINUTES, two cups of coffee and three false starts later, she finally managed to dial Kerry Waldo's number. The pencil between her fingers smacked into the edge of the desk and her knee beneath the desk bounced like a wind-up toy.

Nervous much? she thought, wishing she could laugh at herself. Then the ringing stopped midring and a cold sweat bloomed over her forehead.

"Kerry Waldo," Kerry said in her no-nonsense way.

"Where's Waldo?" Jennifer said, an old joke between them. Kerry was quiet and Jennifer winced in the silence and put her head in her free hand. Stupid joke. It had always been a stupid joke.

"Jennifer?" Kerry asked. "Is that you?"

"It's me."

"You better be calling to say you're ready to go to work, because I don't have time to chat."

Jennifer smiled. Good old Waldo.

"I'm ready to work," Jennifer said.

"Excellent, I've got about four stories I could use your touch on. Two of them are edits, but we'll give you a—"

"I've got my own story," Jennifer said. "I've got a big story."

Kerry paused and Jennifer heard the squeal of her desk chair and she could picture Waldo sitting back, kicking one foot up on the edge of her desk.

"How big?"

"Biggest thing I've ever done."

Kerry whistled. "Gonna need some details."

"It's the Annabelle Greer follow-up."

"Excellent. What's the angle?"

Jennifer swore under her breath. She did not want to do this. Kerry hated sensationalism and everything about Ian Greer was sensational up to this point.

"Okay," she said and squared her shoulders. "Remember you trust me."

"Now you're making me nervous. Give me something or we're—"

"Ian Greer."

There was a long pause, a deadly pause. "Ian 'sexiest man alive' Greer?"

"Yes."

"Ian 'supposed to be in rehab' Greer?"

"Ye—"

"Ian 'son of the former President of the United States of America' Greer?"

"Yes." Jennifer blew out a long breath. "I get it, Kerry, it's not my usual thing. But this is a real story."

"Says Ian Greer?"

"Says Ian Greer and me."

On the other end Jennifer heard something that sounded like a door being slammed shut.

"Kerry, I don't even need a soft yes," she said quickly, trying to stop whatever tirade was coming. "I'll write the piece and send it to you. You get first—"

"What are you doing, Jennifer?" Kerry asked. "And I'm not asking as your producer, I am asking as your friend."

"What do you mean?" She tried to play dumb, but it didn't work.

"I mean, you are tying your name, your career, to a sinking ship. The guy is supposed to be in rehab after showing up drunk at Annabelle's memorial. Two years ago you wouldn't have touched this with a ten-foot pole."

"I know it's risky, but this story is astonishing."

"But is it real?" Kerry asked. "What if this guy is wrapping you up in a lie."

"He's not," she said definitively.

"Be sure, Jennifer. You've already compromised your career, don't do it again for this guy. Be sure that Ian isn't going to drag you down to his level."

Jennifer shook off the sting of Kerry's all-too-true words and the bone-deep worry that maybe, just maybe, Ian was no better than he had to be.

"He's not what he seems," she said earnestly. "Nothing is what it seems with him." And as confused as she was about him, she knew he wanted this story told in a way that was honorable and serious. That at least was true.

There was another long ominous pause. "Jen," she finally said, "you're not…involved with this guy, are you?"

Jennifer couldn't control the flush that swept over her chest, across her face to her hairline, but she could control her voice and she kept it steady. "Absolutely not," she said. "My assessment of him and of this story is as a professional."

Waldo was quiet. Too quiet. "All right. This is me as your boss again. Your boss who shouldn't need to remind you that if this story is big and you break it at my station while having some kind of relationship with the guy, you jeopardize not only what is left of your career, but mine as well."

Jennifer put her forehead in her hand and cursed silently.

"You're good, Jen. One of the best I've worked with, but if you're going to jeopardize what I've worked for, I will cut you loose faster—"

"I'm not," she said, pushing all thoughts of that kiss into the wild arctic of her mind. No more wanting Ian Greer. No more wishing things were different.

No more freaking heart-to-hearts in the moonlight.

"Waldo?" Jennifer asked when the silence went on too long.

"I believe you," Kerry finally said. "You think this thing is going to be big?"

"I think it's huge. I think it's Peabody."

"All right, Jennifer, I won't ask how and I won't ask why. Get me some rough copy by Friday." Kerry sighed. "And please, please be careful. You've been hurt too much."

Jennifer made some garbled goodbye past the lump of emotion in her throat and hung up before she made an idiot of herself in front of Kerry.

Just as she sighed and leaned back in the office chair that was barely held together by duct tape, there was a knock at the door and Ian poked his head in.

"Here," he said, holding out his cell phone. "Suzette would like to talk to you."

Jennifer rallied, readying herself for the next set of questions.

"Careful," he whispered, his blue eyes sparkling. "She's a little protective."

"I can handle it," Jennifer said, taking the phone and wishing she didn't notice that it was still warm from his hand.

Ian ducked out and Jennifer lifted the phone to her ear. "Hello?"

"This is Jennifer Stern?" a voice touched with southern steel asked.

"It is. This is Suzette Williams?"

"Yes. Listen, before we go any further there's something I need to be sure of."

"What's that?" Jennifer wasn't quite used to working with so many conditions on a story before.

"I have been waiting a long time to tell Annabelle's story in a way that is respectful and as gracious as the woman was—"

"I couldn't agree with you more," Jennifer said. "That's my philosophy about this story as well."

"Wonderful. Now, can you control Ian?"

"Control?"

"I don't trust him, Jennifer. Not as long as he is living to destroy his father. It makes him unstable. One minute you believe he is your friend, the next he is turning your life into a circus all so he can wound his father. Can you prevent that?"

Jennifer paused, flabbergasted. Was this a woman being protective? Or was Jennifer just a fool for wanting to believe the best of Ian Greer?

Wow. Life had gotten messy in the last twenty-four hours.

"I can control him," she said, more shaken and doubtful than she wanted to admit.

"All right." Suzette sighed heavily. "Can you give me a day to gather up my journals from those years and—"

"You have journals?"

"And photos," Suzette said. "Like I said, I've been wanting to tell this story a long time. Longer even than Ian."

Mother. Lode.

"I'll call you in a day." Jennifer then said goodbye, her blood humming through her veins. She buzzed with excitement. If she looked in a mirror, she wouldn't be surprised to see she glowed.

"Jennifer?" Ian poked his head back in. "You done?"

His smile was charming. His manner gracious and that dark thought began its march through her excitement, laying waste to it.

Control him? She could barely control herself when she was around him.

And now this story, her career and Kerry Waldo's career seemed to depend on her controlling everything.

"Jennifer?"

She held out the phone. "Thanks," she said.

Carefully, as if he were aware of her doubts, he took the phone from her. "Everything okay?"

"Good," she said, eager to get him out. Eager to come up with a plan, a way of dealing with him that would get her the story without jeopardizing anything. "Everything's fine."

He pursed his lips, obviously not believing her. Still, he left.

Left her alone with all her doubts.

CHAPTER ELEVEN

IAN MANAGED TO put away the clean plates from the break-fast catastrophe without breaking a single one. He managed to stop himself from smashing every single plate and cup against the wall to vent this sudden wild nervousness that flooded him.

He wanted to toss the coffeepot against the office door to make Jennifer come out and talk to him. Tell him what was going on behind those sharp, impenetrable whiskey eyes of hers.

Andille and the kids who followed him like snakes out of Ireland came barreling in the back door.

"Hungry!" the littlest girl howled, jumping up and down in front of Deb, who, Ian noticed, was looking slightly less uptight than she had before. In fact, now that Deb's face wasn't pinched with disapproval, Ian was stunned to see how young she was.

And beautiful.

One day with Dille and the woman practically glowed.

Which wasn't good. At all.

Ian was going to need to have a chat with Andille about flirting with the locals. He cringed slightly knowing that he could have used the same chat, oh, about twelve hours ago.

"I'll get some snacks together and we can head out to the pond," Deb said and the kids flocked to their spots at the table.

It would be best for the women, he thought, watching Deb watching Andille from the corner of her eye, if he and Andille left now.

Not that he was worried about Jennifer after her speech this morning. But he didn't want Deb in danger of getting hurt when they left. And they would leave.

"You did the dishes," Andille said.

"I did." He threw a clean frying pan in the cupboard with other pan-type things. "Don't look so surprised."

"You'll have to forgive me," Andille said, leaning against the counter nibbling on, of all things, some string cheese. "I've just never seen you do that."

"Yeah, well, you've never seen me do lots of things," he snapped, feeling snarly since Jennifer had been locked in the office for hours and he didn't know what was going on.

He leaned closer to Andille so they wouldn't be heard, even though the kids were keeping up a steady stream of chatter. "What the hell are you doing?" Ian asked in a whisper.

"What are you talking about?" Andille asked, mocking his whisper.

"Deb," he said and Andille stopped mocking him. His face turned thunderous.

"Watch what you say, Ian."

"Have you forgotten that we don't live here? That we live in New York? That we have jobs and—"

"I haven't forgotten," Andille said through his teeth.

"Then what are you doing?"

"I could ask you the same question," Andille answered, his voice getting silky.

"I told you," Ian said. "I'm telling my story. Jennifer is helping me."

"Right. Which explains what you two were doing last night and why—"

"Jennifer knows the score," Ian said, not wanting to think about how he'd misread her last night. How he'd missed the moment enthusiasm turned to doubt. "Does Deb?"

Andille's eyelids flinched and Ian knew the truth. "This place," Ian said, feeling bad for his best friend, even though he didn't quite understand it, "women like these women, they're not for us."

"Not for you," Andille said, his eyes flashing. "They're not for you. This could be for me. She could—"

Ian waited for Andille to finish but he looked down at his feet, his throat working hard. Ian cursed under his breath, knowing what Andille was butting up against. It's what Ian himself always butted up against and it was beginning to make him nuts watching Andille fight this.

"You don't owe me anything anymore, Andille," Ian said. "We're paid up and if you want—"

Andille's eyes burned right through Ian and he shut up. This was a seriously, painfully old argument. One that Ian never ever won.

"Fine," he said, curving his hand over Andille's thick shoulder. "You stubborn son of a bitch."

Andille's face cracked in a thin smile and the tension in him, the tension Ian knew was getting thicker and deeper and heavier every day, dissipated just slightly.

"So," Andille asked, "how goes it with the story?"

Ian blew out a big breath and stared at the closed door of the office. She was behind that door working on things without him. He'd noticed the change in her demeanor when she returned his cell phone. Suzette had said something, planted some doubt in her mind, and it was sticking.

This was his story, damn it. His mother. His overbearing nightmare of an abusive father. Without Ian, she didn't have a story. She didn't have anything. He turned slightly, hoping the door might open and she'd appear, radiating that icy all-business attitude that was such a ridiculous and sexy challenge it almost wasn't fair.

To him or her.

Really. The poor woman had no idea the red flag she'd waved in front of him with that whole "let's keep this professional" thing. He agreed totally, and nothing would happen. But he knew, just as she did, that if he so much as crooked a finger at her, she'd be right back in his arms, trying to crawl into his skin like she had been last night.

And her sitting in that office, working on his story and pretending she wasn't interested in him was all combining to piss him off.

"It's going great," he lied, not wanting Andille to know the truth. But his friend laughed.

"Right," Andille said.

The office door stayed shut and Ian thought his head would explode from the pressure of trying to will it open.

"Why don't you come outside with us?" Andille asked. "Take an afternoon off from being Ian Greer and kick around a soccer ball."

"Yeah!" Spencer, Jennifer's son, piped up from the table where he was assembling peanut butter and jelly sandwiches.

"There's no paparazzi out there, Ian," Andille said. "No Jackson, nothing but sunshine and kids."

An afternoon off? Playing soccer instead of turning himself inside out for revenge?

He glanced at the door to the office.

"I can't," he said. This was hardly the time for fun. His life was on the line and if it required him sitting here all day staring at that door, then he'd do it.

His revenge demanded that.

"Sorry," he told Andille, whose old, wise eyes said way too much.

"It's not me who's sorry," he said.

"I get it, Andille, but I can't pretend that my life's not on the line right now."

Andille shook his head. "It doesn't have to be your life," he said.

Ian rolled his eyes. "Well, right now it is."

Right now what was happening behind that office door was all he had.

WEIRD DAY, Spencer thought. Really weird. Probably one of the weirdest days in his life. And it wasn't because he'd watched Andille bounce a ball off his head, like, thirty-five times. What made everything off-the-charts weird was Madison.

First of all, he didn't like her anymore. And he definitely didn't love her. He could cross that stuff out in his book.

She was mean. Supermean when people weren't looking and then she'd turn around and be nice whenever adults were around.

She actually pinched him at the swimming hole when he wouldn't let her go ahead of him. Pinched him!

He looked at the red spot on his arm under the table.

Yeah, they weren't in love anymore. For sure.

"What are you doing?" Madison asked. She sat beside him at the dinner table because everyone thought they were such good buddies.

"Nothing," he said, real fast because he was a little scared of her.

"Here we go, guys," Deb said, putting down plates with pasta and peas and apples on them. "Careful, the pasta is hot." Then she turned away back to the stove.

Andille poured milk and set glasses down in front of all of them and then he looked away, too.

Spence rubbed his arm and glanced toward the closed office door. He really wished his mom would come out now. Then, like she'd heard him, the door opened and his mom walked out with a big smile on her face.

"Mom!" he cried. "Come sit by me."

"Sure, let me help Deb get stuff on the table." Mom leaned over and gave him a big kiss on the cheek and he almost grabbed her hand to keep her right beside him. "Hey," she said, "looks like you hurt your arm. You have to be careful doing those flips off the rope swing."

She brushed his hair off his face and turned to help Deb. And there was Madison, leaning toward him.

"Don't you dare say a word," she said, looking mean and ugly.

"Leave me alone, Mad—"

Madison grabbed his arm—the arm she'd already pinched—and she dug her fingers into his skin and squeezed and pinched and twisted her hands so his skin burned and ached and he gasped with the pain and shock of it.

"Don't say a word, or I'll—"

"Madison?" It was Ian standing right above them and Spence was so glad he nearly started crying. "Madison, what are you doing?" Ian knocked Madison's hands loose and Spence pulled himself away so fast he fell off his chair. He just laid there, holding his arm and wondering why he didn't run like he'd said he would.

IAN WASN'T THE only one motionless. The kitchen was frozen. Everyone was paralyzed with surprise. Daisy stood between Spence and Madison, whining, her canine loyalties divided.

Ian couldn't even be sure of what he'd been interrupting

between Madison and Spencer, but it had looked wrong. And now Spence wasn't getting up and the sound of his soft sob sent everyone into motion.

Madison wrestled her arm out of Ian's loose grip and charged Spence where he lay on the floor and she managed to stomp hard on his foot before Ian grabbed the girl around the waist, lifting her off the ground so she couldn't kick anyone else.

"He's lying," she cried, pushing and flailing against him. "He's totally lying. I never hurt him."

Jennifer was on her knees next to Spence and the boy curled into his mother, cradling his arm and trying to rub his foot at the same time.

"Whoa, whoa," Ian said, feeling the waters come up right over his head. His flight instinct was in full effect, but he knew he couldn't just walk away. He couldn't even let the girl go. "What is going on here?"

Angelina had gone into a sort of catatonic state that had Deb's hands full and Andille was holding on to Shonny.

That left him with the young abuser.

"Let me go!" Madison screamed, moving from pushing to scratching and biting him.

"Ouch, no." He tried to switch positions and the girl got loose and was heading for Spence, who cringed in sudden terror, again.

"Ian," Andille growled. "Take her out of here."

Right. Out. Ian snagged her around the waist and hauled her into the office. Ignoring her screams, he plunked her down in the chair, then turned around and left, slamming the door shut behind him.

Andille looked up at him, appalled.

"I should stay with her?" Ian guessed and Andille nodded, so he ducked back into the office.

Madison stood and tried to make a break for it, but he pushed her gently back into the chair. That game went on for a while. It felt like Ping-Pong, but a bad version of it. Man. He'd give about a million dollars to have Andille or Jennifer in here.

Jennifer wouldn't be bouncing this girl around like a ball.

"I can do this all night," he said when she snarled at him. She kept coming, and he kept putting her back in her spot, until finally she seemed exhausted.

The little girl sagged slightly in the chair, her hair shielding her face.

Ian didn't often have much empathy. Sympathy he could do. Anonymous sympathy from a very long way away was actually his favorite. Handing out money and legal aid was preferable to talking to people and trying to walk a mile in their shoes.

But looking at that little girl, he felt her shame and confusion right in his gut. Like a thousand-pound weight suddenly sewn into his stomach, he felt as if he were fourteen years old again at boarding school for the first time. Ashamed that he'd done something so bad to be sent away and unsure of exactly what it was. And angry with everyone.

The anger in her eyes was painfully familiar.

All worked up with nowhere to put all those feelings.

God, it was his childhood all over again.

Nausea spun through him and he took a deep breath, battling the memories.

"What are you doing?" he asked softly.

She shrugged. The veil of hair didn't reveal so much as an eyeball or the corner of her mouth. But he could feel her glaring at him like a cold wind blowing through the office.

"I thought Spence was your friend," he said.

She shrugged again and Ian felt his own temper rising.

The temper that terrified him. The temper that reminded him he was his father's son after all.

"You don't treat friends that way," he told her, carefully.

"I can treat him however I want." She sneered. "He's my friend."

Man, oh, man, if Madison's mother could see the lesson she'd given her little girl. It was the same lesson his father had taught him.

"He won't be if you keep hurting him."

Madison didn't respond.

"I know you're really scared and worried about your dad—"

"I don't care about my dad!" she said, shaking back her hair, so he could see her snapping eyes.

"You don't?"

"No!"

"But—" Ian was at a loss "—you saw him get hurt."

"I told him we should leave," she said, bristling and furious. "I told him we should leave a million times but he didn't listen. He didn't care."

"Oh," he said stupidly, his tongue and mind in knots. He sat hard in the chair by the desk. He'd done the same thing with his mother. Begged her to leave. Begged her to choose him over Dad. Begged her to keep herself—and him—safe.

And so she sent him away.

Christ, where was this grief coming from? He'd put this behind him. Way behind him. But here it was coming down on him like a landslide.

"I'm sure he—"

"Shut up!" she yelled, leaping to her feet and pushing him so hard he nearly fell off the chair. "You don't know anything! You don't know what it's like! You don't—"

Ian crouched and grabbed her shoulder. Going on some

kind of adrenaline-fueled instinct, he gave her a little shake, and another, until she stopped screaming, and was staring at him wide-eyed.

He saw himself reflected in her eyes and it pushed him over some edge he didn't realize he was so close to.

"I know more than you think. I know you have to do everything in your power to not be like your mother," he whispered right into her face and she stilled. He could actually see her listening. "I know you're angry and you don't know what to do with it. I know you're hurt and you don't know what to do with that, either. But acting the way your mother did is shameful. It's mean and it's wrong. And you have got to spend your entire life—every single day—trying to be better than that. You have to put all that anger and that hurt away."

She blinked at him and he worried in some distant place that he was scaring her. Perhaps his personal motto was too much for an eleven-year-old.

After a moment, she nodded and he stroked her shoulders with his thumbs, terrified that his anger and fear had gotten the better of him.

"I'm scared," she said and her voice broke. Tears filled her eyes and his heart just about shattered.

"What are you scared of?" he whispered, afraid it was him.

"I'm scared I'm just like her," she wailed and threw herself into his arms.

For a second he just crouched there, feeling her hot tears on his neck, feeling the strength and desperation in her stranglehold on his neck.

He wanted to run, to leave. But he knew that was the coward's way out. And suddenly, somehow, he was tired of being a coward.

Awkwardly stroking her hair he thought of his father, of

every decision Ian had made and the fears that woke him in the night. He thought of all that and was suddenly brave enough to whisper, "Me, too."

CHAPTER TWELVE

"WHAT DO YOU THINK he's doing in there?" Deb asked the quiet room. Jennifer lifted her head and glanced at the closed office door.

"I have no idea," she whispered. Spence shuffled around and looked up at her with damp, blue-grey eyes. "You hungry?" she asked and he nodded.

She helped him into his chair and picked up the glass of milk that had spilled, trading it for a full one.

"You okay?" she asked while he drank.

He nodded. "I don't know why she did that," he finally said, so baffled.

"Me neither, sweetie," she said.

The office door behind them opened and Spencer stiffened, his fingers white around the glass. Jennifer stroked his hair and looked over her shoulder.

And time stood still.

Ian, the sexiest man alive, was gazing down at a tear-streaked Madison. Holding her hand, even. And Madison clung to him, like a boat in a storm.

"Madison," he whispered, jostling their linked hands, and she looked at him for a long moment, gathering some kind of strength from something she saw in his eyes.

Finally she nodded and stepped toward Spence, who, still tense, still scared, looked at her.

"I'm so sorry," she whispered, tears in her pretty green eyes. "I understand if you don't want to be friends anymore," she said. "But I promise I'll never hurt you again."

Jennifer was floored and Deb and Andille seemed equally dumbfounded. Angelina wiggled off Deb's lap and threw herself against her sister.

Spencer, her serious little boy, stared at Madison for a moment then nodded solemnly, as if ratifying some international agreement.

Madison's tears shook loose from her lashes and trickled down her cheeks. She hung her head, her shoulders so small, and Ian was right there.

"Good job, kiddo," he whispered.

Deb and Andille burst into action, grabbing more milk and putting kids back in their seats, keeping up a steady and distracting stream of chatter and Jennifer, stunned and awed by this new unexpected side of Ian, stood to give him her thanks.

His eyes lifted to hers and her stomach twisted and plummeted to her feet.

His eyes were ravaged. Haunted. Past his smile and easygoing charm, whatever had happened in that office had scourged him.

"Let's eat," he said brightly, then he sat between Spencer and Madison, acting for all the world like nothing was wrong.

Jennifer sank into her chair, all too aware that he was lying.

"WHAT A NIGHT," Deb said, collapsing into one of the kitchen chairs. "What time is it?"

"Nine," Andille answered, the sound of his thick warm voice like sliding into a bubble bath. He put away the last of the dishes from the dinner that nobody ate and then sat across from her.

"Is that all?" She sighed and his chuckle had the bizarre

effect of making her smile. Despite her bone-deep weariness. Despite her bone-deep anxiety.

She glanced at him from the corner of her eye as she had all day long, as if taking small sips of him was easier than gulping him down in big swallows.

"Thank you for your help," she said.

He waved off her gratitude like he had before whenever she extended it. The man was a pure miracle with that little Angelina, to say nothing of the way Shonny took to him.

To say nothing of the way Deb felt herself softening toward him like butter left in the sun.

"I'm just glad I was here to help."

"Me, too," she told him.

"You wanted us gone," he reminded her, a twinkle in his eye.

"Well." She smiled and looked at her casts, her useless hands, and marveled at what a day it had been. What a few days it had been. Felt like years in some ways and, in some ways, it felt like moments. "I'm glad you didn't listen."

One of the doors to the bedrooms clicked shut and Jennifer appeared in the kitchen like a wrung-out ghost.

"Oh, honey," Deb said, standing. "Let me get you som—"

Jennifer smiled and shook her head. "I'm fine. Spence is finally asleep. Daisy is in bed with him and I didn't have the heart to kick her out." She pushed her hands through her hair, ruining the last of the bun she'd had in all day. She took out the ponytail and shook her hair down around her shoulders.

"What did the girl's aunt say?" Jennifer asked.

"She's coming for them in the morning," Deb said. "Their father is getting released from the hospital either tonight or tomorrow so they'll be able to be home with him. I also called the county child psychiatrist, and Madison and Angelina have appointments next week."

"Good," Jennifer said. "That's good."

Silence fell over the kitchen. A silence that practically hummed, chanted and whispered Ian's name.

Oh, you dummy, Deb thought as she watched Jennifer chew her lips. *Just ask. Just go on and ask.*

"Where is Ian?" Jennifer finally asked, trying too hard to sound casual.

"Outside," Andille said, gesturing toward the back door.

"Still?" Jennifer said, clearly concerned and Deb wanted to tell that woman that her worry plate was pretty much full without adding that man to the mix. But she doubted Jennifer would take the advice.

"He didn't show it, but he was pretty upset," Andille told her, crossing his big arms behind his head—a motion Deb watched and appreciated from the corner of her eye. "And you can imagine," he said with a sly, quiet smile, "getting upset, upsets him."

"I'm going to go check on him," Jennifer said, heading for the door. Deb and Andille stared after her for a long time, watching the white of her shirt cross the dark lawn like an apparition.

Deb, while Andille was watching Jennifer, stared at the man's profile. Deb didn't give two figs about Ian. But what was really obvious was that Ian Greer upset Andille. And that did bother her. He was a good man, too good a man for the likes of Ian.

"Can I ask you a question?" Deb said, breaking the silence.

"Sure." Andille smiled at her. And that smile was seriously the most intimate thing Deb had experienced in years. It made her twitch and burn and look away, embarrassed by how much this man was under her skin.

"Why are you with Ian?"

Andille's whole face shut down, his gracious smiles

and warm eyes vanished and he was a cool—cold, even—stranger.

"I'm sorry," she quickly said. "It's none of my business."

"Why do you ask?" Even his voice was different. Formal, somehow.

She shrugged. "It's not important."

"It is," he said, surprising her. "To me, it's very important. So, please, tell me what you see that made you ask that question."

"He clearly brings you…" She searched for the right word. "Distress. You watch him and you look pained. Like a parent watching his kid misbehave."

Andille stared at her, then slowly smiled. Chuckled, even, though it didn't sound very cheerful. "I suppose that's pretty much what I feel."

"So, why are you here?"

"He needs someone to watch over him."

"He's a grown man," Deb said incredulously. "A rich, grown man. I think he can take care of himself."

Andille's face told her otherwise.

"So, then, why you?" She tilted her head, trying to match the man who so clearly loved and craved children to the man who professionally babysat Ian Greer.

Andille stood and braced himself against the counter, his wide strong back to Deb, and she was stunned by the sudden desire she had to touch his back. Wrap her arms around his waist and press her face to that muscular dip that split along his spine. A woman could get lost in a back like that, be shielded and protected by whatever came.

"I owe Ian Greer," Andille said. "Years ago, he did something for me. He broke one of his rules and helped me. Helped my family."

"And because of that, you are spending your life trying

to keep him out of trouble?" He nodded and looked up, meeting her eyes in the reflection in the window. "That must have been some favor."

He licked his lips, his eyes riveted to hers, and for a second she couldn't breathe for the intensity in his face. The heat in his eyes. Then he turned around.

"My father was the king of a very small African country. We had diamond mines and not much else. When I was eleven he sent me away to boarding school, but kept my mother and seven sisters in Africa. When I was twenty-one there was a very violent coup and my father was killed. My mother and sisters held hostage."

Deb couldn't breathe, couldn't move, couldn't think. She could only sit and bleed for this man. For the pain that poured out of him.

"Ian asked his father, who was president at that time, for help. Something Ian swore he'd never do for any reason. Ever. But he did it for me and his father used his influence to get my sisters and mother out of the country."

"And that's why—"

He nodded. "One of my sisters is getting married next summer. Another is going to law school. Another is a pediatrician. The youngest is a track and field star." He smiled, radiantly. "None of that would be happening if it weren't for Ian."

Deb slumped in her chair.

"So, you see? I owe him eight lives," he said and she nodded.

If someone did that for her, she'd spend the rest of her life thanking that person. It wasn't, oddly, all that different than the way she felt about Serenity. Serenity House and Sam saved her life, and now she was dedicated to returning that favor.

"I know," Andille said, walking toward her and stopping a few inches from her chair, "Ian can be a tough man to like, but he's a good man. Underneath everything, he's a good man."

"It doesn't matter what I think," Deb said.

"It does to me," Andille said. Deb thought she felt his hand on her hair and everything stopped. Her blood. Her heart. Her thoughts. And she just concentrated on that ghostly sweet sensation.

"Can I ask you a question?" Andille asked, his quiet voice ricocheting through her bones, and she nodded, unable to speak.

"What happened?" he asked. "That made it so hard for you to like men?"

Her eyes shut briefly with a sense of the inevitable. Of course, he was going to ask this question. Of course he'd wonder. And somehow she gathered strength from his presence, from that whisper-light touch of his hand, from the sound of his voice.

She opened her mouth, wanting to tell him, feeling the words in the back of her throat like bile, but nothing came.

"Deb?" He sat, pulled his chair close to her and placed his hand over her casts. His big black hand, holding hot pink plaster because it was hers, broke her silence. Broke her heart.

"My father," she said simply, staring at his hand, stretching her fingers out so she could feel his warmth. "He was a difficult man. A..." She sighed, searching for the right word. "Evil man. He was a preacher, but there was something really twisted in him. He hurt me. He hurt my mom and I thank God every day that Mom didn't have any more children."

"Thank God," Andille said earnestly and she smiled at him, feeling a connection with him that she'd never felt anywhere before. Ever.

"It took me a long time to rebel, but I did when I was about nineteen and I got pregnant. He found out and beat me so badly I almost lost the baby. I managed to get out of the house. Mom, I think, intervened and I walked here with two broken ribs, a broken wrist and a sprained ankle. I had a concussion, two black eyes and—" Andille shifted his hand, linking his fingers through hers, and the sensation stole her breath. It had been years, a lifetime ago, since a man touched her and that man, that touch, was nothing compared to Andille. "I got here and I just never left."

"What about Shonny's father?" Andille asked and Deb shrugged, pulling her hand free and tucking both into her lap where they could burn and pulse.

"He wasn't interested in us," she said. "And frankly, I'm glad he wasn't. We're better off without him."

"Not all men are like your father, or like Shonny's dad," he said and she sighed. She'd heard this so often. "Not all men are cruel or indifferent."

"I know," she said but he shook his head, scooted closer.

"I don't think you do," he said.

"No," she said emphatically. "I do. I understand that." *In theory,* she thought. *Until you.* But she couldn't say that. Couldn't even believe she'd thought it.

His fingertip, calloused and hot, touched her cheek and there was a sudden vacuum in the world, until it was just her and this man and this touch.

"You're too good a woman to be alone," he whispered, his eyes searching her face. "You should let a man love you."

Deb couldn't move, couldn't stop him when he lifted her cast and kissed her fingers, like the prince he was. "Good night, Deb," he said. Then, like she wasn't dying, like she wasn't feeling desire and lust for the first time in her life, he left.

JENNIFER FOUND Ian on his back in the yard behind the house. He lay in the tall grasses, silver in the moonlight, staring up at the stars, his hands on his chest.

He was the picture of a man without worries or cares.

And it pissed her off, because it cost her so much to be here. Her pride. Her professional integrity. She came out here because she'd thought, after this harrowing night, he might need her.

But, when he caught sight of her, he smiled merrily.

"Hi," he said amiably. "What are you doing out here?" He tilted his head as if to see her better.

A very good question, Jennifer. Perhaps one you should have asked yourself, before you came running out here to be some kind of emotional Florence Nightingale to a man who was moon-bathing.

"I was—we were worried."

"Not about me, I hope."

She remembered the look in his eyes as he came out of that office. She remembered the tension on his face, the grief that covered him like a blanket. This flip, casual man before her was lying. She was sure of it.

"Are you all right?" she asked. "Really? Or is this an act?"

"Act?"

"None of us knew what to do with Madison, but you just swept her into that office. You said something to her, something that made her unable to let you out of her sight. She apologized to Spencer three times."

He stared up at the stars with perhaps a bit more purpose than before. "Madison and I understand each other."

She laughed incredulously. "I wasn't even sure you knew her name before tonight. I've never seen you look at her twice and suddenly you understand each other?"

"We're the children of abusers, Jennifer," he snapped, his eyes flashing in the moonlight. "We've got a lot in common."

She digested that, along with the emotion he was trying valiantly to hide. She sat beside him in the grass, the blades poking through the cotton of her pants to scratch her skin. "So," she asked, "what did you say?"

He sat up in a quick swoosh, spoiling the image of a man at leisure, which, of course, had been an act. One more act. One more layer to the mysterious and confusing Ian Greer. "I told her she had to fight every day to control her anger and hurt because she had to be better than her mother."

Jennifer struggled to not touch his leg where it rested inches from hers. The story, even Kerry Waldo and her career, seemed so far away from this moment. He was human. She was human. And she could, so easily, put her hand on his knee and tell him she was sorry. Sorry that he'd had to deal with Madison when it obviously caused him such turmoil. Sorry that he had this baseline experience that made him understand that complicated girl inside.

"I told her—" he sighed, staring up at the stars as clouds rolled across the sky "—that she shouldn't be mad at her father. Because she is, you know."

He turned, pinned her with his gaze.

"She feels betrayed by him," Ian said. "Abandoned. Because he chose to stay when she begged him to leave."

Jennifer had the sinking suspicion they weren't talking only about Madison.

"Is that how you feel about your mother?"

He smiled slightly, heartbreakingly. "It doesn't really matter now, does it?" he said, and she didn't believe him. Not a bit. She wanted to grab him and shake him, tell him that of course it mattered. But he was talking. "But I know that when I met Andille, when we were kids and I liked him right away, the first thing I did was give him a bloody nose." He plucked a crabgrass leaf and rolled it in his fingers. "Because that's all I knew about showing someone I liked them. Not effective friend-making."

That was the saddest thing she'd ever heard, despite his efforts to make a joke.

"Andille told me that he could have me killed for punching him." He smiled at her. "He's a prince, you know. A real live one. Well, a king now. Not that he talks about it."

"Really?" she asked, somehow not terribly surprised. There was something regal about the guy, and if there were kings in this world, Andille should be one.

"Yep, and he told me he could have me killed or he could be my friend, but not if I ever tried to hurt him again."

"You chose to be his friend?"

"No, I chose to ignore him for a year. Then he chose to be my friend and I couldn't shake him."

She laughed, imagining Andille doing such a thing. Ian looked truly relaxed for the first time since opening that office door and Jennifer decided to drop the Annabelle questions for now.

It was effective interviewing, the careful circling of the real issues, luring the subject into a truthful discussion, without them ever noticing. But she knew, deep down, that she liked him smiling right now.

"That same tactic must have worked wonders with the girls," she said. "Pulling their hair then ignoring them."

"I've never been on a date," he said, leaning back on his elbows, and she rolled her eyes at him.

"Come on. Half your dates are on the front pages of magazines."

"Those aren't dates."

"Then what are they?"

The look he flashed her was so heated, so filled with dark, carnal knowledge, she actually blushed. She got the very distinct impression that this man made practice things she'd never even thought of. Things she'd never known. "Oh. Well. Those are still dates, aren't they?"

He laughed and shook his head. "They're like doctors' appointments."

She wanted to be disgusted, horrified even. But instead she felt sorry for him, which was ludicrous. He was the sexiest man alive and she'd had two lovers in her whole life. But, that something so special could be reduced to something so clinical was sad.

"That's too bad," she said, leaning back in the grass, unconsciously mirroring his posture. "Dates are fun. All the suspense." She smiled, thinking of Doug and their first date when his credit card had been declined. Then she realized with a sort of breathless wonder the memory didn't hurt. There was no sting, no wild mental shelving of all things Doug.

When had that happened?

It had been so long since she even allowed herself to think of him, in fear of that pain.

But, it was bittersweet to remember those heady days with Doug and awkward to be remembering them while sitting with Ian.

But it didn't hurt. And that was astonishing.

Perhaps it was because she knew that what she'd had with Doug was something totally different than what was happening between her and Ian. Like apples and oranges. Or love and lust.

She cocked her head to study Ian's profile—so handsome and chiseled in the moonlight. It was hard to imagine him not being on a date, he'd be so good at it. So suave and charming. She could imagine him over candlelight, drinking wine, carefully flirting. She could feel the sizzle of his touch, his glance. The magnetic power of his body dressed in something classic across candlelight and white linen.

"Why haven't you dated?" she asked, proud when her voice didn't crack.

"I have made two kinds of decisions in my life. Decisions to hurt my father and decisions to not be like my father."

"Where does not dating fall?"

"Nice girls date, Jennifer. And nice girls want husbands and babies. And private lives and husbands who aren't—" He stopped, sighed. "Angry most of the time. The girls I'm with don't care."

"You don't want a wife and children?"

He opened his mouth as if to answer then stopped. And was silent.

Oh. Oh, Ian. She couldn't stop herself, she was about to reach for his back, that wide muscled expanse hidden behind cotton.

Career. Story. Waldo.

Reality was a wall between them and she could not touch him, because she knew, in her bones, in the throbbing pain in her chest and fingers, what would happen if she did.

That dark knowledge was back in his eyes, his lip curled slightly and she couldn't pull in a deep breath. He knew what she wanted and what she fought against.

And worse, those things she wanted, those dark carnal things that she suddenly longed for with her whole body, he wanted, too. She could see it in his eyes, the sharp lines on his face. The way his breath came fast in his chest.

He put his hand over hers, sending sharp zings of desire through her nerves. Just a touch, one touch on her hand, and she couldn't help but imagine that touch on her face. Her lips. Breasts. Between her legs.

Oh, God. Could she die from this? From wanting this much?

"I thought we couldn't do this?" he whispered, seduction

in his voice, taunting her. Teasing her. "You told me this morning this was against the rules."

"It is," she told him, glad her voice was strong and steady, and she pulled her hand away.

"Ah, but you wish it wasn't," he said, so sure of himself that a spark of anger ignited in the middle of all that heat churning through her body.

"Not everything is about sex," she said. "It can be about friendship. Comfort, Ian."

"Don't lie," he whispered. "Not about this. If you want to touch me, be honest."

"I think you need to be touched," she said and she could tell she'd surprised him. She'd surprised herself. He pulled away. Oh, lord, this was so awkward. So unreal. What was she doing in this situation? She didn't even know the right vocabulary. "I think you need to be comforted."

"You're being a bit melodramatic."

"Your father was an abuser, your mother sent you away, the women you're with don't care. I think—"

"Stop, Jennifer," he said, shaking his head, all that dark seduction he put on like a suit, gone. "You're making me into something I'm not."

This man was not what he seemed. He was better than she even dreamed and the real kicker was that he was so much better than he thought he was.

"That's part of the story, Ian," she told him, her hands securely in her lap. "The whole world is going to find out that you're not nearly as bad as you pretend to be."

"I'm still the same man," he said. "These things I've told you, that stuff with Madison…it doesn't change who I am. You don't want me as a friend, Jennifer."

"You don't get to decide that," she said, stunned that he

would think that after all that had happened between them. They were friends, at the very least. Weren't they? "I do."

He stood so fast she could only gape at him.

"The story is what's important, Jennifer. It's all that matters," he said, his eyes touching on all of her features, a soft sweet touch, a lingering goodbye. "I'm not important. I never have been."

CHAPTER THIRTEEN

IAN WOKE UP TO the sound of someone pounding on a door. He lurched upright, slipping and nearly falling off the couch onto the floor. Something wet brushed his ear and he found himself face-to-tongue with Daisy.

He jerked back, expecting to have his face bitten off.

Daisy followed, jumped up on the couch with her front paws and slobbered all over him. A tongue bath of doggy love.

Apparently she'd had a change of heart regarding her affections toward him during the night.

The door-knocking came again and he shoved Daisy out of the way. Through the open door of the bedroom Ian watched Andille roll over and open one eye.

"What's going on?"

"Someone's here," he said and the dog, sitting alertly beside him, barked once as if seconding him.

"I thought that dog hated you," Andille said.

"It's momentary, I'm sure."

The rumble of voices filtered from downstairs and Andille sighed as if to stand. Ian stopped him. "It's probably Madison and Angelina's father," he said. "I'll go check."

Andille smiled wearily. "Two days ago we were sure we had to leave and today we're making sure everyone is okay. This place has a strange effect on people."

"Probably a good indication that we should have gone

with our first instinct," Ian said, scrubbing his hands over his face. Strange that he truly did want to see Madison off, that he thought it was important. Two days ago the thought wouldn't have even entered his mind.

But he stood, tugged on his jeans and a shirt. His cell phone on the table started to ring, rattling against the table. Both Ian and Andille turned to stare at it.

"You gonna get that?" Andille asked.

Ian shook his head, clenched his fists against the urge to hurl the phone against the wall.

"He's been calling a lot more."

"I need to get a new number," he said and headed for the door, the dog beside him.

He found everyone in the common room. Angelina was happily held in a man's arms. A man with a bandage on his forehead and a doozy of a black eye.

The abused father wasn't what Ian expected. The man was big, strong-looking, like a former athlete. He was handsome, despite the bandages, and certainly didn't look like a man who got knocked around by his one-hundred-and-ten-pound wife.

When he saw Ian he did a quick double take. Ian was familiar with that brief, slack-jawed look—the dude recognized him. And Ian wished he'd never come down here.

But there was a certain tension in the room, something explosive. Ian looked to Jennifer for some explanation of what everyone was so nervous about. Before he could make eye contact with her Madison was across the room and attached to his leg like a leech.

"I don't want to go!" she cried into his jeans and Ian saw Madison's father go even more pale.

"Hey," Ian said, crouching down to remove Madison's tourniquet-strength arms from around his leg. "Madison, you get to go home. You get to sleep in your own bed. Yesterday morning you said that was all you wanted. Remember?"

She stared across the room at her father. "I don't want to go with him," she said.

Her father groaned and approached her from across the room, looking more pained than any man should. "Sweetie, your mom is gone." He glanced at Deb as if checking his script. "She's getting help," he said. "And she won't be back for a long time."

"I don't believe you," she said, sharp-eyed.

Ian caught Jennifer's eye and saw, unbelievably, that she thought he could handle this. That he would. That somehow Ian had the answer to this terrible situation in his back pocket.

Which was crazy because all he had in his back pocket was a law degree and a ton of cash. Neither of which would do any good.

"I swear to you," Madison's father breathed, looking so damn earnest Ian believed him. "Mom is not welcome in our home right now."

He could tell Madison wanted to believe her father, and who wouldn't. But she was stubborn and smart and had spent who knows how many years being disappointed by her parents.

"Tell you what," Ian said. "I believe your dad." Madison shot him a dubious look. "But I'll make you a deal. If your mom comes back, you can come spend the night here."

He had no clue if that was the right thing to say, but Madison looked cheered. "I can?" she asked and Ian looked to her father, who nodded gratefully.

"Absolutely," he agreed empathically. There was a long pause and Madison finally nodded and Ian exhaled a breath he hadn't realized he'd been holding. There had been no Plan B, there was hardly a Plan A, but it seemed like everyone expected him to have an answer right now.

"Go get your things, sweetie," Madison's father said and both Madison and Angelina took off for Deb, who stood in the kitchen, with their backpacks.

"Thank you—" her father started to say and held out a hand to Ian, but Ian shook his head, forgoing the handshake in order to look the man right in the eyes.

"You better mean it," Ian said with far more anger than he thought he felt. But suddenly there it was. This guy was not his mother, not even close, considering his mother had never made such a promise. She'd sent him away instead. But Madison's father was here and Ian's mother was dead and the world just didn't get it right sometimes. "That girl feels betrayed by you. She feels like you chose her abusive, mean mother over her time and time again and a kid doesn't just forget that."

Ian hadn't intended to make the guy feel worse, but he could tell he had, and he reined in his sudden temper.

"I didn't want to lose my family," the guy whispered. "I thought I could make it work."

"Well, you've got another chance to make what's left of your family work," Ian said and the guy nodded, tears flooding his red-rimmed eyes.

Oh, for crying out loud, Ian thought, clapping his hand on the man's shoulder, like they did in movies when men had heart-to-hearts. "Your daughter loves you," he said. Madison's father nodded, sniffing back emotion. "Don't mess it up and you'll do fine."

The guy seemed to buy his half-assed platitudes.

My work here is more than done, Ian thought, his skin feeling too tight. *I gotta get going.* Andille was right, this place had a weird effect on people.

He turned and caught Jennifer staring at him and the look in her eye, like she was proud or impressed, seemed ridiculous. This whole thing seemed ridiculous.

Ian Greer went out with models who didn't wear underwear. He didn't counsel abused men about how to handle their children. It wasn't in his skill set.

"I need to do some work," he told her, thinking of why he'd been called to Serenity in the first place.

"This afternoon, I was hoping we could talk," she said, touching his arm as he passed her.

"About the story?" he asked sharply and she stiffened, her surprise at his tone evident.

I told you, he wanted to say. *I told you I'm not who you think I am.*

"Of course about the story," she said, slightly belligerent.

"Fine," he said, stepping away from the heat of her touch, that no matter how much distance he put between them he could still feel.

He could still almost feel her touch from last night, the smooth slide of her palm that, had things been different between them, he would have felt against his back. And who knows where else.

Comfort! Ha! The woman wanted in his pants so bad she was lying to herself.

And what about you? a little voice asked. *You want in her pants so bad you're playing the benevolent counselor. The child of an abuser who has got it all figured out.*

It was all too complicated. He liked his life simple. Annoying and embarrassing his father had kept him occupied and busy for years. Far too busy to think about good women and hurt children and fathers with their backs against a wall.

Wanting revenge kept him away from anything messy. Anything complicated.

And now he was at Serenity and it was as if his life had just exploded. He was covered in mess.

"Suzette's journals arrived this morning and I'm going through them," she said, all businesslike.

Part of him wanted to take back his harsh words from moments ago. He liked her compassion, the warmth and pride in her eyes. He liked her in the moonlight, pale and earnest, seeming so strong and fragile at the same time.

Friends, he thought. It seemed unlikely.

"I'll be available whenever you need me," he said as apologetically as he could under the circumstances. And, before he found himself volunteering for babysitting or picking up litter or something else totally unlike him, he left.

The dumb dog following him in his wake.

AN HOUR LATER, the phone tucked into Ian's pocket started to ring. Ian swore and pulled it out.

Dad. Again.

"I thought you were going to change the number?" Andille asked from his "office" at the folding table in the upstairs apartment.

"I've been too busy saving the world, Andille," he joked and turned the phone off. Part of him wanted to answer the phone, swear at the old man, like the old days, tell him in explicit detail how Jackson Greer's days were numbered.

But he couldn't jeopardize the story that way. Couldn't jeopardize Jennifer that way.

And it was truly shocking to put the vengeful instinct aside. To be able to put it aside, because two weeks ago the temptation would have been too great.

He supposed he had Jennifer to thank for that. Jennifer, whom he just jumped on with both feet for simply doing her job.

Yeah, he thought sarcastically, *you've come a long way, baby.*

He tossed the phone onto the floor.

"What's the plan with the lawsuit?" Andille asked.

"Settle," he said. It's what he always did. The keyboard of his laptop clacked under his fingers as he e-mailed the paralegal he worked with on these cases. She was discreet, quick and the single mother of two kids who'd grown up in a shelter not unlike Serenity.

"With a mob wife?" Andille asked, looking up from his own laptop, where he was sorting out Serenity's financial woes. "She's fishing, Ian. It's not even a—"

"You know I'm not going to court," Ian said, laughing at the very idea. "Representing Serenity is hardly what a guy like me would do. I've got an image to maintain."

"Ian." Andille sighed and sat back. "Once this story breaks you won't have to pretend anymore. You can just be you. Do what you want." Andille scowled and turned back to his computer. "Should be a relief," he added.

Ian stared blankly at his oldest friend. He fought the urge to ask Andille who he thought Ian was, because he had no clue. For more years than he wanted to count he was the guy who dressed well and showed up at the right parties with the right women. He made not particularly funny jokes that everyone laughed at. He pretended and lied and had no idea what to do if he weren't doing that.

"Won't it?" Andille asked. "I mean, what would you do with this lawsuit if you didn't have to worry about your image?"

What would I do? Ian wondered. Ian Greer? He thought of the thousands of dollars he gave away to overreaching scumbags and abusers just so he could keep things quiet, under the rug. He thought of who he'd been in law school, the things he'd wanted to change, the people he wanted to give a voice to.

Most of the time, that person, the idealistic student he'd been, seemed like someone else. A different man. A foolish guy with big plans who had no idea how cruel the world could be. How those big plans could get squashed.

Idealistic didn't even begin to cover it.

But then, this thing with his dad started. Ian got caught coming out of a bar one night by some paparazzi and the next morning his father called, furious, throwing demands around like he had the right.

And Ian had realized how he could get back at his father for those long years of abuse.

And that idealistic guy got pushed out of the way. Forgotten.

Ian wasn't sure if he would ever be that idealistic again, but he could do the right thing. In the bright light of day he would do the right thing.

Grinning, he deleted the e-mail to his paralegal and began to draft another one.

JENNIFER CLOSED Suzette's last journal and sat back in the office chair.

Ho. Ly. Cow.

Lifting the first journal from the FedEx box that had arrived at dawn this morning, Jennifer had no clue what she was in for. That journal began on the first day Suzette, as a young assistant to the wife of a new governor, noticed something wrong. Something wrong by way of a split lip on the pretty new first lady of North Carolina, which coincided with Ian's arrival from the hospital. Reading about it was like taking that first breath-stealing plunge from the high dive into cold water.

And it didn't stop.

Ten years. Ten journals. Dates. Photos. Everything. It was an insider's look at marriage gone wrong and the hard choices Annabelle Greer made every day.

Jennifer looked down at the journals and thought about

what Annabelle had said two years ago that changed Jennifer's life. *Embrace the pain or cut it out before it overwhelms you.*

Annabelle embraced the pain.

And Jennifer really didn't know how to feel about that. It was impossible to be proud of the woman, not after she'd sent her son away, in effect choosing the abuser over her own kid. But at the same time Jennifer couldn't quite simplify all her feelings into pity. Or anger. Or grief.

She rubbed her eyes and tried to stretch the knots out of her back. No wonder Ian was so complicated, so layered. He was the byproduct of every event recorded in the journals.

He learned how to hide himself, his true self, from a master. His mother.

"Wow." Jennifer sighed, both energized and totally drained. Her stomach growled and, thinking she'd missed lunch, she glanced out the window to see where the sun was.

Gone.

It was night.

Uh-oh.

Deb had knocked on the door a few times asking her if she needed anything and Jennifer had kept telling her she'd just be a few more minutes.

Not so much as a boo from Spence, which bummed her out on one hand, but on the other she was grateful. Grateful for the day to herself, for her career. For this story.

This story that was already bigger and better than she'd ever imagined when Ian had told her.

Ian! She was supposed to talk to Ian this afternoon.

She stood and opened the office door only to find Ian sitting in the dark at the kitchen table, the green-blue glow of the laptop open in front of him, illuminating the clean handsome lines of his face.

He was so absorbed in whatever was on that screen that

he didn't see her in the shadows, and so she watched him, her heart hammering in her chest as it seemed like her past and present collided.

How many times had she come home late from work to find Doug just like that? They'd both be tired, but glad to see each other. He'd have a beer and maybe she'd have one, too, and they'd sit and talk about their days. He'd ask her about whatever story she was working on and she'd ask him how Spence went down, what he had for dinner, if he asked about her.

It seemed that when she let Ian walk in the door she'd let in the past, too. And she was stunned to find that it was okay. She'd spent so long making sure these memories never surfaced and now they were here, seemingly everywhere she turned. Every time she looked at Ian.

And the pain that she'd lived with, the pain that she was terrified of, wasn't there.

"Jennifer?" Ian asked quietly and her head snapped around.

He smiled, the effect sort of sad in the strange light from the laptop and, caught as she was between memories of Doug and the reality of this man, she felt her heart twist. "We were wondering when you'd come out."

A hulking shadow at his feet shifted and sighed and she recognized that sigh as Daisy's. Daisy was at Ian's feet.

"I thought that dog hated you," she said.

"So did I," Ian muttered, crossing his legs and nudging the dog with his toe.

Amazing, she thought. *Lock yourself in an office for a day and the whole world changes.*

"I know it sounds lame," she said, "but time really did get away from me. Where is everybody?"

"Deb is putting the kids down," he said, sitting back in

his chair, crossing his arms behind his head. "Andille is making some calls upstairs and so I'm out here."

"Did Spence eat dinner?" she asked.

"Like a pig," Ian answered.

"Did he ask—" She stopped. Really, the kid was eleven, if he wanted to talk to her, he could have knocked on the door. And he didn't, so wasn't that her answer?

"He asked about you a lot, but Deb told him you needed to do a little work and you'd be out soon. But he got into a game with Andille after dinner and stopped asking. Are you hungry?" He stood, the chair scraping across the linoleum.

"Starved," she said, stretching her back. "But I'd really like a beer, I don't suppose…?"

With a wry grin, he glanced over his shoulder at her. "Despite how I arrived here, I was telling the truth when I said I don't drink. I haven't for years. The best I can offer you is some of the cold coffee I'm drinking or—"

"You don't have to make my dinner," she said, wishing a little that he wouldn't. It all felt a little too intimate. After the journals then finding him in the dark, looking so…normal.

He'd said they weren't friends, so what was this?

He pulled a plate of salad out of the fridge, and a bottle of dressing, and set it on the table. "Dinner," he said with a flourish. "As you can see I slaved away."

"It's perfect," she said. "Thank you."

All too conscious of him watching her, of him being in the same room, she sat down to the salad and hoped she didn't get it stuck in her teeth.

"I'm sorry," he said. "For earlier."

"When you got all snippy with me?" she asked with a smile.

"Well, I protest the word *snippy,* but yes. That thing with Madison—" He shook his head.

"Don't worry about it."

The silence between them was so different than the one between them that first morning, she almost said something, made a joke about how far they'd come. But that would be too personal, and she didn't know how to handle that right now. Everything was so out of sorts.

"What are you working on?" she asked, pointing at the laptop with her fork.

"Your lawsuit," he said.

"Oh, yeah, what are we doing with the mob boss's wife?"

"Countersuing."

She speared a cucumber. "On what grounds?"

"Damages. Everyone here was very scarred by the Contis showing up the way they did."

Jennifer choked on the cucumber. "You think you can prove that?"

"I don't think I'll have to," he said, sitting down with a full mug of what had to be terribly cold and therefore very bad coffee. "She's reaching. With her husband in jail, she's going to be strapped for cash." He smirked at her over the edge of his mug, looking like a little kid getting away with something and her heart went *ka-thunk*. "Not every mobster has money buried in the backyard, and she's trying anything she can think of. She doesn't have a case." He took a sip of the coffee and grimaced.

"If she drops it, will you pursue?" she asked.

He shook his head. "We don't need that money. You have an interest in law?" he asked. "Or just TV law shows?"

She licked her lips and looked down at her salad. Not wanting to bring up Doug, she realized, had nothing to do with Doug and everything to do with the vibe in this room right now. The way she felt so comfortable. The way he seemed so alive. The way her skin remembered so clearly the touch of Ian's skin, the feel of his hands, the bite of his teeth.

"Doug was a lawyer," she finally said.

"Ah."

She chewed and he sipped and the silence weighed a thousand pounds.

"Do you want—"

"Were you—"

They spoke at the same time then laughed, awkwardly. "Go ahead," she said, feeling worse than if she had the whole salad in her teeth and dressing in her hair.

"Do you want to talk about Doug?" he asked, so uncomfortable and so earnest she couldn't help but laugh. "I'm being sincere," he protested.

"I know you are," she said. "And I appreciate it, but no. I do not want to talk about Doug."

"All right," he said, unable to keep the relief out of his voice and suddenly he was so dear. Such a strange and uncomfortable friend, no matter what he thought.

"Thanks, though."

He nodded manfully.

"Do you want to talk about the journals?" she asked, watching him in the half light as all his features tightened.

"I don't know," he said with a sigh, watching her with an inscrutable gaze. "Do I?"

She knew he was shutting down in an effort to protect himself, to stop what had to be a tremendous amount of pain from rushing to the surface. Part of her wanted to push him, force him to deal with this pain.

And suddenly she realized—she saw it so clearly she nearly fell off her chair. Ian had done the same thing she'd done with her pain. He'd cut it out.

"Jennifer?" he asked, no doubt wondering why she stared at him with her mouth agape.

"You know what your mother said to me that changed my life?" she asked.

"I don't have the slightest idea."

"She said, about my grief over Doug, that I had to either embrace the pain or cut it out. I couldn't stay in limbo, grieving for him for the rest of my life."

"So?"

"So, I cut it out. I left my house, my job, my state. I picked my son up and I moved to a place that didn't smell like my husband."

"Sounds like a reasonable thing to do," he said. "Get on with your life. Good for you."

"But you know what I've realized?" she asked, leaning forward. It felt oddly like she'd opened a window inside of herself, and a great clean breeze was blowing through her, picking up all the dust and cobwebs, the small flotsam of grief and loss that had been lingering for too long in her stagnancy. "I'd grieved for him. He was sick for so long and afterward, when Spence and I came here for the first time, I was grieving. All along. Before he was gone. After he was gone. I was ready to move on. I needed to move on. But you—"

"Me?"

"You cut out the pain of your mother's abandonment before you ever got a chance to grieve," she said and he scooted away from the table, clearly horrified by her assessment, and probably her audacity, playing psychologist. But she was right. She knew she was, she could suddenly see him so clearly. He was in crystal-clear focus, the pain and anger that he built around himself and used to strike out at the parent that deserved revenge. "It's all still right there. All the pain. All the grief and anger. It's right beside you like a pet that follows you everywhere. And you've just added it to what you feel about your dad."

"Spend a day with Suzette's journals and suddenly you're an expert on me?"

"Did you ever talk to your mom about sending you away? Have you ever—"

"Stop, Jennifer. Enough." Something in his voice was like the edge of a sword and she shut her mouth so fast her teeth clicked. Ian stood there, no hint of warmth in him. No hint of the friend or the boy getting away with something. He was pure man, and he was purely pissed off at her. So much so she could feel it—an electrical current across her skin. And she realized she'd gone too far. She should have kept her mouth shut. "You said you wanted to be friends but you can't leave well enough alone, can you?"

He towered over her in the dark and an awareness of him slithered through her.

She braced herself for his reaction, knowing him well enough that he wouldn't walk away from this without drawing blood first.

"I think it's pretty laughable," he said, his voice dropping down to that purr that he used when he was slipping into his Ian Greer, sexiest-man-alive persona. That purr that slid like honey over her and she wished she didn't react, but her skin went tight, her belly soft, her legs weak. "You think you're over Doug, but tell me, who were you kissing the other night? In your head, in your imagination, who were you kissing?"

"You," she answered, standing to face him, armed with the truth and a reckless fearlessness.

"You're lying."

"I'm not. I was kissing Ian Greer. The first man I've touched since Doug died. You'll have to cut me some slack if I handled it badly. It has been years, Ian. Years since hands other than my own touched me. And before that it was just Doug for a more than a decade. I freaked out, I admit it. But it was you all along."

That took him aback and she picked up her plate just to

have something to do with her hands. "It's not Doug between us, Ian."

"Seemed like it the other night."

"The other night felt like a betrayal. To him. To his memory. To being a wife. It doesn't mean I'm not over him. It means I'm getting over him."

His laugh was bitter, ragged. "Glad I could be a part of the healing process."

"And what was I to you, Ian?" she asked baldly, not at all sure why she asked that, because she was not prepared for what she knew would be his answer.

Nothing. She was nothing to him.

And she didn't need him to tell her for it to hurt.

But he didn't say anything. He simply gaped at her and she had to guess that the lingerie models didn't ask such questions.

Because he didn't mean anything to them.

"I'd like to be your friend," she whispered, meaning it all the way to her toes. Realizing that she was free from her grief, that she no longer needed her sword, no longer needed to be afraid of living her life the way she wanted. "And what I said earlier, about you and your mother, I said as a friend."

"I don't need a friend." He scowled.

Stupid woman that she was—stupid, stupid woman breaking every rule that mattered in her life—she stepped forward and touched his cheek, touched the rough growth of hair, the smooth skin of his cheekbones, the delicate curve of his ear. "Yes, you do," she whispered, and his eyes fluttered slightly and he appeared half-drunk on her touch and the sensation. The giddy, powerful sensation of touching this man, of affecting him, filled her like smoke, drifting through her body and clouding her vision.

The man did need comfort. He needed friendship and the

good clean love of a strong woman who saw him for what he was. For what he could be.

Not you, she told herself, and she knew that she wasn't the good woman for him. She knew that to her bones, but it didn't change her desire.

She smiled at him, knowing it was bittersweet, and she pulled her hand away, stepped to the sink to try and put distance between them.

"Jennifer—" he whispered and she shook her head, knowing she had to leave. They couldn't do this anymore—dark rooms and intimacies.

"I need to go, Ian," she said, not looking at him.

"I've never had a friend like you," he said, exasperated. "I don't know how to do it."

"Treat me like you would Andille," she said, rinsing her plate, keeping herself busy. "But don't go punching me in the face just because you like me," she tried to joke.

She felt him step up behind her. Every hair on her body, every inch of skin, drop of blood, felt him. Right there. Close enough that if she leaned back, if she let go of all the things that were more important, they'd be touching.

"When this story is over—"

"You'll leave," she said, turning to him, feeling things start to fall apart.

"Not before I make love to you," he whispered.

She wanted to shout at him, call him a liar, but she could see in his eyes, he meant it. He meant it.

And she wanted it.

Time slowed to nothing. The space between them diminished to breath. She could feel him, smell him, taste him, and it made her burn.

"We can't," she said.

He shook his head. "You won't. There's a difference."

"You're right," she said, "there is."

Then, like it wasn't tearing off her skin, she stepped away. "I need to check on my son," she said, heading for the door.

She couldn't stop herself, she glanced back. Just once. To make sure he was okay.

Ian stared at her, his eyes glowing in the darkness, the blue burning like the hottest part of a flame.

CHAPTER FOURTEEN

IT HAD BEEN a half hour and God had no answer for her, which, Deb thought, was weird. God was usually pretty good at offering up some guidance in her time of need.

But maybe He drew the line at prayers about sex.

Tell me what to do, she prayed for the hundredth time. *Lead me in the right direction. I am so scared of bringing pain into my life, but at the same time I am so tired of being scared. I am so tired of being alone. Of being on the outside of what everyone else in the world takes for granted.*

Shonny played beside her with his backpack of toy cars and she reached out to stroke his hair. They sat under the willow tree, the singing long over, but still he sat beside her, quietly being himself, while she came apart at the seams.

He was a blessing, this boy. A gift.

But his conception had been anything but holy. Or really very pleasant. It had been rushed and messy. Something frantic that had always seemed to Deb like it was unfinished.

She'd laid in her bed, her underwear around her ankles, her blood pounding like a freight train through her breasts and in her ears and she'd wondered, *Is this it? This is what the whole world goes crazy for? This is what my daddy tells me will send me to hell?*

It hardly seemed worth it. And it hardly seemed capable of bringing about the blessing of Shonny.

But Andille…

Oh, Lord, please, please tell me what to do with this man. Tell me what to do with these feelings.

She wanted to rock and clutch herself, like the women used to while Daddy preached. She wanted to throw herself across something, offer herself up for the Lord.

Anything. Anything to ease the fever in her blood that Andille had put there.

His touch. His hands. His grace. His gentle strength. The knowledge in those dark eyes. The knowledge that assured her, promised her, *swore* to her, she would not be left on a bed, her underwear around her ankles wondering what the fuss was about.

Andille would open doors for her. Show her secrets. Set a part of her free.

Please, she prayed, *I do not want to be hurt.*

He would never hurt you, her internal voice answered.

I do not want to be cheap.

You? Please, woman. You are gold and rubies, nothing you do with a man could change that. But with the right man, it might just make you shine brighter.

She'd seen that happen, women so well loved they shone like pearls.

Her internal voice was smart and she wondered if God wasn't here, leading her after all.

Daisy's big snout broke through the willow branches, busting into their cocoon. And where the dog went, Spence was sure to follow.

Shonny leaped to his feet, church and cars forgotten.

"Hi, Deb," Spence said, stepping into her sanctuary, looking glum.

"What's wrong, hon?" she asked, sweeping Shonny's cars into the backpack.

"Mom's talking to Ian. She's been talking to him all morning and I'm bored."

"Me, too," Shonny cried, when he wasn't the slightest.

"I was thinking of taking care of the garden," Spence said, scratching at a doozy of bug bite on his knee.

"That's a good idea," she said.

"I'll come, too!" Shonny cried, jumping. Daisy barked as if agreeing and Spence smiled.

"All right," he said, ducking back under the willow branches, letting in bright sunlight and fresh air and taking her son with him.

"Spence?" she cried.

He ducked his head back in. "Yeah?"

"Keep an eye on Shonny, will you?" she asked, wondering if the heat in her cheeks was visible to the boy. "For like an hour?"

"Sure," he said with a shrug, since he was probably going to do that anyway. Spence was a good kid.

The willow branches swayed and danced behind him, glittery light playing with the shadows.

Deb sat in the closed quiet of her church and really thought about what she was going to do. If Spence was with Shonny and Ian was with Jennifer…Andille was alone.

Sometimes, she thought, standing up and brushing off her black capris with the glitter butterflies all along the sides, *God doesn't come straight out and answer prayers.*

Sometimes He just gives you the opportunity to do it for yourself.

Courage and fear in hand, she went to find Andille.

HE WASN'T HARD to find. Her whole body was a dousing rod tuned to the man. Deb simply listened to the vibrations that filled her whenever he was around. And she followed those trembles, up the stairs to Sam's old apartment.

He stood at the kitchen window, looking over the backyard, his cell phone pressed to his ear. He wore those khaki shorts, low on his hips. So low it seemed like his round butt was the only thing keeping them on his body. She watched, breathless as he hitched his shorts up with his free hand.

On top, he just had on a white undershirt.

He was barefoot.

Her body was flooded by him, bombarded. There was simply no way to look at him and hold onto rational thought. So she let it go, just like she'd let go of her fear.

Spying on him, watching him not only with her eyes, but also her whole body. All of her skin. All of her muscles absorbed the perfect reality of him. The way the sunlight made his skin look like polished black stone. How his muscles bunched and layered in his shoulders and back, turned his body into something so earthy, so voluptuous and almost indecent. She blushed just seeing him.

Either she made a noise or he felt her staring at him, because he turned, swiveling at the waist, and saw her there, sick with lust, in his doorstep.

"I have to go," he said into his cell phone and immediately closed it. "Deb?"

Something foreign was in charge of her body. Something hot and willful and reckless. Unaware she'd crossed the room until she felt his heat like a radiator all along the front of her, she leaned forward and kissed him.

Oh. It was awkward. Her lips weren't actually on his. But pressed to the corner of his mouth, where the smooth skin tasted like sugar and coffee. And her nose dug into his cheek. And she wasn't touching him, not enough. But he wasn't really touching her. Or kissing her back.

She pulled away, burning with embarrassment.

"I'm sorry," she breathed, stepping back. "I'm so sorry."

Turning away, she could not get clear of that room fast enough. And to think she'd probably have to see him again. Maybe she should go home for a few days. Put her head under her pillow and try not to die of shame.

His palm touched her shoulder, slid down over her skin to her elbow, and he stopped her. She didn't look at him. Oh, no, she wouldn't ever do that again. But she did stop and she felt the heat and heft of his touch in her womb, where it curled and quivered.

"Deb?"

Oh, lord, his voice was in her ear and she felt it more than heard it. The deep bass sparked up nerve endings all along her shoulder, up into her hair, across her scalp, like a brush fire.

"Why are you leaving?" he asked and her eyelids could barely stay open. His fingers were making little circles in the crook of her elbow. Little circles that were making her crazed.

"You're on the phone," she whispered.

"Not anymore."

The laughter in his voice obliterated her weak-kneed desire and she turned around, pulling her arm free. This was one of the hardest things she'd ever done, coming up here. And if he was going to laugh at her, then he could take his muscles and his voice and beautiful skin and go torment some other woman.

She opened her mouth to let him have it, but he slid his hands across her face, up into her hair, and suddenly her head was so heavy. All the bones in her body gone.

His gaze danced over her face, touching her lips, her chin, the scar above her eye.

"I don't want you to leave," he whispered without a trace of laughter. "I've been waiting for you a long time."

He leaned in and she waited for his kiss, the press of his lips to hers like a starving man waits for food. Instead the tip of his tongue touched the corner of her mouth. His breath fanned her cheek.

He licked her. Just a little. Just enough.

Her body spasmed. And suddenly this desire was painful. Shocking. She stiffened in his arms and he gentled her with small brushes of his lips against her skin, her neck and face. His thumb pressed the tight muscles of her neck as he calmed her.

"It's okay, Deb," he whispered. "It's all right."

"I don't—" She didn't have words for this. Nothing about this man or what she felt was in the realm of her experience. Her hands, immobilized by the casts, were in fists at her side.

He leaned back and waited. Instead of putting words in her mouth and pretending he understood what truth was being pulled from her, he gave her the time to find it herself.

"I don't know what to do with you," she said. "With this."

"We don't have to do anything," he said and she laughed, exasperated.

"Well, that's not really why I came up here."

"Why did you?"

"I want to…" She licked her lips and looked away from his eyes, the intimacy suddenly too much. *Have sex. Make love. To you. With you. I want you to put out this fire. Show me what I'm missing, what it seems more and more like I need.* "Feel more of what you make me feel."

Andille sucked in a deep breath and his hand, when he touched her face, shook a little. And knowledge, like sliding into a warm bath, embraced her.

He feels it, too.

Emboldened, she unclenched her fists and put one hand on his waist. Because of the cast, just her fingertips felt the thin cotton of his shirt and beneath that the hot, glorious living flesh of Andille.

Her other hand she placed over his heart.

"Deb." He sighed, his heart pounding under her hand, she could feel it through her cast. "I can't be the man who loves you. Not like you deserve. I can't stay."

But I'd let you, she thought. And even though she'd never thought it before, never even dreamed of having this man in her life for real, she knew it was true. If Andille gave up what he owed Ian Greer, she'd welcome him right on into her heart.

She smiled, knowing somehow that his obligations to Ian were what was eating him. "Honey, I know that," she said, stroking the smooth skin of his face. He'd shaved this morning and his skin was satin. "And I don't need you to stay. I just need you."

He searched her eyes then—oh, sweet heaven—he kissed her.

She expected his mouth to open. She expected that licking flame of his tongue, the gentle bite of his teeth. She expected to be overwhelmed, swallowed up, caught up in his tide.

But it didn't happen.

His mouth brushed her lips. Her nose. Her eyebrows. He took off her glasses and kissed her eyes shut, licking the corners, tasting tears that his poignancy commanded.

"You're so strong," he whispered against her neck. "You are like rock. Like the ocean. Or a mountain. I can see it. Here." His hands settled on her shoulders, his fingers finding soft spots in the muscles, places that he touched and it felt like he touched inside of her. Her belly and womb. Her breasts and heart. "And here." He kissed her chin. "And here." He licked her lips. "And here." He returned to her eyes. "I look at you and I want you so much I can't stand it. I can't stand it that someone has hurt you. I can't stand that

I am not the man to make you smile. To make you cry out and laugh for the rest of your life."

"Andille—"

"So, I will do it now," he whispered into her ear. "Right now I will love you enough for the rest of my life."

And there it was, his tide, reaching out for her. Sweeping her up. Washing away her words and thoughts. Until she was simply Deb. A creature of instinct and need, reaching out for Andille.

His touch was warm. Gentle. A breeze through an open window. In its wake she had flames and goose bumps and the combination made her feel at odds. Conflicted.

"Shhh," he whispered when she tensed and she realized he was pulling her, carefully, slowly toward the bedroom. The bedroom was flushed with light, it seemed almost to glow over his shoulder.

Suddenly she recognized this precipice that she stood on.

I have no control here, she thought. Sure, she'd read those articles that said a woman was in charge of her own sexual pleasure. She'd read them hoping for some play-by-play help. A map even. But the articles might have been written in Greek for all she could understand.

"Don't disappoint me," she said, staring right in his eyes, which flared at her words.

"Oh, woman," he said, leaning down slightly to pick her up under her hips, pressing himself full-tilt to her. "You've got nothing to worry about."

CHAPTER FIFTEEN

IT WAS FRIDAY. D-day. Waldo would expect copy e-mailed to her before the end of the day.

Which was why Jennifer was up at dawn and already on her third cup of coffee by 8:00 a.m. She chose to work in the kitchen, hoping some sunshine would keep her awake and on task, but there was no luck today.

It was one gloomy, gray day out there. Thunder cracked in the distance and it was only a matter of time before a storm crashed down on Serenity.

Which threw further monkey wrenches into her plans. With bad weather Spence was going to go stir-crazy and she had so much work to do without a whiney, bored eleven-year-old at her elbow informing her that there was nothing to do.

"Hey." Ian's quiet voice behind her made her snap around.

"Hi," she said. It had been odd between them throughout yesterday when she'd interviewed him. At dinner she'd felt him seething slightly. He was a pot set at simmer.

And he stood in the doorway, braced against the wall like he'd been there a while, watching her.

I am going to make love to you.

His words hummed in time with her heartbeat, unavoidable and unforgettable.

Her heart pinged, her body sang at the sight of him and

she wished desperately she didn't care about Ian Greer, as a person, an unlikely friend…and a man. She wished he was just a story.

SHE SAT AT THAT TABLE, her hair in a messy knot, circles under her wary eyes, and he had to clench the doorframe to prevent himself from reaching for her.

He realized he shouldn't have told her he planned to make love to her. Not because it wasn't true—he hoped to God it was—but because it made everything between them, every moment, every word, so damn hot.

He couldn't breathe for the tension rolling off the woman, ribbons of this frustrated longing wrapping around him, circling him only to weave back to her—binding them.

He wanted to stand her up, run his hands down that lithe body, find and claim her secrets, even those things she hid from herself. He wanted all of her. All of her wrapped around him, crying his name, begging him.

Fantasies of power struggles in bed usually left him cold, but not with this woman. Not with her forthright eyes and her mantle of stern respectability.

Stripping that from her, finding her naked and panting and needing him, seemed like such a good idea.

Even this early in the morning.

"You're up early? Or didn't you sleep?" he asked.

"Up early. Today is my deadline."

Ignoring the end-of-the-story countdown pounding in his crotch, he whistled. "How is it going?"

"Well, it's not pretty, but my editor will understand."

"When do we tape?" he asked, pouring himself some much needed coffee.

"My producer has to approve the story and send down a camera crew."

"What if she doesn't approve it?"

"She will," she said with assurance. "She'd be a fool not to. What are you doing up?"

"Andille and I are setting up a trust for Serenity, so Sam won't have to call every time she wants to buy a computer." He sloshed coffee into a cup and took a sip without sugar or milk or waiting for it to cool. It hurt and he winced. "We should have done it years ago, but turnover at these shelters can be pretty significant and it's hard to know who to trust."

Story of my life, he thought.

"I'm sure Sam will appreciate it," she said.

He took another long drink from his mug then refilled it.

"Long night?" she asked and he knew it wasn't a leading a question. That wasn't her style. But the rough edge of her voice sent lightning through his bloodstream.

He was bold. Bolder than any man she'd ever met, he knew that about her. He knew he was bolder than her husband, and he loved that. Wanted that. So, he watched her, memorizing the mess of her hair, the elegant line of her throat where it arched into her chin. He wanted to spend a half hour on her collarbone, learning her. Studying her.

Her eyes clashed with his and he invited her right into his dirty little mind.

Her entire face went red, her lips parted on a deep breath and she tore her gaze from him, before the whole kitchen went up in flames.

Turning away so she wouldn't see him smirk, he added sugar to the tar she called coffee.

When it happened between them, and it would, it was going to be so good.

Behind him, she coughed, discomfited, and he felt a prickle of guilt. The woman wanted to be his friend. She'd said it and he believed her. She was too honest to lie about something like that for the sake of an interview.

But he didn't know how to be her friend.

"Were you able to use anything from yesterday?" he asked, referring to their three-hour conversation.

"It was perfect," she said. "Once we do tape, you'll see how it all works out."

"It was harder than I thought it would be," he said, the words coming from some unknown place, but once out there he realized how true they were. He spent the night working so he wouldn't have to think of all the things they'd talked about, the way she'd carefully led him through his childhood, reminding him of things he'd forgotten. "All along I've had these memories, but when you started putting dates on things and attaching the abuse to events…" He trailed off, wishing he could shut up. "Made it real again," he finally said and drank more coffee, burning his lips on purpose.

Was this friendship? Talking about things he never ever spoke about? Was that what it took to be her friend? He'd much rather peel that T-shirt off her back and spread her out on the table. That was his kind of friendship.

"We're spilling all your family secrets, Ian," she said. "That would make it hard for anyone to sleep at night."

He laughed, despite the pain in his lips and the heat in his pants. "Actually, that spilling I'm excited about. Thrilled about it. Can't happen too soon," he said.

"Well," she said turning back to her laptop, "it won't be much longer."

Spence came into the room, rubbing his eyes and yawning. What was it with kids when they woke up? Ian wondered. They looked so little. So lost. Something pinged and rattled in his throat. When Jennifer had asked him if he wanted kids he didn't have an answer because he'd never ever considered the question.

When was he supposed to meet a nice girl, a woman who'd make a good mother and have some kids with her? He was too busy going to parties and clubs, pretending to have fun.

"Hi," Spence said to Ian, watching him with guarded eyes and, honest to God, Ian started to blush. The things he was fantasizing about that kid's mother were filthy, and when the boy looked at him like that, it was like Spence knew Ian was up to no good.

"Hi yourself," he said, playing it cool. But still the kid watched him.

"What are you doing up so soon?" Jennifer asked her son, clearly panicked. She was up early probably hoping to get a few hours of work in before Spence woke.

Spence shrugged, blissfully unaware of deadlines and family secrets. "I just woke up. What's for breakfast?"

"Cereal," she said, saving her file and standing to get a bowl and the cereal for him.

Ian sat next to Spence and took a deep breath, wondering how one went about arranging fun with the side benefit of Jennifer getting the story done. Andille seemed to do it pretty easily. How hard could it be?

"What do you say we play some soccer today?" he asked.

"You're not too busy?" Spence asked, shooting Jennifer a toxic look and she sighed.

"Not busy at all." Ian shook his head, crossing his ankle over his knee. "Your mom is going to be stuck inside all day, but I can play soccer. It will be…fun." The word bubbled up from someplace neglected and sad. Someplace ignored and forgotten for the past twenty years.

"Can you teach me how to pass the ball off my head?" Spence asked. "Andille said you knew how to do it."

"Of course," Ian said, wondering if he still had that particular trick up his sleeve. It had been years. Eons. Since he'd touched a soccer ball.

A huge crack of thunder practically shook the house and Spence looked outside, his smile fading. "But it's gonna rain."

Fat raindrops, as if summoned, began to splat on the window. A drizzle warning of wetter things to come.

Spence and Ian groaned at the same time.

"What are we going to do, Mom?" Spence asked.

Andille came downstairs, looking sleep-deprived but calm. Happy. There was a certain looseness to his walk, a little I-just-got-laid.

The hairs on the back of Ian's neck went on high alert.

"Good morning," Andille said, his voice even darker, rougher in the morning.

"Morning, Andille," Jennifer said, watching him. She smiled, Andille's glow spreading to her, which was ludicrous since Ian knew for a painful fact Jennifer had not just been laid.

"Paperwork done?" Ian asked, a little sharper than he intended, but the last thing he needed was Jennifer catching Andille's glow, for crying out loud. Things were complicated enough.

He glared at Andille and the man didn't seem to care. He'd clearly seduced Deb, a woman with roots so deep to this place it was a wonder she could move, and he was grinning about it.

Andille wasn't usually a cad. The guy was more of a monk, but there was nothing good about what he'd done. Not from Ian's perspective.

"Sent the last e-mail last night about 2:00 a.m.," Andille said and yawned, nearly splitting his face in half.

"Mom." Spence's voice had a good chunk of whine in it and it set Ian's teeth on edge. "What are we going to do all day?"

"We should celebrate," Ian said. "Hey." He turned to Spence, creating a coconspirator in the boy. "Is that arcade still open in Northwoods?"

"The one in the bowling alley?" Spence asked.

"They added a bowling alley?" Ian asked, as if the news were the greatest thing he'd ever heard. "We need to check this out."

Jennifer stared at him, coffeepot poised over mug as if she were watching a magic trick. Or a car wreck.

"That okay with you?" he asked her and she nodded. She was so cute, with three pencils caught in her sloppy bun and a coffee stain on the sleeve of her oversize blue button-down shirt. She was so cute, he winked, just a little, to let her know he was trying to help out.

Just to let her know they were friends, despite what he wanted to do to her on the kitchen table.

"You're going to a bowling alley?" Andille asked, sitting at the table with his coffee cup. He sounded skeptical.

"I bowl," Ian said, defensively. "I am, in fact, a very good bowler. Why don't you come, too?" Ian asked Andille. "See for yourself."

Andille hesitated and Shonny burst in the back door, Deb not far behind him.

"We need help!" Shonny yelled, jumping with both feet.

"Groceries," Deb said, with a smile. "I can't—"

"I got it," Andille said, standing.

Deb blushed. She actually blushed. And when she looked at Andille, she smiled, a soft womanly smile. A glowy smile.

Ian gritted his teeth. The woman was clearly halfway in love with Andille, which, of course, was what always happened with Andille. The man smiled at a certain kind of woman and they just fell in love, right then and there.

What a mess, Ian thought. He'd expect this kind of behavior from himself, but Andille always acted as though he was above flirtations. Above string-free relationships.

And now here he was embroiled in one at the worst possible time with the worst possible woman.

Deb had strings everywhere.

"Wait," Deb said, stopping Andille at the door. "I think you should see this."

Deb pulled from her purse three magazines and tossed them onto the table in front of Ian.

People. Star Magazine. The National Enquirer.

All of them had cover stories about Ian.

"'Where in the world is Ian Greer?'" Jennifer read from one of them, flipping to the story. "Is that your apartment? And your mother's grave?" She was horrified. "There is an interview with the actress you took to the funeral." She skimmed the article, paraphrasing for everyone's benefit. "She claims you just disappeared, leaving her stranded in New Hampshire. Is that true?"

Ian shrugged. He was too drunk to remember. Too heart-broken to care.

"I gave her plenty of cab fare," Andille said, finally meeting Ian's eyes.

Don't you dare judge me, Andille's eyes said. *You have no right.*

And Ian didn't. Not really.

"*The Enquirer* says you were either abducted by aliens," Deb said, "or the mob."

"Slow news day," Ian said, not touching the newspapers.

"I could not take this," Jennifer said, shuddering. "People outside my house. Thinking they have rights to me? How do you handle this?"

As if he needed evidence of how different they were, of how she would not fit into his life—there it was.

"I used them and they used me," he said. *Parasites,* he thought. *All of us.*

"They're looking for you," Andille said, flipping through one of the papers.

"They won't find me," Ian said, laughing at the idea. "They wouldn't even know where to look."

"Maybe you shouldn't go into Northwoods," Jennifer said.

"In case the paparazzi are there?" he asked, incredulous. "I think I'm safe."

"There weren't any at the grocery store," Deb joked, adding further proof that something had happened to lighten her up.

Andille crossed his arms over his chest and smiled at Ian. "Two weeks ago, the paparazzi wouldn't have had to look for you."

There was something smug in Andille's voice and Ian wondered why everyone thought they knew him so well all of a sudden.

"What's your point?" Ian muttered into his mug.

"Something's different. You're different," Andille said, his smile growing. "Coming here was a good idea."

Ian's eyes bounced from Andille to Deb. "Certainly was for you."

Jennifer gasped, Deb went bright red.

"Why don't you help me with the groceries?" Andille said through his teeth, all but hauling Ian up by his shirt and leading him out the back door.

THE DOOR SLAMMED and the silence behind the men rocked and shook.

"Whoa," Spence said. "What's going on?"

"Andille and Ian are getting groceries," Jennifer said, craning her neck to see out the window. "And arguing."

"What are they arguing about?" Spence asked, hooking his feet on his chair and propping himself up on the table so he could see out the window, too.

"Nothing new," Deb murmured, her eyes soft and sad when they looked at Andille. "And nothing he's going to change."

"Does this mean we aren't going to the arcade?" Spence asked and Jennifer smiled. Ian volunteering to take Spence off her hands for the day was one of the nicest things anyone had done for her since long before Doug died.

He just wants the story out, she reminded herself when she wanted to take the gesture and wrap it in hearts and flowers and make it about her.

"No," she told him, "I'm sure you're still going to the arcade. Eat up, buddy."

Spence dug into his cereal, flipping the box so he could study the word puzzles on the back.

"Deb?" Jennifer asked quietly. "Everything okay?"

Deb watched the back door for a second then looked down at her casts, her fingers. She pressed the hot pink plaster to her stomach and took a deep breath.

When she finally looked up her smile was radiant. It was as if Deb were shot through with bright white sunlight.

"Everything," she said, "is just fine."

"You want to elaborate?" Jennifer asked, dying for details. Spence was occupied with his cereal, Shonny was going through one of the drawers—if they spoke in adult code, the kids would never know what they were saying.

"I'll just say…" Deb sighed, her eyes so knowing and womanly that Jennifer suddenly felt like the last virgin on earth. She felt old and dry and withered, compared to Deb's sudden lushness. "That I finally know what all the fuss is about."

CHAPTER SIXTEEN

SPENCE CAREFULLY wrote a four in the box for frame two then glanced at the big lit screen above their lane to make sure the four was there, too.

So cool how that worked.

Ian sat, after rolling that terrible four, and grabbed his red cup of Coke, slurping the last of it through his straw.

And then, because they had a pitcher—*a pitcher* of pop—he poured himself some more.

Mom would have a heart attack.

"Hey," Spence said, swiveling his chair all the way around to face Ian. "You lied."

Ian choked on the pop. "About what?" he asked, setting down the cup.

"About being a good bowler. You suck."

"I do?" Ian asked, grabbing some of the french fries from the basket on the table. "Go get 'em, Shonny!" he yelled. Andille was helping Shonny hold the ball. Shonny sucked, too, but he was three. And while Andille wasn't as bad as the rest of them, he certainly wasn't great.

Spence won the last game.

"Yeah, you do," Spence said, reaching for some fries before Ian ate them all. "So, why'd you lie?"

Ian leaned forward and whispered, "Isn't this more fun than hanging out with your mom and Deb?"

"Of course."

Ian shrugged and poured a little more pop in Spence's glass, even though it was half full and Spence already felt like he could run around the bowling alley, like, a billion times without getting tired. "Welcome to your first guys' day out," Ian said.

Spence liked the sound of that. Guys' day out. Not that Mom wasn't fun, but she was Mom. But now she was Working Mom, which did make her less than no fun.

Ian, on the other hand, was a blast. He had never-ending quarters for the arcade and a cool car and he and Andille made fun of each other all the time.

Ian was wearing a ball cap, pulled real low over his eyes so no one would recognize him and call the magazines.

Ian said he was going incognito.

Spence wished he'd brought his ball cap.

It was really cool to hang around guys.

Shonny's ball went right into the gutter and Ian applauded anyway, like the kid had hit a strike. "Way to go!" Ian yelled. Then it was Andille's turn, which took forever because Shonny thought he had to help him carry the ball.

Babies. Sheesh.

But it gave Spence a little more time to talk to Ian. Which was good, because Spence had a question he was dying to ask, but couldn't seem to work up the guts.

He'd been wanting to ask his mom the same question, but she'd been in her office nonstop and he didn't have the chance.

Or maybe he was just a big chicken.

But now was the time. The question had to be asked.

"What's up, Spence?" Ian asked, brushing the grease and salt from the fries right on his jeans, which would make Mom dive for the paper towels. Another reason to like hanging out with the guys. No paper towels. "Something wrong?"

"Nah," Spence said and stared down at his blue and red shoes. They were slippy, these shoes, and he slid them over the floor.

"Now *you're* lying," Ian said, real quiet.

"Do you like my mom?" Spence blurted, then winced. Not the coolest move ever.

There was a long pause and Ian finally said, "Of course."

Spence rolled his eyes. "No, I mean, do you *like her* like her?"

Ian's mouth hung open.

"I know you're spending a lot of time together. And sometimes when you look at her—" Spence stopped. Probably too late, because it looked like Ian was going to kill him or his head was going to explode.

"When I look at her what?" Ian asked, his voice sharp and Spence wanted to crawl under the table. He knew this was a bad idea. He never should have said anything.

"Never mind," he whispered, swiveling around and lining up the little half pencils along the top of the scorecard. His stomach felt sick. Too much pop.

Behind him, he heard Ian swear.

Oh, man, Spence thought, *that's a really bad word. Mom would flip right out.*

He heard Ian move and Spence's whole body went tight when the guy came and sat next to him at the score table.

"I'm sorry, Spence," he said. "You just surprised me."

"Sorry."

"It's not your fault, but…" Ian sighed and spread his hands out on the table, palms down, fingers wide. "Finish what you were going to say."

"You look at Mom like my dad used to," Spence whispered, feeling like the biggest bonehead in the world. "And sometimes she looks at you like she used to look at my dad."

Ian didn't say anything. He didn't even seem to be breathing.

"It's okay," Spence said quickly. "If you are. It's totally okay."

"How's that?" Ian asked. "How is it okay if I'm in love with your mother?"

Whoa, Spence didn't say anything about love, and there was something weird in Ian's voice that made Spencer feel careful, like when he and Dad went to visit Grandpa in Wisconsin in the winter and all the water was frozen over. Spence, when no one was looking, walked out on the ice and heard it crackle under his feet.

This conversation felt like that.

"I'm just saying that I'm not mad. My friend Ed's mom started dating a guy after his parents got divorced and Ed hated that guy, was really mean to him, and I'm letting you know that I won't do that."

"Be mean?" Ian asked, with what sort of looked like a smile on his face.

"Nope." Especially if the pitchers of pop kept coming, but he didn't say that.

"Well—" Ian laughed "—glad we got that taken care of."

Spence could feel Ian watching him, but he was too embarrassed to look at him. He played with the light for the scorecard projector.

"Do you miss your dad?" Ian asked.

Spence's heart hammered hard in his chest. Once. But then it went away. "Sure," he said. "But not like I used to." Ian didn't say anything and so Spence kept talking. "I used to think about him all the time. And Mom used to talk about him all the time, and we—" He darted a quick look at Ian. "We cried sometimes. But it's gotten better."

"Do you think your mom misses him?" Ian asked.

Spence shrugged. "Yeah. She says part of her will always miss him."

"That makes sense," Ian said, and Spence didn't want the guy to get the wrong idea.

"But she likes you now," he was quick to point out.

"Spence." Ian shook his head and his voice, for the first time all day, sounded like an adult voice. Which was weird. He didn't always think of Ian like an adult. More of like a big kid. It would be easy to be his friend, eventually. "You don't know that—"

"Of course I do," Spence insisted. "She's my mom. And I told you, she looks at you like she used to look at my dad."

Andille finally finished his turn and somehow, even with Shonny attached to his hip, managed to bowl a spare. Spence made the careful slash in Andille's row and leaped to his feet.

"My turn," he cried. "Watch and learn," he said to Ian, giving him his best smirk. "Watch and learn."

IAN WAS LITERALLY dumbstruck. He sat in the uncomfortable plastic chair, sick to his stomach from the junk food he'd been eating all day, and felt like Spencer had just taken a crowbar to his head.

"You all right, man?" Andille asked, practically filling the whole bank of seats in their lane. Shonny was dwarfed as he sat by Andille's side. "Someone recognize you?" he asked, glancing around. "Should we get going?"

Ian shook his head, scrubbing his face with both hands. He knocked off the ball cap and just left it on the seat next to him. No one was going to hassle him here, and the whole thing was beginning to feel ridiculous.

"Then what happened? You look sick."

"Spence said it's okay for me to like his mother," Ian said, a tad too loud and Andille sat back, his eyebrows in his hair. "And apparently it's okay for Jennifer to like me."

"Boy's got it all worked out."

"The boy is delusional."

"What's wrong with Jennifer?"

"Nothing!" Ian snapped. There was not a thing wrong with her, from head to toe. One side to the other, the woman was amazing. What was wrong was that she wasn't for him.

Andille spread his arms across the top of the chairs and crossed his legs at his ankles. He had his "the doctor is in" look on his face that always made Ian want to start a fight. The impulse was particularly strong right now.

"What are you going to do when this is all over, Ian?" Andille asked.

"When what is all over?"

"Your revenge mission against your father. Because this story is going to end it, right?"

"That's the point." Ian felt defensive. There was something about Andille's tone that made him feel pressured.

"So what are you going to do?"

"Go back to my life."

"Your life that was all about the revenge? You're going to go back to the clubs and the women and the tabloids?"

His whole body, everything in him, shuddered at the thought. Recoiled. It had been no way to live before and after the story, after Serenity, it would be worse. Emptier. Lonelier.

"What am I supposed to do?" he whispered, knowing what Andille was getting at. "Pack up Jennifer and Spence and take them to my apartment? Introduce her to the pack of photographers who live outside my door?"

"They'll leave you alone once you stop giving them something to photograph. You settle down with a woman like—"

Ian laughed, waving his hands. "There will be no settling

down. Not with Jennifer, not with anyone." Settling down was what his parents had done—and he wanted nothing to do with what his parents had.

"This is so hard?" Andille asked, holding his arms up indicating the bowling alley and Spencer and the junk food.

Ian was giving Jennifer a break. He was giving Spence too much pop. It wasn't real. Or normal. Not in the trenches, day-in-day-out normal stuff. And what Jennifer felt for him, it wasn't what she felt for Doug. Not at all. It was sexual. She was alone and lonely. She was, in a word, horny. That's all. It wasn't real, either.

"This isn't real life, Dille," he said. No more junk food, he thought, it was making him sick to his stomach.

"It's more real than what we've been living," Andille said.

AT FOUR IN THE afternoon Jennifer hit Send on the e-mail to Waldo and sat back. Hot-cold waves of relief and excitement rolled down her spine, from the top of her head to her feet, making her giddy.

This is it, she thought. She felt nothing but pride about the story. It was good, she knew it in her gut, and she could not wait to tell Ian.

She wanted to celebrate the return of her career, the return of Ian's life to himself. And she wanted to celebrate with Ian.

"Deb!" she cried, rising from the office chair. She stumbled slightly because her feet were numb.

Deb didn't answer right away so she went to the class-rooms, where she found Deb at the round table in the back of the classroom she used the most, going through paperwork.

Gospel music poured out of the radio at her elbow and Deb was humming along. Deb's whole vibe was different, lighter. Before, it was as if she wore what had happened to her like an invisible coat. Always there. A shield against the whole rest of the world getting too close.

The coat was gone and it was just Deb sitting there. Radiant.

"You about done?" Jennifer asked.

"Sure, I just—" Deb's eyes narrowed and she turned off the music. "You look like you swallowed a lightbulb. What's with you?"

"Finished the story," Jennifer said, stretching in the doorframe, feeling every muscle grow and pull. She wished she was the dancing kind—like in the movies, when good things happened to women and they pranced around their apartments, singing into hairbrushes and dancing with their cats.

"Congrats, Jennifer. You must feel great."

"I do." She tried clapping her hands and striking a little pose, but it felt so stupid she immediately stopped. She'd have to find another outlet for all this joy bouncing around inside her. "Let's go meet the boys in town and celebrate."

Deb blinked at her, the papers still in her fingers. Something terribly sad crossed her face and she looked away, setting down the paper carefully on a stack. "The boys," she murmured. "They've been here a week and it feels like they've always been here, doesn't it?"

Dread crept along the edges of Jennifer's celebratory mood. "Deb?" she asked, coming to stand beside her. "What's wrong?"

Deb's lips curled cruelly. "What do you think?"

"Andille? This morning you seemed happy about him—"

"I'm happy, I'm sad. I'm angry." Deb sat back and blew a dreadlock off her forehead. "I'm sick about the man and I barely know him. He took my son today, for the whole day so I could work, and he acted like it was no big deal."

"I don't think it was to him."

"Of course it wasn't, because he's a good man. One of

the best I've ever known and he's going to walk out those doors one of these days and never look back."

"Ah," Jennifer sat down heavily. No more desire to dance, she felt like lead had been poured in her shoes. "I get it."

"Do you?" Deb asked. "Really? Because I don't even get it. I barely know the man and I'm trusting him with my boy. With my body. My heart. My—" She shook her head. "I'm just going to get hurt."

Me, too, Jennifer thought but didn't say. And the lead crept up her legs to surround her heart. When Ian walked out that door with Andille, part of her would leave with him and it made her terribly sad. And anxious. Anxious to have him for as long as she could. Anxious to break herself open on him, unlock the parts of herself that had been locked away for a long time.

But she couldn't.

"It sucks," Jennifer groused and Deb laughed.

"Truer words have never been spoken." After a minute Deb sighed and stood. "Let's have some fun while we can," she said. "I'll call Andille and tell him to meet us with the kids at Eastside's."

"Excellent idea," Jennifer said. Because nothing said celebration like a big cheeseburger and onion rings eaten on a picnic table. And maybe she'd get that beer she'd been craving. "I'll go get the Rolaids."

DINNER HAD BEEN a rousing success. She'd had her beer and her son confessed to massive sugar consumption. Ian and Andille had kept them all in stitches with stories of boarding school hijinks. Andille, it turns out, had been quite the devious kid.

They finally decided to leave when the sun set and Shonny curled up on Andille's shoulder like he'd been doing it all his life.

Jennifer had reached under the table and squeezed Deb's knee, knowing the sight must have delighted and wounded her in ways she'd never even considered.

Deb, Andille and Shonny left in her car and now Spence was passed out in the back of Ian's car. The sugar had finally worn off.

"I really don't think he'll throw up," she said, trying to convince Ian that his leather was safe. "He's not much of a puker."

"That's a relief," Ian said, smiling tightly at her.

Something was wrong with the guy and she didn't think it had anything to do with the double cheeseburger he ate. He'd been odd since they'd gotten in the car.

"Thank you," Jennifer said, touching his shoulder and he flinched slightly. Guilt settled hard in her stomach. "For taking Spence today. I wouldn't have—"

Ian sighed. "For about the hundredth time, it was no big deal. Really." His eyes pierced the darkness that filled and surrounded the car. There was nothing darker than night in the rural South. The darkness felt tactile, thick, like something she could pull over them and they could hide underneath. "We had a lot of fun."

"Deb was very relieved to have a day to catch up on work, too."

"Andille's a saint," Ian said, sarcasm rolling off the words.

"You don't approve of them?" she asked.

"Approve?" Ian asked. "I'm hardly in a position to approve of anything. I just don't want anyone to get hurt." He unrolled his window slightly, the scent of the low country—marsh and mystery—filling the car.

Her stomach squeezed low in her belly.

"Deb's a big girl," Jennifer said. *And so am I. We're all adults.*

"Maybe it's not Deb I'm worried about," Ian murmured.

"Andille?" she asked, nearly laughing. "He's the one who is going to leave. If he wanted to stay with Deb, he should stay."

"Sadly, it's not that simple." Ian sat forward, craning his neck to see out the windshield. "Wow, that's a lot of stars."

"Why doesn't Andille stay if he wants to?" she asked, refusing to talk about stars. "Why does he have to leave with you?"

"Because he thinks he owes me."

She waited for him to elaborate but when he didn't she nearly rolled her eyes. "What does he owe you?" she asked as if he were a simpleton.

Annoyed, his eyes flicked to her then back to the road. "I asked my father to get his mother and sisters out of Africa while there was a violent coup in their country. He thinks his sisters are alive because of me."

Jennifer slumped in her seat, astonished once again by this man and his many secrets. Just when she felt like she had things under control, or at least labeled correctly, he went and messed up everything.

"It's not a big deal," he said. "Don't look at me like that."

"Like what?" she whispered.

"Like I'm something I'm not," he yelled, then swore, glancing in the rearview mirror at Spence, who slept on, oblivious. The kid slept through hurricanes. A little yelling wasn't going to faze him.

I don't think you know what you are, she thought, but didn't say. *I don't think you have the slightest clue.*

The silence between them was tense, had been since they climbed into the car together and she, at first, attributed it to having spent the day with an eleven-year-old. But now she wasn't sure what was wrong with Ian.

The phone on the console between them buzzed and Ian

glanced down at the readout and swore before turning it off. The oppressive atmosphere getting worse by the moment.

"Who—" she said then stopped. It wasn't her business. It felt more and more like nothing about him was her business.

"My father," he said through clenched teeth. "My father keeps calling. My father won't leave me alone."

Oh. She turned to stare out the window. When it finally felt like her head was going to pop from the pressure inside his fancy car, she broke down and asked him. "What's wrong? I mean, I get your dad. But all night you've been acting…different."

Muscles along his jaw and neck flexed and pulsed and she suddenly wanted to suck back her question.

Suddenly, Ian jerked the wheel and they veered over to the shoulder, the wheels spitting gravel against the car.

She braced herself against the door and looked back at her son, who slept on. Still oblivious.

"What's wrong—"

His lips crushed hers, his hands gripped her face like she was about to run from him. His lips, his tongue, his teeth. The heat of his breath, the taste of mint, all of it tidal-waved over her and she could only brace herself against him. Her body, of its own volition, opened itself up, every nerve ending, every blood cell, every single inch of her skin stretched wide to get as much of Ian Greer as she could.

Her hands cupped the muscles of his shoulders, feeling the sweat under his shirt, the pounding of his heart. Her fingers bit into his flesh as if he might run away, pull back and leave her.

"Tell me," he said. He nipped at her, sucked at her, like she was something delicious. "How am I supposed to act?"

She had no answer, no words. If she opened her mouth she'd simply groan. He pushed her away, his lips bright and wet and lush in the light from the dashboard.

Again, her body yelled. *More,* her sex screamed.

His eyes were flinty and hard and after staring at her, staring at her as if he could strip her with just his gaze, as if he could suck and bite and penetrate her with his eyes, he turned away and drove them back on the road.

Headlights sliced through the night toward home.

CHAPTER SEVENTEEN

IAN WAITED FOR HER. In the shadows. In agony. He stood in the corner of the kitchen, his eyes trained on the hallway where Jennifer had disappeared with her son.

If she comes back out, it's on, he thought. *She knows. She's not stupid. If she doesn't want me, she'll stay in her room.*

God, please let her come out.

He thought he'd be so much more in control here. Those fantasies of breaking down her common sense and barriers, of revealing the panting woman beneath all that logic and reason, were frayed. False.

Instead he was the one panting. Running out of control.

Please, please walk out that door.

He fully understood why this was a bad idea. He simply didn't care anymore. There were bigger, harder, more pressing demands right now.

The time for doing what was right was gone. He felt, desperately, as if he needed Jennifer. Needed her. And he didn't need anyone. Not anymore.

Suddenly she was there, in the doorway, her lithe silhouette a long shadow across the kitchen floor, and up his legs.

His fingers pulsed, twitched with the need to touch her.

Her eyes met his and he saw that she was as caught up in this painful desire as he was. He could see it in her face, the curl of her lips. But he could also see that she was going to be sensible. She was going to tell him all the reasons they couldn't be together.

And he couldn't let her do that.

He crossed the room before she could talk.

"Ian," she breathed, putting up her hand, and he stepped right up to it, grabbed her palm and put it over his heart. His thundering, pounding heart. He saw her defenses get pierced, her rationale wavering. "Ian, we can't—"

No talking, he decided, and he pushed his hands into the silk ribbons of her hair, tangled his fingers in the long blond strands until he was sure she couldn't pull away.

Then he kissed her. Softly. Slowly. A seduction. He teased the resistance from her, the stiffness from her lips, her chin, the curve of her back. He breathed across her face, stroked the pulse points in her neck.

Gentling her. Making her his.

He swallowed her gasps, her logic and reason, and gave her fire instead.

His hands slid from her neck to her back then down to her hips. Sliding one leg between hers, he pressed her high and hard against him and she cried out into his mouth, her fingernails raking the skin of his neck. He wanted to grin with delight.

He had her. Oh, he had her.

"Ian." She pulled away, pushing against him.

No. No. Not when he was so close. When they were so close. He couldn't even put into words why this was so important, but it was. She was different. With her, he was different. He liked who he was and he wanted to keep that version of himself for as long as he could.

"Please, Jennifer," he breathed, stunned and embarrassed the words had come out of him. He tried to look away, but she wouldn't let him. She cupped his face, forcing him to meet her eyes then she stopped. As if someone had hit Pause on her, everything about her was held in suspended animation and he waited, not wanting to push any more than he had.

Miraculously, she smiled. And his whole body rejoiced.

"We can't do this here," she said, her fingers like cat's claws, digging and releasing into his shirt, his skin. Her hips arched slightly against his leg and her eyes dilated.

She bit her lip and it was so damn hot, it blew out the last of his control. So hard he hurt, he couldn't stop himself from pushing against her hip, and she groaned. Her hand slid down from his chest to his pants, her heel pressing against his erection.

"Get us out of here," she whispered.

He bent, picking her up beneath her hips, holding her tight, and she wrapped her arms around his neck, staring into his eyes for a moment before she kissed him. And everything got blown to hell.

"Where?" he asked, heading outside.

"Office," she said into his mouth.

He turned, bumping into the door frame but finally getting the door shut behind him. He hated that he was going to make love to her here. They should be someplace fancy. As elegant as she was. As refined and clean. She should have the best sheets, soft lights. Flowers. At the very least, some place not filled with storage boxes. "I'm sorry," he murmured, leaning her against the wall, pressing wet kisses to that supple, elegant neck he loved so much. "You deserve better than this."

"Than what?" she asked, twisting against him until she slid down his body, her hand back to the front of his pants, pressing and squeezing against him.

"Than up against a wall in an office," he muttered and she

pushed him away slightly. Her grin was pure Eve and he groaned, straining against her devilish hand. Seriously, he wasn't going to be able to take much more of this.

He slipped a hand under her shirt, cupping her breast. His fingers found the hard crest of her nipple and, to let her feel a slice of what he was feeling, he pinched her, just hard enough.

She laughed and groaned, her back swaying off the wall in invitation and he bent, pressing his mouth over her shirt and bra to her other nipple. He sucked. Hard. Her fingers abandoned the front of his jeans to find his belt buckle.

"I love it," she said. "I love that you can't wait. That I want you this much. I feel like a kid. And I have never, ever felt this way."

Some new emotion surged alongside the lust in his blood-stream, but he didn't have time to analyze, because she got his pants open and was kissing her way down his chest, her knees bending.

Oh, dear—

"Sweetheart," he said. "You don't—"

She looked up at him, her eyes glittering, her mouth a wet, warm oasis. "Yes," she murmured with a smile, "I do."

She slid him into her mouth, her hands cupping him, teasing him. Bracing his hands against the wall he tilted his head to watch her, the most erotic thing he'd ever seen in his life, and he wondered if he was going to survive making love with Jennifer.

Power surged through her. The more he groaned and arched, the more lush and alive she felt. His shaking hands touched her chin and she leaned back, letting him slip from her lips.

Oh, his face. Ian was a man barely in control and she'd brought him here. Heat and damp throbbed between her legs and if she didn't get some relief soon, she thought she just might die of wanting Ian Greer.

It was wrong in a million ways, but oh, boy, right now, did it ever feel right.

She leaned against the wall and lifted her shirt with the damp spot over the breast over her head and he fell on her like a starving man.

Her bra was gone, her breasts pushed high and together as he tongued the nipples.

"You're killing me," he groaned.

"You feel pretty alive," she said and he stopped, for just a moment. But before she could say something he had his hand between her legs, pressing the seam of her shorts against her.

Pleasure laced with pain arced through her and she welcomed it. She welcomed whatever dark and depraved thing this man had up his sleeve for her. One night. One night that would warm her and keep her for the rest of her Ian-free life.

Their eyes locked and it was the hottest thing she'd ever been a part of. His finger twitched and rubbed against her shorts, and her eyelids slid shut.

"No," he said, an iron edge of command in his voice. "Watch. Watch what I do to you."

Oh, it was thrilling. His eyes—so dark they were almost navy—bored into hers and she spread her legs and let him do what he wanted.

He yanked her shorts, a button popping off and rolling around in the dark, and his violence delighted her. She smiled and he growled. He ripped her underwear off and she laughed but suddenly his fingers were inside her. Lancing her, piercing right through to her heart and she sobbed once, breathless and wanting.

Lifting her leg, hooking it around his hips, she opened herself, waiting. Needy and mindless.

His thumb brushed **her clitor**is and she gasped, shaking as if on an electric wire.

"You like that?" he asked **and** she nodded, unable to speak.

He pulled away just **long en**ough to roll a condom on, then he was back. **Pressing, sliding,** easing into her as if she were made for him.

Ian Greer made love **to her like** a man possessed. He held her against the wall, **arching into her,** whispering dark praise into her ear, urging **her to new place**s. And when she thought she couldn't take any **more, he** proved her wrong.

And finally, when his **body, s**lick with sweat and shaking, reached the end of his control, she wrapped her arms around him and held on tight.

Wishing as hard as she could that things were different.

IAN, HIS BACK against the wall, his legs boneless and tired and stretched out in front of him, simply watched Jennifer. She sat in the office chair and tucked her torn underwear into the pocket of her shorts that no longer closed properly.

Thanks to him.

He would have apologized and meant it, but the secret womanly grin on her face and the light that gleamed in her eyes told him no apology was necessary.

The woman had a hidden appetite for dirty things and he loved it about her. Wished they had a week in this closet to see where her boundaries really lie.

"You're so lovely," he said, resting his head against the wall.

She laughed, the husky sound of it delighting him. "You say that to all the girls you screw against walls." He couldn't stand that she would even joke about that. He reached out and grabbed the rolling office chair and pulled her to him. Somehow he found the strength to get off his butt and cup her face in his hands.

"There has never been anyone like you," he told her, honesty coming easy in this post-orgasmic state. He brushed the hair from her face, tucking it behind her pretty ears. Funny how he never noticed how pretty her ears were. "I am honored you even let me touch you."

"I'm so glad you did," she said, pressing a kiss to his nose. "And there has never been anyone like you," she said and then laughed. "No one even close."

He stroked her hair, kissing her forehead. He didn't know how true that was, her brain was shorted out and she didn't remember her husband as clearly. When she'd told him he felt alive, he'd felt her husband's ghost, his own shortcomings. The truth was the years she spent alone had more to do with her having sex with Ian than he did.

But she was here and she was deluded and he was going to take advantage of that while he could.

He eased her off the chair, settling her in his lap, her legs curled around his hips. He was hard again and he knew she could feel it, but wasn't sure what she'd want right now.

Were they back to business only? Was she going to tell him that this was a mistake? That it should never have happened?

Seemed the wrong way to end things.

So, he kissed her. He kissed her until she was putty in his hands, until she arched slightly into him, growing damp through her shorts.

"Ian," she breathed, pulling away. She flipped her hair over her shoulders and ran her fingers across his face, slowly, carefully, like she were memorizing him.

"You look happy," she breathed, smiling slightly.

"You make me happy," he told her simply, cupping her bottom in his hands, flexing his fingers in that warm curve of flesh.

"This never happened," she said, tracing the lines around

his mouth. "If this got out, it would jeopardize everything. You understand that, right?"

"I do," he murmured.

A certain shyness entered her eyes and she dropped her hands to her lap. "But when it's over. When the story is out. Maybe—" She laughed, staring down at her hands. "I'm so bad at this."

"Maybe what?" he asked, tipping her chin up to meet her eyes. And what he saw there eviscerated him—hope, loyalty and something that looked too much like love to be believed.

"Maybe we can try this again. Maybe we can try it for real."

He was speechless. For real? She wanted something real with him?

"We could go on a date," she said, trying to joke and he couldn't respond. His heart was beating a mile a minute. "Or not," she muttered and shifted as if to stand and he couldn't have that.

Couldn't have her leaving when she'd just gotten here, just found her way to him. He pressed his hands on her thighs, keeping her close, pulling her to him. He couldn't look at her, afraid of what she'd see in his eyes, afraid she'd know how close to the edge he was.

She melted against him, catching fire in his hands, burning both of them right through the night.

JENNIFER WASN'T sure if she slept, but when her eyes opened at dawn she was wide-awake, engaged in what could only be called a full body smile.

And it wasn't just the sex. She was hopeful. Hopeful about Ian and a life that included him. A life with him.

She thought of Doug, like pressing a tentative finger against a bruise, and was relieved by the absence of pain.

Her life came together—her past, her present, her potential future. Nothing was shut off. No part of her shut down.

She rolled to her side and laughed into her pillow, feeling like a teenager. Her body was sore, bruised and full in the best possible way, as if she were full of life.

But, before there could be any more Ian, there was the story.

Spence was still sound asleep in the single bed on the other side of the room and so she stood, grabbed her laptop and snuck out of the room, trying not to wake him.

There was a very good chance she had an e-mail from Waldo and she couldn't wait to see her producer's reaction to the story. Stepping into the kitchen she saw Daisy standing at the front door to the common room. Growling at the closed door.

"Daisy?" she called, but the dog only glanced backward. The ruff went up on the dog's neck and she growled harder, throwing in a menacing bark.

There was probably an opossum hanging out on the front stoop and Jennifer stomped over to the front door and threw it open to scare the beast away.

An explosion of lights blinded her and a thousand voices screamed at her.

"Who are you?"

"Where is Ian Greer?"

"Is this an alcohol treatment facility?"

"Are you sleeping with Ian?"

Daisy was going berserk at her knee. Suddenly the door was yanked from her hands. It was Ian, she knew it before she saw him.

And the flashbulbs doubled in their intensity. Or course it didn't help that he was standing beside her without his shirt on.

"Ian, where—"

"We're calling the cops," he said, his voice iron-plated. "You've got five minutes to clear the property."

"Come on, Ian," one of the men whined. "Tell us—"

"Who called you?" Ian barked.

"A woman at a bowling alley," the guy said, snapping pictures. "Why don't you smile, little lady—"

"Ian." A fat man elbowed his way to the front of the group. "Any comment on your father's announcement that he will be running your mother's foundation and that he is going to cut funding to—"

"What?" Ian asked and Jennifer felt as if lightning had struck them, that's how tense he was. How charged.

"Your father is taking over New Horizons—"

Ian slammed the door so hard the house rattled.

Shell-shocked, Jennifer blinked. "What was that?" she asked, trying not to stare at his chest, or the hard curve of his lips.

"My life," he said, harder than she'd ever seen him. "Are you okay?" he asked. "I'm sorry if they scared you."

"I'm fine. Ian?" she said. "Are *you* okay?"

Ian's pocket began to ring and he pulled out his phone, looked at the call display and right in front of her eyes he changed. He became a different man. Cold. Callous. Made of stone. Her lover was gone. The vulnerable man-child— gone. The lawyer, the silent benefactor, the man who played video games with Spence—all gone.

He was a stranger to her.

He lifted his eyes and looked at her for a long time, as if studying her. Memorizing her.

"Ian?" she asked, feeling as if there was something happening, something pulling him away.

"I'm sorry," he said.

Ian flipped open the phone and pressed it to his ear.

"Hello, Dad."

CHAPTER EIGHTEEN

"IT'S ABOUT TIME you answered my calls," Jackson Greer said, his cultured, modulated tone sounding like a snake hissing in Ian's ears.

The rage, the anger he'd beaten back during these days at Serenity, surged through his veins. If he could have reached through the phone and strangled his father, he would have.

That Jennifer stood watching him, her mouth tense, her eyes worried, made it all worse.

So, he turned away, unable to look at her face and talk to his father at the same time.

"There's no way you're taking over Mom's foundation. No way."

"You're in no position to make demands like that," Jackson said, chuckling softly, and Ian felt a familiar madness coursing through his bloodstream.

Ian would do anything, *anything* to shut that man up.

"You're all over the Internet," Jackson said. "You and that woman."

The photos taken minutes ago would be all over the world by now. That's how the parasites worked. Their web was perfection, all-encompassing.

"She doesn't look like your usual slut—"

"Not another word, Dad. Not another word."

He nearly ran from the room. It wasn't enough that he

couldn't see her, he didn't want his father's poison in the same room. The same building.

"Perhaps it's time you came home," Jackson said. "I wouldn't have to take over New Horizons."

"You won't. You won't get your hands on it. I will fight you every step of the way."

"You should be in rehab. You are a drunk. You are incompetent and your mother deserves better than this, Ian. You should be at—"

Ian's dams broke and fury burst through him, drowning good sense. "Do not talk about my mother," he whispered, clenching the phone so hard his hand hurt.

Jackson laughed. "Is this your attempt to show the world you care about her? Getting drunk at her funeral and running off with some woman—"

"Don't you recognize that woman?" he asked. And here he was, pulling Jennifer into the mud of this conversation. Into the mud of his father's sickness. Because he was weak. Because he would do anything, anything to hurt his father. "She's a journalist."

"Right," Jackson scoffed.

"She was the reporter you and Mom talked to two years ago. Your last interview as a couple. Camelot, the golden years, don't you remember?"

There was a long silence. "What have you done, Ian?"

A sickening glee filled him. Satisfaction like a thick oil oozed down through him. "I told her the truth, Dad," he said, nearly laughing. "Every bit of it. About the abuse and the rape and—"

"The rantings of an alcoholic," he said, dismissing everything, like he always did. "No one will believe you."

"She did," he insisted, feeling like the teenager he'd been standing up against the most powerful man in the world.

"Because, no doubt, you're screwing her."

Ian braced his shoulder against the wall. It was too close to the truth not to sting and he suddenly realized what he'd done last night. The damage that he'd caused to himself, to the story, to Jennifer. All because he was exactly what his father thought he was. Weak.

But still Jackson kept talking and Ian kept taking the punches, his defense weakening. Always weakening. "You've spent years ruining your reputation. You are a disgrace, Ian. A shame. Your mother would loathe you for doing this. She'd—"

"I will destroy you," Ian said and, shaking, he hung up.

His brain was imploding. Anger and pain, the past and present converging, and he turned, hurling the phone against the wall, where it cracked and split.

Somewhere Shonny started to cry.

"Ian?" Jennifer whispered, her hand a firm warmth against his arm.

"My father is right," he said, broken somewhere deep inside. He couldn't look at her. "No one will believe me. I'm a drunk throwing rocks at the former president of the United States. I'm a fool trying to ruin the great American marriage."

"You're telling the truth, Ian." Jennifer tried to put her arms around him, but he shook her off.

"It won't matter. I shouldn't have pulled you into this," he said.

"You want to give up?" she asked, her whiskey eyes hurt and worried.

There was a yell outside, laughter from the photographers, and Ian felt a new idea form. A new plan come together.

"It won't matter what the truth is," he said. "But, if I open the door and tell every one of those parasites out there what my father did, it will be all over the papers in minutes. It will be a scandal so huge that whether it's true or not it won't matter. The world will judge him. Damn him."

"No, it won't," she said, holding on to him with a new fierceness. A new strength. Horror and disbelief dawned on her face. "The story will be dismissed in a matter of days. It will be what everyone expects of you."

He ignored her, victory snowballed in him, destroying reason, and he stepped toward the door.

"Ian!" Jennifer cried and he had to ignore her. He knew what she was going to say. He knew how he was hurting her, but it didn't matter. Nothing mattered but revenge. He saw suddenly, his mother's black-and-blue eye. The bruises the size of hands on her arms, the blood on a marriage bed's sheets.

"Take a deep breath, Ian. Think about what you're doing." Jennifer grabbed his arms, throwing him off course.

Don't look at her, he told himself. *Do not look at her.* But he couldn't help it. Her eyes were swimming in tears.

"Please, don't do this," she whispered. "Please, let's do this the right way. Don't make it a rumor, make it a fact."

"It doesn't matter," Ian told her. "He's right, I have more power this way."

"What about me?" she asked.

"You're better off not getting involved."

"Don't you think it's a little late for that?" she cried, heartbreak vivid in her eyes.

"The story—"

"This isn't about the story! It's about us. It's about last night."

"Last night never happened, remember?" He saw his cold words slide right through her. Watched her shrink. He saw her pain and anguish and he told himself to keep watching. That was his gift. That is what he had to give her. Not love. Not a life. Just pain.

"This isn't you, Ian," she breathed.

He grabbed her arms, lifting her on to her toes. "I am not who you think I am," he told her. "I've tried to make you see that. I am not Doug."

Her eyes narrowed, anger burning in her cheeks. "This isn't about Doug," she said. "It's about you. It's about who you really are."

"This is who I really am," he said.

"No, it's not. You're a good man." She kept trying, he had to give her that. Relentless, his Jennifer. Though she had never truly seen him for what he was. She'd been wearing rose-colored glasses all along. "You could have another life—"

"With you?" he asked, the words tripping over themselves. "You honestly think you would let me into your life?"

Tears spilled down her cheeks. "I would have let you in," she whispered. "I would have let you all the way in."

His foundations shook and rattled and he felt himself wavering. Trembling. *Not for you, Ian,* he told himself. *You know that. It's always been that way. This woman is not for you.*

To prove it he thought of his father. Their blood that tied them. Their eyes and height. Their hair. Not so different, in the end.

"You deserve better than me," he said. "You wanted me to be someone else so you wouldn't feel so cheap when I touched you. Well, guess what? We're both cheap. The only difference is I have always been that way."

He grabbed the doorknob and Jennifer closed her eyes for one second and he watched, spellbound as she gathered herself up, picked up every piece he'd just ripped away from her.

She opened her eyes and she was reborn, made of steel and rock. Iron and earth. Implacable. Immovable. An enemy where moments ago she'd been a friend.

"Pack your bags and get out of my house," she said.

"Right after—"

She shook her head. "No right after. You want to destroy your life and mine, you're going to have to do it another time. Some other place. This is a women's shelter, Ian. Respect that."

"This has nothing to do with you," he told her.

The breath she pulled in shook as if he'd sucker punched her. "You have twenty minutes," she whispered.

BETTER THIS WAY. *Better this way. Better this way.*

Ian threw the meager amount of crap he'd brought with him to Serenity back into his duffel bag. While Andille, slow as molasses, carefully folded and packed.

"Say it," Ian yelled. "Just say it."

"What?" Andille asked, his voice so slow and careful.

"Say I'm an idiot. Say I'm a bastard."

"You're a bastard."

"I had no choice!" Ian yelled.

Andille turned, an old man, weathered and beaten and sad. "There's always a choice, Ian. That's what you've never seen. I'm sorry for what happened to you as a kid. I'm sorry that all your freedom and decisions were ripped away from you. But what you're doing now doesn't make up for that."

Ian jabbed his finger in Andille's chest. "I am doing—" he wanted to fight, tear down the wall, punch Andille in the face, but the guy wasn't cooperating "—the only thing I can."

Andille shook his head and turned around, zipping his bag. "I'm sorry you feel that way." He hoisted his bag onto his shoulder and headed for the door. "Let's go say goodbye."

Ian yanked the zipper pulls so hard they broke off in his hand.

JENNIFER STARED at the journals through tears that would not fall. There would be no more crying. Not for Ian. Not for herself.

She grabbed the story off her printer, folded it and placed it in the last journal. A little going-away present for Ian. So he'd see what he was losing when he chose the easy way out.

Upstairs, the floors creaked and she knew she only had a few minutes before Andille and Ian left. Two days ago she'd thought, stupidly, that when he left she'd be sad. Sorry. She had no idea how devastated she'd be.

Because that's what she was—torn to the ground, burned to ash.

She picked up the journals and headed to the kitchen, where it seemed like there was a funeral taking place. Deb's eyes were stone dry, but she and Jennifer couldn't look at each other very long or they'd both break down. And Jennifer knew neither of them wanted to watch these men leave through tears.

But it certainly wasn't stopping Shonny, who clung to his mother and wailed, letting it out for all of them.

Spencer sat at the table, looking baffled. "Why are they leaving, Mom?" he asked.

Because I told them to.

"Because they have to get back to their lives, honey," she said, cupping his head. He ducked out of the way, his emotions making him a little belligerent.

Wonderful.

Andille came through the door and stopped at the sight of Deb with Shonny. For a second he looked like he was going to just fall to his knees in grief, then the moment was gone and he was carved out of stone.

Shonny reached for him, crying his name, and Deb, as if ripping the skin from her body, let him go into Andille's arms.

Andille turned slightly, whispering something private in the boy's ear.

Jennifer grabbed a paper towel and handed it to Deb.

Ian barreled through the door a million miles an hour, no doubt ready to leave. Ready to open the door to all those "journalists" and ruin the rest of his life, with no regard to the rest of hers.

God, he'd taken such care of her the other night. Held her as if she were made of gold dust, looked at her as if he couldn't believe his eyes. And now he was trashing her dream, her future, as if it meant nothing to him.

And clearly it didn't.

Her anger had the lucky benefit of burning away her tears and she was grateful, at least, for that.

"You're leaving?" Spence asked Ian as he slid from the kitchen chair to stand in front of him.

Ian's throat bobbed as if swallowing something painful. "I am."

"Are you coming back?"

Ian's eyes skipped to hers and she raised her eyebrows. Was he insane? Like she'd welcome him back with open arms? Please. She was dumb, she wasn't stupid.

"No," Ian said, standing awkwardly in front of Spence, before crouching. "I won't."

"I thought we were going to be friends," Spence said. "You were going to show me how to pass a soccer ball off my head."

"I'm sorry, I can't. I—"

"That sucks!"

Jennifer didn't even bother to check his language. Nope, Spence got it right on the nose. Spence stomped over to stand next to her. She patted his shoulder before approaching Ian, who, she had to admit, was looking as if someone were pulling him apart. Which, she supposed was true, but he was doing it to himself and he was just too blind to see it.

"Here," she said, handing him the journals. "You should have these."

He didn't reach for them. "I don't want them."

"Of course you don't," she said, pulling the broken zip on his duffel and stuffing them inside. "Which is why you should read them. If you're ever going to make sense of your parents' marriage, you need to read these journals."

"I don't want to make sense of it," he told her.

"If you ever want to make sense of your own life," she snapped, so tired of running her head into the brick wall that was Ian's past. *If you ever want a normal relationship, if you ever want to come back to me,* she wanted to say, but it was a moot point. He would not be coming back around.

"Jennifer." He sighed. "I never meant it to go this way."

Tears scorched the inside of her skull and she curled her hands into fists, distracting herself with the pain of her nails biting into her palms.

"I hope you read those journals and are able to put the past behind you," she said. "Because, if you don't, you won't be able to get on with your life. With or without me."

And that was as close as she was going to get to telling how she really felt under this betrayal.

"Goodbye, Ian," she breathed, her chest crushed by grief and anger and regret—for him. All for him.

"Let's go, Dille," Ian said, stepping toward the common room where Daisy growled at the door, ready to see him out, no longer friends.

But Andille didn't move. He looked at Shonny then, slowly at Deb. A smile, so radiant, so filled with love and joy, spread over his face and he reached out a hand for Deb's cast. "I'm not going," he said to her and her head bowed, as if the strength it had taken to not show her sadness simply did her in.

Andille towed her in, curled her to his side and pressed a kiss to her dreadlocks. The tears Jennifer had refused to shed ran down her cheeks.

"I'm not going," he said to Ian, a thousand things unspoken between them. A dozen years of friendship boiled down to this moment. All debts repaid. "I'm making my choice."

"Right now?" Ian asked.

"This very minute."

Ian's smile was bittersweet and his eyes touched Jennifer's face briefly. "It's a good choice, man," he said. "A really good choice."

They shook hands, a long hard squeeze. "Take care, Dille," Ian whispered.

"I'll be in touch," Andille said, looking like a young man. A young man in love. "Just because I'm not going to be your babysitter anymore doesn't mean you're rid of me."

"Good," Ian said, the same sad smile on his face. "I don't ever want to be rid of you."

He opened the door and the photographers were no longer on the front stoop, instead standing on the road, off Serenity property.

"Ian, what are you doing here?" one of them yelled and Jennifer held her breath. Closed her eyes.

Here it comes, she thought, bracing herself for the worst.

But Ian didn't say anything. The wind blew. A car honked. But Ian was silent. And finally she opened her eyes, the suspense killing her.

Ian was watching her and she couldn't read his expression. Couldn't make heads or tails of what he was thinking.

He lifted his hand, opened it, closed it.

And left, without a word to the press.

"Deb," Andille whispered into her ear. They sat together on the couch where they'd collapsed after Ian left. Jennifer and Spence were in the kitchen, talking in low tones. Somewhere in the mix of emotions pounding through Deb's body she felt bad for Jennifer, that the disappointment Deb had seen coming had actually arrived. Jennifer didn't deserve this.

But Deb wondered, her body curved along Andille's like they'd been sitting together on couches all their lives, did she deserve what she was getting?

Shonny ran laps around the couch, shouting, "He's going to stay."

Andille was so solid beside her, an odd reality where before there had been nothing. Empty space for so long, that she'd gotten used to it, grown attached to it. He was staying. And she didn't know what that meant.

"Deb, please," he whispered, "don't freak out."

"I'm not freaking out," she said. She didn't, as a rule, freak out. She handled things. Dealt with stuff. Snakes excluded.

"You are." He laughed, pulling a dreadlock from in front of her eye. "I'm not moving in," he said. "I'm not expecting—"

"What if I'm expecting," she said, surprising both of them.

He leaned back, smiling at her like he already knew all those things about her that she was just figuring out. "What," he said, his fingers a butterfly caress up her arm, around her elbow, "are you expecting?"

"I don't know," she said, "but you're staying." She reached for him, suddenly dying for the feel of his skin under her hand. He was staying. He was here. Right here. "For me."

"For you," he agreed, nodding solemnly like taking an oath. "And Shonny."

She pressed her hands to his beautiful face, pulling him

forward, kissing him in front of her son, God and everybody. "Then I'm expecting a lot," she said, laughing against his lips.

She didn't know if she deserved this, but she was taking it. She was grabbing Andille with both hands and she was not going to let go.

CHAPTER NINETEEN

JENNIFER SAT ON the floor, her back against the wall of the office. It was where she'd made love to Ian last night and it was only fitting that she make this call from here. Ground zero.

"Waldo here," Kerry said, in the office even on a Saturday. And Jennifer winced, swearing silently. The chicken in her had been hoping for voice mail.

"Hi, Kerry," she said.

"Jennifer." Jennifer could hear something hit Waldo's office door with extreme force and the resulting slam made her jerk the phone from her ear. This was not going to be pretty. "Do you want to tell me why there are pictures of you with a half-naked Ian Greer all over the Internet?"

"It's not how it looks," she said, bracing her head in her hand. She hadn't counted on the photos, one more layer to this crap cake she was eating.

"You and I both know that it doesn't matter. How it looks is all that anyone cares about."

There was nothing Jennifer could say so she was silent, taking her lumps like an adult.

"I read your story," Waldo said and Jennifer's heart leaped. "It's good. It's brilliant. But there's nothing we can do right now, not with these pictures all over the place."

Jennifer sighed and looked at the ceiling. "We might not

be able to do anything," she said. "Ian may leak the story to the tabloids."

"Is he an idiot?" Waldo asked in her customary frankness.

"He's consumed," Jennifer said, not sure why she defended him. "Revenge against his father is all that matters."

"Well, we won't scrap it," Waldo said. "Let's see how this plays out."

"Waldo," she said, emotion nearly choking her, "there won't be any interview. I won't be seeing him again."

Waldo was quiet for a long time. "Well," she finally said. "This sucks."

"I know," Jennifer said, pinching the bridge of her nose as if that would make her feel better. "I'm so—"

"What's done is done," she said. "You want some editing work? I'm swamped here, and I could use your touch."

Jennifer didn't even think about it. She didn't think about money, or time constraints. The past or Doug or the sword were no longer factors.

"Yes," she said. Sitting at ground zero, imagining the wall still held the heat from their ill-fated passion, she decided to get on with her life.

IAN LOCKED HIMSELF in his apartment. After a week most of the photographers went away, the sidewalk in front of his house practically a ghost town. He never did talk to them. Every morning he woke up and planned what he was going to say, how he was going to tell them all about his father's abuse. But every day he looked out the window at the seething sea of parasites waiting for one word from him to broadcast around the world. He looked at them and felt Jennifer's ghost haunting him.

And he didn't do it.

He heard her voice confidently telling him she knew who

he was. The real him. And as the days passed, he began to wonder if maybe she was right. Since he'd been a prisoner in his house he didn't know who he was anymore. Revenge was right outside his door and he couldn't do it. And that wasn't him. Not the him he'd created these last dozen years. Not the him he recognized.

At night, he felt her kiss, her hands, her weight against his chest, and it got so bad he stopped sleeping.

He was convinced, in the pit of his stomach, he had made the biggest mistake of his life walking away from Serenity. Away from Jennifer.

Today, his eighth day of exile, he pushed aside the drapes of his window and there was only one photographer out there. A flash went off and Ian gave the guy the finger before letting the drapes drop back into place.

If he wanted revenge, it looked like this might be his last chance.

I should go down there, he thought halfheartedly, knowing he wouldn't. Jennifer's ghost made sure of that, sitting on his shoulder, convincing him he was better than that.

He turned and stared down the long hallway toward his guest room, where he'd stashed the journals. They pulsed in his empty house. A constant whisper. A lure. A beckoning finger.

"This is ridiculous," he muttered, because he was crazy. A week alone in a house with nothing but regrets, ghosts and pulsing books will do that to a guy.

He was going to end it, finish it. He'd read the journals and call *The Enquirer.* Today. He'd banish all the ghosts and go sleep with an actress. Because he could. Because that's who he was. That was the life he deserved.

He stomped through the house, stopping in front of the guest room, staring at the ebonized door like he was engaged in combat.

The doorknob was hot in his hand as if whatever energy made those journals so hard to resist was filling the whole room like smoke from a fire.

I'm not strong enough, he thought, suddenly, his momentum deflated. *I'm not strong enough to change.* His anger and his resentment, his need for revenge, all felt comfortable. Believing he didn't deserve Jennifer kept him safe from wanting her too much.

"Right." He nearly laughed. "If this is not wanting her too much, I'd hate to see what love looks like."

He pressed his head against the door, hard enough to hurt.

I would have let you in. He heard Jennifer's words. *I would have let you all the way in.*

The courage it must have taken her to say that astonished him now, maybe because he lacked the courage to even walk out the door of his house.

Sick of himself, he twisted the knob and stepped inside the cool room. The journals were stacked on the foot of the bed, a dark splotch, like blood on the white duvet.

He sat, picked up one of the journals.

December 2, 1972—Ian's fourth birthday. Jackson stayed for pictures and left. We covered Annabelle's split lip with lip liner. No one asked any questions, except for Ian and I.

"Oh, God," Ian groaned, collapsing backward on the bed, pulling the journals close.

IT WAS DUSK by the time he put down the last journal and picked up the folded papers that had been tucked in the last one. Jennifer's story. Jennifer's brilliant work that took his family's shame and mess and crafted a story about forgiveness and hope. His mother was a victim, sure, but on her terms. As stupid as that sounded.

His hands flopped to his side. If these were the events that made him, the events that he allowed to shape every single thing he did day in and day out...then she did know him better than he knew himself. If she was able to look at those journals and the things that he'd told her and still see a bright side, why couldn't he?

I don't want to be like this anymore, he thought. *I don't want to lose the rest of my life the way I've lost everything up to this point.*

He picked up the phone beside the bed and dialed the house in New Hampshire while the impulse was irresistible.

"Jackson Greer's office," some anonymous assistant said.

"This is Ian," he said, his voice a rasp from disuse. "I'd like to talk to my father."

"Right away."

Ian smirked. *Right away.* They must all be on tabloid watch, everyone waiting for the shoe to drop.

"Ian?" His father's voice still sent chills down his spine, and he imagined it always would. But the bloodlust was gone. Mom had made peace somehow. With everything that he'd done to her, she'd managed to still find beauty. To still hope and dream. Her decision to send Ian away had been harder than staying with Dad all these years. The price, Suzette had said, for all of her concessions was to lose the trust of her only child.

"Dad." Now that he was at this moment he didn't actually

have a plan, and his instincts, long ignored and abused, kicked in. "I haven't talked to the tabloids," he said.

"I've noticed."

"And I won't." Ian sighed and let go of revenge. Let go of hate. Let go of his father. He welcomed Jennifer's words right into his heart and let change take place. "But I want control of Mom's foundation. I don't want you as a spokesperson for her anymore."

"Suddenly you're a philanthropist?"

Ian ignored the jibe. "And I'll be using that foundation to help literacy as Mom intended, but I'll be giving a lot of money to women's shelters."

There was a long pause and Ian, for the first time in his life, realized he had all the power. Right now. This moment. The power was his.

"She'd like that," Jackson said quietly. "She would... approve."

"Damn right she would," Ian said, refusing to be touched by the old man's concession. "But you're out, Dad. You're not on the board, you're not an advisor, nothing."

"Or what?"

"Or I will give this story back to Jennifer Stern and she will destroy you."

"Blackmail?"

"Learned from the best, Dad."

"What are you going to do?" he asked.

"I told you—"

"About your life?" Jackson asked. "More actresses?"

Jennifer's lithe, strong body, her passion that infused everything she did, the way her hair slipped out of those intricate knots she tried to keep it in, came to him.

"It's none of your business," he said. Something thick and bitter stuck in the back of his throat and he needed to get off the phone. "I'll fax over papers today and I'll expect them signed and returned to me by week's end."

"And then?"

Ian blinked and sat up, wondering if his father was asking about them, about what would happen between father and son. As if this cease-fire might give them a chance to have something even resembling normalcy? Ian couldn't imagine, frankly couldn't even stomach the idea. But he could imagine Jennifer over his shoulder, telling him to keep an open mind, to see where his father was going with this.

"The story, those journals?" Jackson said, true to character to the very last and making Ian feel a fool for thinking his father would ever be different. "What happens to them?"

"I get the papers and you stay out of my way and the story and journals won't see the light of day."

"All right," Jackson said. "It's a deal."

A *deal*, Ian thought, shaking his head. Not even bothering to feel sad or angry, just glad that he was getting this cancer, this toxin, out of his life. Finally.

He hung up, pressing the phone down as hard as he could in the cradle.

Over. Finally. Over.

The muscles all over his back twitched and he stood, shaking his hands as adrenaline tripped through his system. He needed to jog. Run.

He stepped to the window, yanking open the curtains. Sunlight bathed him.

Like Andille said, there was always a choice and he was making a choice right now to let go of the past.

He closed his eyes, letting the sunlight warm his face, sift right through his body, burn away everything that was too heavy to keep carrying. He felt himself change. Those things he'd carried for so long, the baggage that kept him from Jennifer, were gone.

The air he breathed was cleaner, the clothes on his back were lighter. The thoughts in his head...all about Jennifer.

His eyes popped open. *Jennifer,* his heart sighed. Suddenly his house was too small and North Carolina too far away.

"HEY, MOM, THERE YOU are again," Spence said, pointing at yet another picture of her in the tabloids at the checkout aisle in the grocery store. It had been a week and Ian hadn't been in a single picture. It was like he'd dropped off the face of the earth. She, on the other hand, had to fight off the photographers to leave her house here in Asheville.

She didn't understand this new life he'd left her with. And she had the terrible feeling that even if she wasn't on the cover of newspapers and being stalked by paparazzi, she'd still be lost.

She missed him. She wondered how he was. If he'd read the journals, dealt with his father, his mother. If he was finding peace at all.

And then she was pissed with herself for caring.

But he hasn't told the tabloids, a little voice in the back of her head whispered. *What does that mean?*

She realized she could spend the rest of her life unraveling the mystery that was Ian Greer, but he'd left. And she needed to move on.

"Can we get it?" Spence asked, while she threw a can of chickpeas onto the conveyor belt harder than was totally necessary. For crying out loud, her son was wearing sunglasses and a ball cap like some kind of convict on the run. "Mom?"

"No, honey," she snapped. "We cannot get *The Enquirer.*"

"But—"

"No, buts, Spence. We're—" Her cell phone rang, cutting off her irrational tirade. She blew out a long breath. This situation was getting the better of her in every possible way. "I'm sorry. I didn't mean to snap."

He shrugged. "I just think it's cool," he said.

Of course he did. He was eleven. He was on the cover of *The Enquirer.*

Her cell rang again and she dug through her purse, answering it while still putting groceries on the conveyor.

"Jennifer?" Waldo's familiar bark was a surprise.

"Waldo?" Jennifer asked. "Is there a problem with the file I sent you?"

"No problem," Kerry said, sounding distracted. "Look, can you get to Serenity this weekend?"

"It's Saturday." Already the weekend.

"Right, can you get there later?" she asked. "Today?"

Jennifer considered the paparazzi outside of her house and decided a few days away from them would do her and Spence some good.

"I guess, why? What's up?"

"Story" was all she said. "Big. The person I need you to interview lives near there. We've got a crew heading down there now."

"Can you give me a name? A hook?"

"Well, it's no presidential abuse scandal."

Jennifer rolled her eyes. Every conversation with Waldo had some dig about the story that wasn't. Jennifer had apologized so many times, in so many ways, there was nothing left for her to do but ignore it.

"But we've got a victim of abuse and a man with a lot of money to spend, that's all I know. Check in when you get there. And Jen?" Something shifted in Waldo's voice. "In advance, I'm sorry. Or, you're welcome, however it pans out."

Waldo hung up and Jennifer stared at her phone. She was sorry if the story was a dud, or a blind alley. Which, chances were, it was.

But, even if that were the case, the trip would not be in vain. It would be good to see Deb, and J.D. and Sam, now that they were back. And perhaps Andille would have talked to Ian. Not that she'd ask him, but if Andille offered some kind of information, that would be okay.

"We're not going to get those," Jennifer said, stopping the clerk from scanning the Popsicles.

It was a long drive to Northwoods.

CHAPTER TWENTY

THEY ARRIVED AT DUSK, fireflies illuminating the low grasses in the twilight. Jennifer was surprised she'd missed Serenity so much. Shonny burst out the back door, Andille not far behind him.

Her heart spasmed at the sight of the man since all he reminded her of was Ian. "Hi," she said, unfolding from her car and immediately getting wrapped up in Andille's strong arms.

The man was nearly unrecognizable. The joy that lifted off him replaced all that weariness, illuminated his eyes, his skin, his smile. He'd been magnetic before, now he was nearly otherworldly with his grace and looks.

She leaned back. "You seem happy." Understatement of the day.

He considered her face and she was simply too tired to try and hide all her grief and anger. "You do not," he whispered.

"I'll get over it," she said with a halfhearted shrug.

He hummed low in his throat then grunted as Spence ran straight into him. "Hey! Dille!" he cried, passing the blue-and-red ball over to Andille. "I brought my soccer ball."

"Excellent," Andille said, bouncing the ball up to his knee. "Let's see if you've gotten better."

And the boys were off chasing the ball toward the yard.

Jennifer grabbed her purse and headed for the open back door and this mysterious big story.

Deb was in the kitchen, cutting vegetables for a salad, the plaster casts gone, replaced by flexible air casts.

"Upstairs," she said, gesturing with her sharp little paring knife. Deb always acted like no time had passed whenever they saw each other. A week, two days, three months, it didn't matter—everyone just picked up where they left off with Deb.

Another thing Jennifer loved about her.

"Where's the crew?" Jennifer asked, looking around for the equipment crews traveled with.

"What crew?" Deb asked.

At long last Jennifer's instincts kicked in. This was beyond fishy. "What's going on?" Jennifer asked.

"Upstairs," Deb said, turning back to her salad. "That's all I'm going to say."

Jennifer threw her purse down on the table and headed for the steps. All the hair on her arms stood at rigid attention as she stomped upward, telling herself that the odds were highly against Ian being up there.

She practically kicked open the door and there he was, blond and blue eyed, wearing jeans and a cautious smile. More handsome than she could stand. Her body lurched and reached for him, wanting him despite everything.

"Hi," he said.

For a second her mind was a blank. Empty. Then her anger kicked in. He'd been pulling her strings ever since she met him and now he'd recruited her friends.

"You've got to be kidding me," she said, turning away for the stairs and outside and her car. There was no air to breathe in this place. No air when he stood so close. He sucked all of her will from her, every thought. And she knew if she was going to hold onto her anger, stand firm against the seductive charisma of Ian Greer, she had to get out of here.

"Jennifer. Jennifer, stop, please." His hand caught her

elbow and she whirled, slapping at his hands, unable to stand the burn of his flesh against hers.

"Is this a joke to you?" she cried. "My life, my career, is it just a game you can play whenever you want?"

"No." He honestly looked horrified. But the guy was a consummate actor, and she'd be a fool to believe him. "Not at all, Jennifer. I wanted..." He stopped, pulled in a deep breath. "I needed to see you and I knew if I called you, you wouldn't talk to me."

"So, you pulled some strings and I came running."

"I didn't think of it that way, Jennifer."

"Of course not," she spat, so angry, so hurt, so half in love with the man that she couldn't see straight. "You don't think of anyone but yourself."

Tears burned in her eyes, tears she really didn't want to shed in front of him, and she turned away, searching for composure.

He circled her, standing in front of her with his hands out. "All I've been thinking about is you for the past week. You've been...haunting me."

"Good," she muttered.

"I didn't spill the story," he said.

"I noticed."

"I read the journals."

Oh, she thought, *don't do this. Don't make me care again. I can't survive getting hurt by this guy again.*

"And I called my father," he said, his voice so ravaged. "It's over."

"What do you mean?" she asked, wiping at the tears that clung to her lashes.

"I mean, I told him I would take over my mother's foundation, without his involvement in any way, and I would never tell the truth about my parents."

"Blackmail?"

He smile was so crooked, so endearing, that she just couldn't stand it. "It needed to end," he said. "It was killing me."

A different man stood in Ian's place. Someone more careful, someone less frantic. Less angry. There was a stillness in him, an empty place where all that frenetic anger had been spinning.

This was the man she'd seen in him. The man she'd hoped he'd become.

"I'm glad," she said honestly.

"Me, too," he whispered and she made the stupid mistake of looking into his eyes, being caught like a fly in a spiderweb by all she saw there. Regret, earnest compassion, worry, doubt.

She'd never seen doubt before, not in him, and she knew everything about him was different. Suddenly the ground she stood on was not so stable anymore. Not so sure.

Anger seemed stupid. The past a million miles away. Nothing mattered but what he was about to say.

"You said you knew me," he whispered and she couldn't breathe, much less speak. "That I was a good man. Better than I thought I was."

She nodded, still unable to speak, cautious hope inflating her slowly.

"I want a chance to be that man," he said. "I want a chance to be your man." The words melted her. Destroyed any lingering doubts. The tears slipped down her cheeks. "I know you don't know me—I barely know myself. But I thought maybe we could try," he said.

It sounded so good, it sounded like exactly what her heart wanted.

"Try?" she croaked.

"I thought I could get to know you and Spence and you could get to know me. We could play soccer and go bowling and argue about how much pop Spence drinks. We could rent movies and sleep in on Sunday mornings. I could help out when you were on deadline and you could help me with the foundation and we could…" He shrugged, his smile brief and sharp, a spark in the center of the world. "Try."

"Try," she whispered.

"Unless—" He glanced at his hands, balled them into fists. "Unless I've ruined this, and I know there's a good chance I have. I know I don't deserve—"

"Luckily," she whispered, stepping closer, reaching for his fist, "you don't get to decide what you deserve." She wasn't going to waste any more time. Not when happiness stood right here. Within reach. "I want to try," she said, laughing slightly. She was queen of understatements today. "I really want to try."

He laughed gruffly, from the back of his throat, and she watched as tears filled his beautiful eyes. His beloved eyes. "Thank you," he whispered and as she leaned up to kiss him, he met her halfway. "Thank you," he whispered against her smile.

Everything that stood between them—the story, the secrets, the past—all turned to dust and blew away, leaving only them and the bright clean vision of the future. Together.

EPILOGUE

"Defense, Spence!" Ian yelled from the sidelines and Spence heard him through the screams of the fans as if Ian were right in his ear. Practically in his head. Spence turned, positioning himself to guard the goal.

"Watch ten, watch ten," Ian yelled and Spence wiped sweat off his forehead, searching for…there he was. Ten was barreling down the sidelines. Baker wasn't fast enough and ten cruised right past him, dekeing left around Max, leaving him in the dust.

"You can do it!" Ian yelled and Spence realized it was just him and ten. Just him and ten and the state championship at stake.

Ten leaned left and Spence nearly grinned. *Nice try,* he thought, sprinting right and sliding under the feet of the surprised ten as his toe clipped the ball, sending it back, away from the goal just as the buzzer rang.

We won! Won!

He laid on his back and realized how incredibly blue the sky was. How big the clouds. How bright the future. Then he was yanked to his feet.

Max hugged him and Baker jumped on both of them. But Spence pushed past them, looking for Coach. Looking for Ian.

And there he was, jogging out onto the field, his arms up in victory and his eyes right on Spence.

"You did it!" Ian yelled, pointing right to him.

Spence leaped up, nearly knocking the old man on the ground. But Ian was strong, and he grabbed Spence, swinging him around, like he used to when Spence was eleven.

Spence was going on to college next year, on a partial soccer scholarship. And he knew it was because of Ian, who'd been coaching Spence's high school team since Spence was a freshman.

Mom and his six-year-old sister Katie came running out of the stands, followed by Andille and Deb and Shonny and he nearly started to cry. And then he did cry. He just let himself cry.

"I'm so proud of you, son," Ian whispered.

"Thanks, Dad."

* * * * *

Harlequin is 60 years old,
and Harlequin Blaze is celebrating!
After all, a lot can happen in 60 years,
or 60 minutes...or 60 seconds!
Find out what's going down in Blaze's
heart-stopping new miniseries,
FROM 0 TO 60!
Getting from "Hello" to "How was it?"
can happen fast....

Here's a sneak peek of the first book,
A LONG, HARD RIDE
by Alison Kent
Available March 2009

"Is that for me?" Trey asked.

Cardin Worth cocked her head to the side and considered how much better the day already seemed. "Good morning to you, too."

When she didn't hold out the second cup of coffee for him to take, he came closer. She sipped from her heavy white mug, hiding her grin and her giddy rush of nerves behind it.

But when he stopped in front of her, she made the mistake of lowering her gaze from his face to the exposed strip of his chest. It was either give him his cup of coffee or bury her nose against him and breathe in. She remembered so clearly how he smelled. How he tasted.

She gave him his coffee.

After taking a quick gulp, he smiled and said, "Good morning, Cardin. I hope the floor wasn't too hard for you."

The hardness of the floor hadn't been the problem. She shook her head. "Are you kidding? I slept like a baby, swaddled in my sleeping bag."

"In my sleeping bag, you mean."

If he wanted to get technical, yeah. "Thanks for the loaner. It made sleeping on the floor almost bearable." As had the warmth of his spooned body, she thought, then quickly changed the subject. "I saw you have a loaf of bread and some eggs. Would you like me to cook breakfast?"

He lowered his coffee mug slowly, his gaze as warm as the sun on her shoulders, as the ceramic heating her hands. "I didn't bring you out here to wait on me."

"You didn't bring me out here at all. I volunteered to come."

"To help me get ready for the race. Not to serve me."

"It's just breakfast, Trey. And coffee." Even if last night it had been more. Even if the way he was looking at her made her want to climb back into that sleeping bag. "I work much better when my stomach's not growling. I thought it might be the same for you."

"It is, but I'll cook. You made the coffee."

"That's because I can't work at all without caffeine."

"If I'd known that, I would've put on a pot as soon as I got up."

"What time *did* you get up?" Judging by the sun's position, she swore it couldn't be any later than seven now. And, yeah, they'd agreed to start working at six.

"Maybe four?" he guessed, giving her a lazy smile.

"But it was almost two…" She let the sentence dangle, finishing the thought privately. She was quite sure he knew exactly what time they'd finally fallen asleep after he'd made love to her.

The question facing her now was where did this relationship—if you could even call it *that*—go from here?

* * * * *

Cardin and Trey are about to find out that
great sex is only the beginning….
Don't miss the fireworks!
Get ready for
A LONG, HARD RIDE
by Alison Kent
Available March 2009,

CELEBRATE
60 YEARS
OF PURE READING PLEASURE
WITH **HARLEQUIN**®!

We'll be spotlighting a different series
every month throughout 2009
to celebrate our 60th anniversary.

Look for Harlequin® Blaze™ in March!

0-60

*After all, a lot can happen in 60 years,
or 60 minutes...or 60 seconds!*

Find out what's going down in Blaze's
heart-stopping new miniseries *0-60!*
Getting from "Hello" to "How was it?"
can happen fast....

Look for the brand-new 0-60 miniseries in March 2009!

www.eHarlequin.com   HBRIDE09

You're invited to join our Tell Harlequin Reader Panel!

By joining our new reader panel you will:

- Receive Harlequin® books—they are FREE and yours to keep with no obligation to purchase anything!
- Participate in fun online surveys
- Exchange opinions and ideas with women just like you
- Have a say in our new book ideas and help us publish the best in women's fiction

In addition, you will have a chance to win great prizes and receive special gifts! See Web site for details. Some conditions apply. Space is limited.

To join, visit us at
www.TellHarlequin.com.

THBPA0108

SPECIAL EDITION

TRAVIS'S APPEAL

by *USA TODAY* bestselling author
MARIE FERRARELLA

Shana O'Reilly couldn't deny it—family lawyer
Travis Marlowe had some kind of appeal. But
as Travis handled her father's tricky estate
planning, he discovered things weren't what
they seemed in the O'Reilly clan. Would
an explosive secret leave Travis and Shana's
budding relationship in tatters?

*Available March 2009
wherever books are sold.*

REQUEST YOUR FREE BOOKS!

2 FREE NOVELS PLUS 2 FREE GIFTS!

HARLEQUIN®
Super Romance®

Exciting, emotional, unexpected!

The Inside Romance newsletter has a NEW look for the new year!

Same great content, brand-new look!